David is a cockney by birth, but was brought up and resides in Diss, Norfolk with his patient wife, Sally. He made his career in technology, but likes to not be boring and so is always on the lookout to get involved with anything else in his spare time. After hobbies, including Wood turning and Bee Keeping, he decided it was time for that one book everyone has inside them to come out—and so it did…

Dedicated to my wife, Sally, for being my sounding board throughout.

David Crawford

Hook, Line and Scammer

A Story about Relationships, Cybercrime, and Justice

Austin Macauley Publishers™
London * Cambridge * New York * Sharjah

A CIP catalogue record for this title is available from the British Library.

ISBN 9781398428751 (Paperback)
ISBN 9781398428768 (ePub e-book)

www.austinmacauley.com

First Published 2022
Austin Macauley Publishers Ltd®
1 Canada Square
Canary Wharf
London
E14 5AA

Table of Contents

Prologue
Reel Him In

"I don't understand?" Paul managed with increasing bewilderment.

"I know it's a shock, darling, but they sent me to the wrong country. I don't know how I got past the gate without them spotting it on my ticket—I mean how hard is it to spot a ticket that says the United Kingdom, not Australia."

"And how is it that you didn't realise?"

"I told you, I took my heavy sleeping pills because I hate flying—I missed all the announcements!—it's not my fault," Julia started to cry.

"OK, OK. Let's not panic—we can sort this out."

"But you paid so much money already for me to come and be with you—I just want to be there," she wailed.

"I know. Don't get upset, my love—I have more money, it's not a problem."

Paul felt lucky to have 'met' Julia via the 'Expats Reunited' dating website. He had been unlucky in love so far and needed some help. Well, in truth he had spent too much time focussing on his career—he was a farmer and he was good at it. He had not only turned his Dad's farm around to be successful but had taken over 2 other neighbouring farms and merged them with his into a 'super farm'. As with most farmers, his time was dictated by the needs of his crops and cattle—so he had little time left for socialising. He had been part of Young Farmers since his late teens and had met plenty of 'ladies' there. But they all had something to do with farming or the countryside—Paul felt he wanted someone who had lived a little and was a bit more 'out there'.

That's what attracted him to the 'Expats Reunited'—the brand strapline was 'Adventurers ready to come home to your heart'. He liked that. He imagined some English Amazonian like Goddess, who had travelled the world but was ready to settle down in the strong arms of a local yokel farmer—clearly a fantasy but wasn't that what the site promised?

Julia had immediately jumped out of all the women on the website—she looked tall, slim and slightly wild. She listed her interests as 'Travel, Cooking, Gardening and fun!'. He hadn't really travelled and wanted a guide. He couldn't cook, so wanted a wife that could. He hated gardening (too close to his day job) but had a large overgrown garden, and of course, he wanted fun—it was a match made in heaven!

Her description said, "I have lived life on the open road (currently in Singapore) but I want to come back to my beloved Isle of Britain to settle. I need a man who will look after me but also let me share with him my experiences of travel. If you want excitement in your life and can provide comfort and love for me—then ping me!"

Paul knew you had to be careful about online relationships, but she was basically being upfront about wanting someone to provide her with a life of comfort—she had clearly run out of money travelling and didn't have a job—he appreciated the honesty. So, he 'pinged' her.

It was a nervous 48 hours before Julia responded—initially through the website chat system (as per the rules—both parties had to agree before direct contact details could be shared). She was tentative in her response—asking the obvious questions about where he was and what he did and what he liked to do in his spare time. Paul thought it was pretty much like being back at school—tentatively stepping your way through a conversation with a girl you fancied. He was glad he was sitting at his laptop in his farmhouse kitchen, with its roaring fire and old beams—he felt less silly and school-boyish here.

Quickly, (well 7 days because that was the time the website said they had to wait as a minimum to allow the relationship to 'grow'), they got to the point where they exchanged direct contact details. Julia immediately sent a more revealing, sexy picture by Facebook Messenger (which she had assured Paul was the best way to communicate as it was secure and private) and Paul was initially shocked and then thrilled. There was a fair bit of flirting back and forth—'sexting' was the term the kids were using—and he did feel young again.

Paul wanted to talk—to hear her voice to complete the picture. He was sure he was falling for her but needed to have that last piece of the jigsaw. Julia was a little coy at first but then agreed to talk the next day at 10 a.m. Up until that point, they had mainly communicated late at night UK time, which was early morning in Singapore—Paul supposed she wanted to be more awake and alert so she sounded at her best.

Julia didn't want to make sure her voice was at its best. She wanted to make sure her voice was in the office—more specifically, that Gloria would be in the office to be the voice of Julia. Julia was actually a five foot eleven, overweight, unshaven Nigerian man, with several teeth missing, who had never left Lagos.

The job always got to this point and Julia (Azi in actuality) had to use Gloria for this bit—she sounded like the persona he had in his mind for Julia. Although he didn't always use Julia—there was Evie, Kate, Tasha and his personal favourite Melanie—they were all the same character basically but meant he could run multiple 'projects' at the same time—although he had to be careful to remember who he was at any one time. He normally acted the persona of a man but had started doing female personas originally and had stuck with his 'punters'.

Paul had almost said 'come and get my money' in his profile statement… 'Strong but lonely farmer who has spent too much time building up my successful business and not enough time on love—wants an interesting, sexy and fun woman to share everything I have'.

After talking to Julia (Gloria) on the phone, Paul had been hooked or more aptly, 'Catfished'. They continued messaging and having telephone calls (at specifically scheduled times) for a few more weeks, just to really bed the relationship in and make the next stage certain.

The trick was to make it think it had been their idea. Paul got there at the end of week 3, which was not uncommon but was fast—this one was going to be easy work.

"Listen Julia. You said you wanted to come home and I know you don't have much money. Please, can I help? I would love to buy you a ticket to bring you home and meet properly."

"Again, this bit was always a little tricky and needed some careful wording…."

"Babe, there is nothing more I would love than to hold you tight. But I can't ask you to do that—I respect you too much."

"I don't mind—it would be my pleasure."

You then wait a day or two—don't appear to have already known about the ticket thing… "Babe. You know you said the other day that you wanted to help me come home—to you." Carefully does it.

"Well, I contacted the airline people and they say the ticket has to be booked in my name and paid for by me—so you can't buy it for me."

Wait, wait. "It's OK Julia, I will just send you the money and you can buy the ticket yourself in your name—problem solved!"

"Oh, how silly of me. I didn't think of that. Are you sure? It's a lot of money to send."

"It makes no difference to me—giving it to you or the airline. Shall I send it to you via PayPal."

"I don't have a permanent address and so have never been able to set PayPal up. I think you can send money via Money Exchange...."

"Oh yes—that will do it. I can do online. If you can get to one of their outlets where you are."

"I think I might know one," JC Money Change, 221 Boon Lay Place, 01 128 Boon Lay Shopping Centre, Singapore, Singapore 64022.... To be precise!

"OK, well, find out the details and I will transfer the money. I can't wait to see you!"

"And me you my darling—we are nearly at the end of our wait!"

A day later, Paul transferred £1200 to Julia via the Money Exchange branch she had given him. He felt it was the best investment he had made and couldn't wait to see her. Julia called Paul from Singapore Airport on the day she was going to meet him at last—only half a day stood between them—she sounded so excited and nervous.

Paul was obviously going to meet her at Heathrow, and he had a huge bunch of flowers lined up and was wearing his best outfit. He watched the flight arrivals boards and could see Julia's flight from Singapore had just landed—so waited right near the arrival's doors with his best smile, flowers and a sign saying, 'xxx Welcome home Julia xxx'. He waited an hour before he started to get worried. He went and found the Singapore Airlines customer service desk and asked if all the passengers from Singapore had come through and if there was anyone called Julia Jones on the flight. They didn't have a record of someone of that name boarding the flight—panic started to set it. They couldn't tell him if someone of that name HAD been booked onto the flight but just not boarded as that information was held in Singapore—they could get it but not until later in the day.

Paul just didn't understand what was going on—had she chickened out at the last minute? Had she been too nervous to board the plane? Had she become sick and had to postpone the journey? If it was any of these, then why hadn't she called him? He waited, checking his phone every few seconds. Eventually, none the wiser, he left Heathrow five hours after his new life should have started.

Azi was having his afternoon break when the flight landed at Heathrow. It wasn't like there were strict office hours and routines, but he still liked to have a break to make it feel like it was a proper job. Anyway, he wanted to talk to Jem and see what he thought about a double-dip on Paul.

Jem 'ran' the scammer unit, which meant that he was the guy who thought up the idea (well, borrowed it from other similar gangs) and took most of the money. Everyone else was sort of employed by him, although there was no sign of contracts or HR or office ping pong tables. The place was a dive, a disused old office from a time when business had been better in the area, but it had good power and internet connection.

As best mates, you would think that Azi resented Jem being 'the boss', but Azi knew Jem was the clever one and a leader to be followed. Azi was fiercely loyal to Jem, having been friends since high school, and kept everyone else in the office in line for him.

Azi approached Jem's office, which was no more than a corner of the room with a curtain pulled across one edge and asked if he was free for a chat. Azi quickly explained his current project with Paul and explained how 'hook, line and sinker' Paul had been—Azi felt his was a prime candidate for the double-dip, but it had to be quick before Paul could speak to Singapore Airlines in Singapore. Jem didn't like the double-dip, although he liked the money it brought in. He always felt it was one contact too far and risked an otherwise clean transaction, but Azi seemed really keen, so he said to go for it.

Paul's phone rang when he was halfway around the M25 on his way home—still a mixture of worried and puzzled. He didn't recognise the number but answered on the first ring.

"Julia!"

"Paul. Oh, Paul. (sobbing). I have messed up so bad."

"What is it my Darling?" Azi, who was listening on a separate headphone whilst Gloria did her act, knew with this response that Paul had not yet allowed himself to think beyond some kind of mistake or illness. Azi knew the double-dip would work and pushed the details of a Sydney based Money Exchange across the desk to Gloria…

Chapter 1
Good People. Good Times

In the UK, Eb (short for the traditional Nigerian name Ebhaleleme) would perhaps have gone to the park or into town with his mates to celebrate the end of High School—writing each other's names and silly stuff on their white school shirts as a memento of their time together. Maybe even have had a crafty can of cheap lager bought by a mate's older sibling. Then later with Mum and Dad, have gone to Pizza Express and had the official end of school family celebration.

But Eb wasn't in the UK, he was in Lagos City, or rather on the outskirts in a poor area near the slums. Lagos High School life was similar to school in the UK in some ways—there was pre-school, primary and secondary and even sixth forms; teachers (some good, some bad); exams etc, but it had as many differences as similarities. Being at High School in Lagos was a privilege—whilst there was some funding from the government, there were other costs—you had to buy books, equipment, school lunches—so to afford that privilege you had to have the support of your parents or in Eb's case, just his Mum, Amelia.

His Dad, Dev, had died long ago during a raid on the motorbike repair shop on the outskirts of Lagos city that he had built up as a small business. Eb had been Eleven and had long learned to suppress the memories. Well, sort of. He could remember helping his Dad in his workshop by fetching tools and spare parts. He would be allowed to answer the phone sometimes and his Dad always insisted he called people Sir and Madam, with lots of 'pleases' and 'thank you' thrown in—he developed quite a posh telephone voice for a boy covered in grease most of the time.

Eb had loved working with his Dad—it was good honest work and his Dad charged people fairly. Eb learnt how to strip a motorbike to remove the engine (removing the seat, gas tank, fenders, exhaust system, side cover etc) and how to earn an honest living at the same time. He always hoped he would be able to continue working with his Dad when he grew up.

Eb's Dad hadn't. Nor had Eb's Mum. Dev loved the time they spent together and although she wished he was at home a little more, Amelia loved the fact that father and son had such a strong bond and Eb was learning how to be a decent human from the man she loved, trusted and believed in. His parents wanted a better life for Eb and his little Sister, Su (short for Somtochukwu). It wasn't that his parents had a bad life, but they were undereducated and didn't have much spare time or cash between running a business and running their family life.

The family home was a small 2-bedroom bungalow on the outskirts of Lagos, with a roof made of reed and walls made from poorly made clay bricks from the local quarry. The windows and doors did not have glass but shutters—once made from reed as well but now patched up with wood and plastic. The inside was basic, with a clay brick tiles floor, some furniture, a kitchen which had a fire stove for cooking and doubled as the dining room and living area. It was very small and had no real garden—just a yard where the outside toilet stood.

This was actually considered to be a fairly decent home for the area and for a family such as Eb's. Amelia had kept it as nice as their money would allow and made a real effort with the internal decorations—it was all a bit haphazard in terms of furniture (they recycled whatever they could), but the whole place was always bright, had aromas of either baking or flowers, and was welcoming to visitors.

His Grandad had worked in the local quarry and had got the bricks on the cheap as they were rejects. His grandparents had built the bungalow themselves over two years back in the late 1970s and it had been handed down to Amelia when she got married—her parents choosing to retire back to their home village after a hard-working life in the suburbs of Lagos. Although they owned the house, Eb's parents didn't own the land it was on—this was rented on a long lease.

They had made it a family home by doing typical family things together—They had eaten together every day at breakfast and for dinner, they had played games in the evening (they had no TV of course), read books and they had even been on occasional picnics to Eleko beach. Then there had been Church on a Sunday of course. Eb had a special shirt and shorts for that. Su had a nearly white frock, that she was also allowed to wear for birthday parties and carnival day.

As with so many working-class families in Lagos, it was Eb's Mum that had kept their spiritual life alive. Dev had often been heard mumbling about a bike he wanted to tinker with rather than being all smiles to people he didn't even like for two hours every Sunday morning. Overall, they had been thankful for their home and family life together.

But that was five years ago, and things had gone downhill a little since Dev died. For Amelia, the children were the only thing that mattered, and she had done her best to give them a good upbringing. Now, as a grown-up sixteen-year-old, Eb was about five foot eight inches, which he must have got from his Dad as his Mum was only five foot. He got his hair from his Mum.

His Dad had black curly hair as most Nigerian men do, but Eb's was long curls, not tight curls and this was more common to Nigerian women. Eb had bright blue eyes and good teeth (not something to be taken for granted in his community). His face was almost a permanent smile and he liked to tease his sister, in common with most older brothers. Despite Amelia's best efforts, food had always been on the cheaper and less plentiful side of things and so Eb and Su were both slender.

They were both healthy but not overly strong in body. Despite this, Eb was fit and never rested—he held down two jobs and poured his remaining hours into his schoolwork. He was not particularly attractive yet, a bit of a gangly teenager with spots, just like teenagers the world over, but he told himself that meant he wouldn't be distracted from his education by girls.

As well as doing her best to look after their physical health, Amelia had tried to give them healthy minds—she had kept up the Church going with them, still read regularly at home with them, made sure they did their homework and generally did everything she could do make sure they got a decent education.

Family life wasn't what it had been, and they all missed Dev terribly, but they stuck together and made the best of it, which was all that Amelia wanted. Eb, however, wanted more for his family and felt an obligation to deliver a better future—he didn't know how he was going to do that but felt sure opportunity would present itself.

Chapter 2
Down, but Not Out

Elizabeth didn't like being called 'Liz', but people would insist on using it. Similarly, she liked to be called 'Mrs Gresham' by people she didn't know or who weren't on familiar terms with her (it seemed not many were). It wasn't that she was especially in love with her name, it was just that she liked things to be as they should be.

Something else that wasn't as it should be was the timing of her Physiotherapist. He was a lovely young man (except that he called her Liz!), but he would come at the most awkward times—his early calls on her seemed to clash with *Lorraine*, his midday calls would clash with *Loose Women* and if he came in the evening, which fortunately he rarely did, you could guarantee that it would be just as *Coronation Street* was about to start.

Although he was coming to see that she had done her various exercises and given her massage and manipulation to relieve her pain, he would invariably help out by doing some household chores. Elizabeth partly liked this as she found them so tiring, but she also felt a little helpless and even ashamed that she couldn't manage by herself.

Elizabeth wasn't 'old', she was only 67, just a little let down by her body of late and without any support from family. Her husband Edward had died 3 years earlier. He had been killed whilst they had been out on one of their country rides on his Honda CB77 (or 'Super Hawk' as it was commonly known). He was 2 years older than her and had only been retired a year.

They had really been embracing the English countryside since they both retired, going out for long summer days on the bike and sometimes packing an overnight bag and stopping wherever they reached by the end of a day, finding a little B&B for the night, before setting off home the next morning. They had enjoyed it so much that they kept going into Autumn on the days when the weather wasn't so bad. They wouldn't have normally been out on the bike on the day of the crash, but they had started out the previous day in good weather and with the forecast promising sunshine for the next 48 hours—so they had done a long run and found a B&B. The next morning, they set off early as normal, but as the promised sunshine was not yet high enough in the sky, some patches of early morning frost had not quite gone.

Elizabeth didn't like to think about that day when she lost her one true love, but she was painfully reminded of it day in and day out by the injuries she had sustained in the crash. She had been left with a spine that was broken in a few places and had to undergo several hours of operations to pin it all together. She also suffered muscle damage to her lower legs. The legs would eventually get better through the Physio, but the doctors had said she would always have mobility problems because of the back.

For the first year after the accident, she had been able to get out and about with the aid of a wheelchair and a carer that the hospital provided as part of her rehabilitation. However, she had another operation after the first year and it had set her back. As a result, she was now more or less housebound and with no hope of living the life she had hoped for in her silver years.

But she consoled herself with memories—Elizabeth and Teddie had indeed had a wonderful life. Everyone called him Eddie, which you would think would annoy Elizabeth, but she didn't mind as long as no one called him Teddie—that was her pet name for him, and she wanted it all to herself. Whilst they were not blessed with children, they had been able to travel the world due to Teddie's job as a Salesman. He had sold drugs to Doctors and Hospitals. This was in a time when everything was done face to face, not an order form submitted through the internet—so he had to go where the work took him and he always took Lizzie-pops with him (of course Teddie didn't have to call her Mrs Gresham!)—they travelled to Hong Kong, the USA, all over Europe and even parts of the African continent. They were never more than a few hours apart, wherever in the world they were—it was bliss.

Elizabeth had been a bit of a stunner in her younger days and you could see much of that carry through into her later years—she was tall, slim, curvy in the right places and her defining gloriousness was her long Auburn hair. Since the accident, the tallness, slimness and curviness may have diminished a little, but the hair was still vibrant, showing no signs of grey (at least her body had not let her down there!). Having followed a bedtime skincare regime for years, she had lovely clear, pale skin with hardly any lines—she didn't look sixty-seven for certain. She had been a bubbly character and still showed signs of this when she forgot her misfortunes. She looked best when she laughed, that's when any strict upbringing or adult snobbishness or regret about her current situation disappeared and you could see the real Elizabeth—beautiful, lively, fun and generous—all just in her smile. It's a shame she didn't seem to laugh so much these days.

It was no wonder that Elizabeth had been lonely ever since Teddie died. She wasn't depressed and before the last operation, she did go out on her own sometimes. She would meet friends for lunch and several times a month she had more than one club that she belonged to—Knitting club, Mothers Union, Bridge and slightly more out there, Motorbike enthusiasts club! This last one had been a joint interest with Teddie—he loved Motorbikes and everything about them.

He joined the Motorbike enthusiasts club before they were married, and Elizabeth loved riding on the back with him so much that she joined the club also. She liked the social side of it mostly, but she knew the difference between a straight twin engine and a flat-twins engine.

Of course, now she wasn't able to go to the clubs and her pain relief drugs meant she got tired of playing bridge or even chatting with people for too long, she didn't see many people. Visitors stopped coming because they didn't want to tire her out. So mostly she sat in her comfy recliner chair and watched TV. That is when she wasn't buying stuff on the Internet or playing Bingo online.

Just before she had become housebound, she had taken the courageous step of going to computer lessons at the local library. She wanted to know what all the fuss about this Web thing was and she had heard you could find old friends through something called Social Media. Four weeks later she was all clued up and decided she wanted an iPad—so she got the biggest one she could get and a headset so she could talk to people online. She hadn't expected to be able to play Bingo and was pleased because it was her guilty secret that she had always liked Bingo but always been too snobbish to go to the local Bingo hall to play.

The iPad had been expensive and signing up for 'Fibre' had added to the cost, although the man at the library had said was the faster version of the internet. Elizabeth could afford it—Teddy's company had looked after him and she had a very generous Widows pension. Not to mention that she had inherited money from her parents when they died. She was nicely well off and could afford to spoil herself a little if she wanted.

She didn't like people to know she had money, and so when Philip the Physio came around, she would shove the iPad into her old knitting bag. Philip was a young man and had grown up with the internet and iPads—he could see her superfast fibre broadband hub and had seen her iPad pop up on his iPhone for a Bluetooth connection under the name 'Lizzie-pops' several times. Philip would often try to coax her into telling him, but she would always just dismiss talk of 'this web thingy'—so he just let her get on with it.

Chapter 3
Norfolk Cyber Crime Unit

Always thought of as a flat, boring landscape, with some random rivers called 'The Broads' and family DNA being 'shared' so to speak, it had come as a surprise to locals to hear that the Norfolk Constabulary had a Cyber Crime Unit.

There had been a special 'Boating' unit for years due to the Broads. The vast and complex array of waterways that opened out at intervals into big lakes, took a lot of patrolling and the illegal fishing and boats going over the 5mph speed limit took a regular team of 6 to keep in check. In fact, the current Chief Constable himself, Chris Bradley, had started this unit when he was a section leader in Wroxham, the centre of the Broads community. He tried to convince the then Chief Constable of the need for a very powerful and flashy 'police boat' to ensure these water criminals could be tackled.

In the end, the then Chief Constable opted for a more stylish boat—complete with walnut interior and brass fittings, and a two-ring stove to make a brew when not fighting aquatic hoodlums. He said that it was more befitting to the polices image and would give the public confidence in them. The fact that he regularly commandeered it during the summer evenings and weekends to take Mrs Chief Constable and their friends out in, was neither here nor there.

In fact, Norfolk was a hotbed of cyber-crime—maybe it was just far enough away from London to not be stepping on the toes of major organised crime or maybe it was there was not much to do in the long winter evenings. Whatever the cause, online fraud, identity theft, hacking, and even online grooming of children for paedophiles had not been left behind in the East of England.

Recently there had been a lot in the press about Stephen Fry being caught out with a phishing scam on Twitter—if a Norfolk statesman as clever as Stephen Fry could be a victim of cybercrime, then anyone could!

The big businesses in Norwich and the various towns around Norfolk were obviously on top of Internet Security and lots of local councils were starting to run free seminars for the community—the police had supported these by sending along a tech-savvy (normally young) constable, but they were under pressure to do more.

Chris had met with his peers countrywide at a recent 'Police and Cyber Crime' event in Manchester and had become aware his lack of interest in the Internet had perhaps clouded his judgement about how serious a breeding ground it was for crime.

It was this and a sketch by Alun Partridge on Cyber Crime in his latest show that made him finally do something.... Alun was suing the police for failing to help him arrest a local 22year-old man, who had made Alun the victim of a 'Catfishing' scam. Basically, Alun swore blind the lady he fell in 'cyber love' with, was a mature 42-year-old dinner lady from Cromer and when she asked him to lend her £3000 to help her get a 'nip and tuck' he had willingly sent her the money.

Admittedly Alun had only seen pictures of the 'lady' via social media and although attracted to her, he felt he didn't want to go further until she had the cosmetic work done—it just made sense for the future of the relationship Alun said. After he sent the money, he didn't hear from her again, so got suspicious and contacted the police to help track her down. The police were made to look idiots for not understanding how the internet could make a fit, young 22-year-old man appear to be a past her best, 42-year-old woman when really it was Alun who was bemused by how he had been duped.

The whole thing ended up with Alun blaming the police for letting anyone under the age of 30 use the internet and for failing to track down the elusive 'Bren-the-Dinner-lady-#42' and retrieve his money—it all got very heated when Alun suggested the police were 'in' on the whole thing and questioned what kind of 'nip and tuck' the young man was having at his expense!

Suffice to say, whilst great comedy from the man who put Norfolk back on the map, it made the Norfolk police look inept at understanding and dealing with the reality of Internet fraud.

A few conversations with his old school friend at the Home Office and 3 months later, some budget was found for 'The Norfolk Cyber Crime Unit'. Initially, officers were asked to volunteer to become part of the unit, but when it became clear that all the volunteers were under 25 and only joined because they thought they would spend their time messing about online rather than on a rainy beat, a re-think was needed.

What was needed was someone who was internet savvy but experienced enough to put some structure and meaning around the unit. They would also need to be able to promote and 'sell' the unit to the public and people of influence in the area.

Jane Porter fitted the bill. A distinguished officer of some 25 years, who had teenage children and therefore was tuned into the modern world automatically. She had often caused the Chief Constable embarrassment by pointing out how out of touch with the youth the Norfolk police were and now she could help tame those very same youth (he assumed it must be them doing this internet messing about crime).

Chris had seen Jane at a conference last year speaking for Norfolk on crimes against senior citizens—she had passion and charisma and a loud voice, which was exactly what would be needed to champion the new Cyber Crime Unit in the community and beyond. He felt sure that Jane would be able to wax lyrical about catching criminals online (or whatever a Cyber Crime Unit actually did) and that she would take these young police officers and get them into some kind of effective fighting force against the evils of the web—yes Jane Porter was his man he thought (showing once more that his mind was stuck in the past!).

Chapter 4
Good People? Hard Times!

The raid was clearly the work of a gang—one of the increasing numbers of small-time (often teenage) criminals that ripped off small businesses that operated on cash. It was a quick and normally violent free way to get their hands-on money. Even though these gangs were looked upon as evil, it wasn't like UK gangs where they would be doing it for money for drugs or other mindless pursuits. It was to feed their families and clothe their brothers and sisters. Clearly, a society caught in a vicious loop. That didn't justify their actions, but it made them seem like victims of a kind as well.

In fact, the raids almost seemed to follow a pattern of 'give and take'—the gang would come at night, break a window, take some but not all of the cash and leave the premises without significant vandalism—almost a gentleman's burglary if you like, where they understood the business owner was probably in as bad a position as them in life and didn't want to overdo it.

That wasn't how Dev's workshop was raided. The gang didn't mean him any harm. They expected to do a standard 'gentleman's burglary' and be home within the hour with something for the family to eat that night. But Dev had promised a good customer their bike would be ready by 10 a.m. the following day and he was struggling with the transmission; it just wouldn't smoothly change gear without a sort of crunching sound. So, he was working late, which was unusual as it would mean missing their daily family dinner.

'Filly' was the gang leader. He didn't look like a gang leader—tall, skinny and with no tattoos or piecing's—he looked like an awkward teenager with a bit of attitude. His clothes were old and worn, he was clearly not very well off—so perhaps not an established gang with much experience yet. At nineteen he was older than the other two gang members. Gil was his thirteen-year-old brother and 'Gums' was his sidekick from school, only seventeen as Filly had been held back a couple of years. Whilst not the most academic student, Filly had earned his nickname from his ability to pinch food from market stalls and shops and keep his ever-hungry schoolmates 'filled' with food—hence 'Filly'.

Filly felt the pressure that his nickname and therefore reputation had burdened him with—he couldn't fail people and let them go hungry. At first, it was just the odd bread roll or apple from a local market stallholder—he told himself they expected a bit of light theft and tolerated these young boys who were desperate for food. This attitude built in his brain and started to justify more significant theft to Filly.

Filly and Gil no longer had parents—their mum died giving birth to Gil and their dad went out one day to get a job and never came back. Filly was thirteen by then and considered a man in their culture—so told himself that his Dad was just letting him stand on his own two feet. Which proved difficult and his petty crime became his career that supported him and Gil. Gil needed the support as he was small and often got bullied at school but not when his brother was around. Gil was also a bit 'emotional' and his brother often tried to toughen him up to play fighting and by making him do football with the other kids in the neighbourhood. Gil just liked to keep himself to himself and like to spend his time thinking about what his mother had been like.

However, Gil, as most younger brothers do, worshipped Filly. Filly loved Gil and would do anything for him. Gil knew what Filly had to do to make some kind of life for them both and helped however he could. Often this meant being the one who climbed through the small window after Filly had broken it, but he didn't mind as Filly asked him to. Gil liked it when Gums was with them as it made them seem like a family and they would protect him from the world.

'Gums' had a better home life, with parents who had good jobs and loved him, in the way they knew how—spending money on gadgets, clothes etc. There weren't many meals together and he had never had a picnic at the beach. Gums grew to despise his parents for their 'throw money at it' parenting and just longed for some attention. He got this attention from Filly. Filly gave him time and involved him in things—this felt like a family to Gums.

He just couldn't control his anger—he wasn't sure what he was angry at, but the red mist descended on a frequent basis. He got into lots of fights with other boys and the loss of teeth that came with these bouts is what led to his nickname—which he wore as a badge of pride every time he grinned. Eventually, his anger bubbled over with a teacher and he got expelled from school having hit them. Well, throwing the teacher across the classroom is more accurate. He was a big lad, with not much control. It was this dangerous combination that surfaced during the raid on Dev's workshop.

Chapter 5
Username = "Lizzie-Pops"; Password = "Teddy1#"

According to the internet man who ran the course at the library, you couldn't be too careful when it came to protecting your identity online. As Elizabeth didn't yet have an identity online, she wasn't too worried about this. Anyway, as long as they got her name right and didn't mistake her for a lesbian, she didn't really mind what people on the internet did. In truth, the internet seemed to her to be this magical place where you could find anyone, to talk about anything for as long as you wanted—it seemed like one of her ladies lunches and there was nothing wrong with the bit of gossip they used to have at them.

Elizabeth started out on Facebook—she had heard of it on the news and Philip the physio said he had found some old school friends on Facebook once. She was going to resister on Facebook as 'Elizabeth Gresham (nee Wilding)' so that her old friends could find her if they were on it. But then she wondered how many of her old friends would be alive, let alone on Facebook. She decided old friends were old and she wanted to interact with young, modern people to make her feel... well, young and modern she supposed.

With this in mind and knowing that no one on the internet 'knew' her, she registered on Facebook as 'Lizzie-pops' and with a password of 'Teddy1#'—the course had taught her that you must choose a password that you could remember well enough not to write it down, but that no one else should be able to guess it. The course tutors top tip was to put a number and special character on the end of your chosen word. Well, no one knew her Husband was Teddy, as everyone called him Eddie and the 1 and hash sign surely made it safe.

She put her age as 58 (only 9 years out) and used an old picture of her from Teddie's retirement party when she had just had her hair done and bought a new outfit. She knew that she looked a bit older now, but miraculously she still had her auburn hair—she just hadn't gone grey at all, so felt she could get away with using a younger photo without feeling too guilty.

She put in her email address that the Fibre Internet people had given her and put her hometown as Norwich. She actually lived in Beeton a little way outside Norwich but didn't think anyone would know where that was. She listed her hobbies as Motorbikes and put her relationship status as 'Single'. Elizabeth had no intention of using the internet to find love or any of that silliness, she just didn't want to be labelled as old and out of touch—and so her 'identity' was formed, and she started to browse around.

Instantly Facebook offered her 'friends' that were local to her. She hadn't seen any reason not to put her real address into Facebook as online people didn't come to visit in person—it was all just online stuff. However, she didn't want to risk being uncovered about her age and so ignored the local friends. She then got offered friends based on her hobbies—so lots of motorbike enthusiasts—this really excited her, and she accepted all the friends that were offered to her. Then she sat back and waited for everyone to start talking to her—the loneliness would soon be over.

Chapter 6
The Right Wo-Man for the Job!

Maybe Jane shouldn't have pushed that last point with the Judge. Maybe she should have just accepted the verdict and the sentence—5 years for child neglect was fairly normal. It's just, well, she wasn't very good at accepting things she thought were not quite right. She guessed that was what drove her to have been a police officer for 25 years anyway—well, that and the fact she had been mercilessly bullied at school for only being four foot eleven inches and needed to show people what she could achieve. Anyway, she could always have another go when the perpetrator inevitably appealed. Maybe she would get a Judge who was a bit tougher on those kinds of crimes.

The Judge had raised his eyebrow and said nothing else at her outburst, but she knew it would come back to bite her in the arse and now it had. Sitting outside the Chief Constable's office always reminded her of being at school outside the Headmasters office. It's funny how the naughty children often become Police Officers or Nurses or priests—must be something about their upbringing that starts them out naughty and then rescues them from themselves with a career that is basically their penance for earlier misdemeanours!

She suspected it would be a quick lecture on insubordination, followed by the old 'disappointing in such a long-standing, senior colleague who continues to insist on collecting black marks on a significantly distinguished career'. That would be the telling off. Then would be the caring bit—'You have done so much for this force and that doesn't go unnoticed. We want what you want', with no actual follow-up on that to show what she did want and if it was what 'they' wanted as well. Then the penalty—'I would like you to do some PR work for us Jane—just some local visits to community centres to raise our profile. You know the people love your… bubbliness. It would mean a lot to me. Thanks'. The 'thanks' being the closure of that conversation—not so much thanks as 'them's your orders'.

Chris opened the door and beamed, which Jane took to mean the Judge really had it in for her. He invited her into his office and asked his PA for coffee, unusually asking Jane if she wanted biscuits. She was not slow to respond when offered these kinds of treats—Jane was a foodie, as her size perhaps indicated. She was not obese in the way that you just can't stop staring even though you know it's wrong, but rather a bit of a little 'round' ball type shape.

In fact, her short stature almost made her seem less fat. She had a big head physically and made it bigger with an unnatural wave in her hair that meant she looked permanently liked she had been in a fight. It gave off the impression, not a million miles away from the truth, that this was a woman who you didn't want to get on the wrong side of. She accepted the biscuits; however, she knew that they were just 'good cop' to the community visit's 'bad cop' in this routine.

"How are things with you these days Jane? We haven't spoken for a while," Chris gently opened the conversation. This threw Jane off a bit; he wasn't normally the small talk type. She figured he must have been on one of these Leadership courses recently and she was getting the immediate after-effects, which would no doubt disappear within a few days.

She nearly decided to call his bluff and tell him how she actually was… 'My seventeen-year-old son Toby is constantly telling me I am not fair to him because I won't let him go to the pub with his mates or stay out later than 11 p.m. at parties, and keeps telling me that when he is eighteen in three months he will be able to do whatever he likes and I won't legally be allowed to do anything about it; My fifteen-year-old daughter thinks she is the next YouTube sensation and I keep getting other Mum's asking me if I have seen her latest video with a worried look in their eye—When I ask Ester about it she just shows me some video of her playing with kittens, which I know is not what she is posting by I can't work out how to find her real 'work' on YouTube; My Husband still thinks I don't have a real job and should have his tea on the table every evening, just because he has stood on his feet at the Auction rooms all day talking his arse off for a living—he would ask me to give up work but he likes the uniform fantasy too much; My mother is driving me crazy by calling me round to her house all the time on some kind of emergency, just to discover she has run out of shower gel; and I have missed the last three girls nights out because you bastards keep me so hard at it with this poxy job!'

However, wisdom prevailed, and she decided to tackle the subject at hand…

"Well fine, until that dipstick of a Judge gave too light a sentence yesterday." She felt it would be good to get into the meat of the conversation quickly—get it over with. Chris looked at her clearly perplexed.

"Oh yes, were you in court yesterday." She wasn't falling for that.

So, she stayed silent, waiting for him to say something like, "Of course I know you were because Judge McCall spent thirty minutes bending my ear about it last night when I should have been watching Top Gear!" But he didn't. Maybe this was about something else. Maybe Judge McCall had put it down to her passion for Justice and had overlooked it. Hoorah, she got away with her outspokenness for once!

"Well, sorry if things didn't go the way you wanted. Perhaps next time. Anyway, as I say, how are you? Are you happy in Domestic Crime? We can't have you getting bored—not one of our most accomplished officers."

It dawned on Jane that this was going to be worse than a telling off—she was getting a new assignment. Damn those biscuits, she walked right into it—call herself a Detective, tch! "Erm, well I have been there a while and the team have come on great—we seem to be making a dent in the stats, I hope you will agree?"

"Yes, yes. Of course. All very good… No, I mean really, we are very pleased with what you have done there over the last couple of years." Here it comes…

"Do you feel ready for a new challenge yet, do you think?" Chris tried to say with as much lightness as he could muster.

"Well, I think there is still lots of work to be done in Domestic Crime, Sir."

"Of course. But you did say the team were coming on—perhaps time for that young lad Stevens to get the next step up to unit head there—no?"

"Stevens is a fine Detective and would be great in my post. Might I know what you have in mind please, Sir?"

"You have teenage children don't you Jane?" Please not youth drugs squad, thought Jane.

"Yes. Toby 17 and Ester 15. Why do you ask?"

"And I expect they keep you on your toes, erm, Technology wise—do they?"

"I am not sure I follow, Sir?"

"You know, the internet, video games, porn, sexting etc.," Chris stammered whilst looking very hard out of the window.

"I can assure you, Sir, that my children don't watch porn or send text messages of that nature!" rebuffed Jane with slightly more aggression than she had intended. Although in truth she had been wondering if Toby had looked at some porn online with his mates, but surely that's just boys-being-boys she had thought.

"Sorry, Jane! I wasn't suggesting anything like that—goodness me. No, I just meant that it's a world you must have at the front of your mind as a mother of teenagers in society today and all that? I didn't mean to suggest, well, you know. Sorry." Chris meant that last sorry, he was out of his depth and struggling to compose the conversation correctly—he must get it back on track.

"Anyway, what we need is a new Head of Cyber Crime to establish and run the unit. I think your past achievements and passion for Justice for those less able to defend themselves, plus you have children of the 'internet age' as it were, makes you suited to this role—what do you think?" he rushed out in one breath.

What did Jane think? Was it a set-up for her to fail or was she being trusted (at last!) with something really meaty and important? She decided to do the dance… "That's very kind of you to consider me, Sir…," she demurred.

"Now none of that Porter. You know I wouldn't ask if I didn't think you couldn't do it." OK, so he was serious, and she wasn't on a list, he wanted her to do it.

More dancing…. "Head of Cyber Crime—a new unit for Norfolk—that's going to involve a lot of PR inside and outside. Particularly with senior local dignitaries…. I am not sure I have the credos, Sir…." She tried to blush but couldn't.

Now to let him lead the dance…. "Any thoughts on how best to tackle that aspect, Sir?"

That caught him slightly off-guard "Ah, well now yes. There was something I thought about to help with that."

He started thinking quickly…. "I think this post requires a, erm, Detective Inspector—do you think you are ready?" Chris grinned with a knowing smile as he re-took the upper hand in the conversation.

"Yes, Sir. I know I am. I have worked hard and feel I have earned it. Thank you for this recognition, Sir," Jane said calmly but with no little feeling.

They discussed the unit a little more and Jane relaxed enough to help herself to two more biscuits. She had made it and was going to command her own unit with a decent title and salary to match—it felt great. She thanked the Chief Constable for his confidence in her and did the cliched 'I won't let you down' thing as she got up to leave.

As she reached the door and without looking up at her, Chris said, “and Porter… if Judge McCall calls me at home once more on your account… it will be traffic duty for you—Inspector or not!” He smiled to himself.

Jane replied, “Yes, Sir. Sorry, Sir. It won’t happen again, Sir,” but was smiling as she said it because she knew he wasn’t really angry with her; he was just restoring the balance of power that came with his privileged office—she was OK with that as it goes.

Chapter 7
The Raid

Dev was in his pit. This was a simple rectangular hole that he had dug out in the middle of the workshop so that he could work under the bikes with good access. The trouble was when he was in it, he couldn't be seen at first glance when entering the workshop. Similarly, he couldn't really see or hear what was going on beyond the bottom of the bike.

When the gang broke the window in the office at the back of the workshop, Dev didn't hear it. The whole building was no more than a corrugated iron shack really—some iron girders concreted into the ground, with the walls welded to them and a roof put on the same. Some sliding doors big enough to get a car through competed the building. Dev had made it into a workshop of sorts by adding the pit, a big workbench and a couple of stud walls with a window looking into the workshop that formed the office.

Nor did he hear Gil cry out when he cut his thigh on a jagged piece of glass as he crawled through the broken window. He nearly heard Gum's swearing when he could hardly fit through the small window but happened to be low in the pit looking for a heavy-duty wrench that was proving elusive in the bad light.

Filly and the gang had done loads of these kinds of raids and they knew a good small businessman would be home with his family by now. Whilst they didn't make unnecessary noise, they moved freely around the small office thinking they were the only ones there.

Gil was at that age where a motorbike held mystery for him and he immediately started looking at the various bikes around the workshop, hopping on and pretending to race them along some imagined back alley. It was Gil's "brrrrmmmm, brrrrrmmmm, nnneeeewwwww…" sound effects that first alerted Dev to their presence. Knowing what they were after, he decided to sit tight and wait it out, hoping they would take the small amount of cash he kept in the office and then leave.

That was when Gil spotted the bike that Dev was working on. It was a beauty—jet black with the word 'Norton' written in gold along the side of the tank—it looked old fashioned but great. Gil rushed over to the bike and jumped straight on. He didn't notice it was over a pit or that someone was in the pit.

"Stop buggering about on that thing," chided Filly.

"Let the boy have his fun," responded Gums. "Go on Gil—fire her up!"

Dev knew what the boys didn't, this bike would start but quickly catch fire as he still had the manifold off. Dev didn't fancy his chances in the pit with a bike leaking petrol that was on fire.

"Alright boys, you have had your fun. Now take what you came for and bugger off!" Dev said with more confidence than he felt he actually had.

The gang all gasped together at the shock of this disembodied voice. Gil just held onto the bike more firmly. Filly was the first to recover and realise the source of the voice. "Come out from there old man or else."

Dev didn't like the idea of being in the open with these boys and found himself saying "Or else what?" his bravery again surprised him.

"Or else you will regret it!" hissed Filly, not really knowing what he meant by that.

Gums grew quickly tired of this intellectual back and forth and as a man of action decide to move things forward. "Oi, Gils, get off that thing and stand back." Gils dismounted shakily and went to stand just behind his brother.

Gums moved over to the bike and sensing it would be his only chance of getting clear, Dev ran up the small steps that led out of the pit—straight into Gums trademark grin (or more accurately his gorilla size chest). Aware that Filly and Gils were watching him, Gums grabbed Dev by the collar of his overalls and threw him back down into the pit. In truth, Gums had only intended to throw him to the floor, but that lack of control of his strength meant Dev tumbled back down into the pit, knocking the bike over as he fell.

Gums started shouting the odds and was telling this old man to stay down there if he knew what was good for him. Filly joined in and then Gils got his confidence back and also started to mouth off. Dev did not retaliate. In fact, it was a good minute or two before the boys realised, they were not getting anything back from the pit. Dev, or more precisely Dev's head, had found that previously elusive heavy-duty wrench.

Death had come instantly. So said the doctor who examined the body the next day. Eb was not sure if the doctor was saying this because it was true or to make them all feel better—surely hitting your head on a wrench actually hurt? Eb thought about this for a good 10 minutes but really only to avoid thinking about his dead father.

The police said it was probably an accident but couldn't explain the broken office window. Nothing was missing, so it wasn't a burglary as far as they could conclude.

The funeral was a week after Dev was killed. Amelia stood silently with Su and Eb by the side of the open grave and the few mourners there were filed by whispering appropriate condolences. Eb recognised relatives, family friends and even a few regular customers from the workshop. He didn't recognise the tall, skinny young man or his younger companion, who cried when the coffin was lowered. He assumed they were customers he didn't know. But then he knew that young boy wasn't old enough to ride a motorbike and yet he was clearly very upset.

Chapter 8
Digital Life

Elizabeth wasn't lonely anymore, but she wasn't enjoying the internet as much as she had hoped. Having accepted every friend offered to her that said they shared her interest in all things motorbike related, she did start to get people to talk to her—well, send her instant messages. The trouble was that they all seemed a little sordid. Lots of grey-haired Hells Angels offering to 'take her out for a spin' or 'help her strip down her bodywork'!

She was sure there were one or two people reaching out for genuine reasons, but the whole thing spooked her a little and she didn't reply to anyone. It was the internet man from the library that helped her out when he sent her an email asking how she was getting on (he had helped set her up on the iPad when she first got it). She told him that she was dabbling with Facebook and was moaning about the unsavoury types who seemed to frequent it—she was thinking of giving the whole thing up.

The internet library man knew that for housebound people, the internet could actually be a good lifeline and help to keep them feeling part of a community, even if it was a digital, one not a physical one. So, he encouraged her to keep at it and introduced her to Pinterest, the photo-based notice board where you were able to follow topics that interest you. It wasn't that Pinterest didn't have its own share of perverts but in the main, you could find genuine groups and people to follow.

Elizabeth found people on Pinterest and then could see they had Facebook profiles as well and slowly she started to trust the community she found herself in. She actually drew some attention herself as she started to post old pictures of her leaning against or sitting on an array of Teddie's motorbikes that he had bought and done up over the years, before selling them on and getting another. Teddie liked to have her pose with each bike, which she thought was cute of him.

Although her Auburn hair (it had been long and flowing out under her open face helmet back then) and her pretty face often caused comment from a fellow Facebooker or Pinterester, it was the motorbikes that caused the attention. Teddie had collected some real gems over the years and with his skill, had brought them back to life.

There was one connection, a man called 'Bike-Crazy-321', who knew all the names of all the bikes and would comment with lots of detail about the various parts of each bike and the particular engineering problems they had or what their top speed was. He was a keen follower of Elizabeth's posts, and she decided to follow him.

'Bike-Crazy-312' and Elizabeth struck up a friendly relationship based around discussing bikes. It was fascinating how much he knew about these old machines—apparently, his Dad used to own a motorcycle repair shop in London.

He wanted to send her a picture of his father with one of the bikes he was very proud of, but he didn't want everyone to see it online and so he asked if he could send it to her via Facebook messenger. Elizabeth had not used instant messaging since her initial bad experience, but she was keen to see the photo and so agreed. After this, they would regularly chat on Messenger and swap pictures relevant to their conversation.

Elizabeth realised that she had been lonely and messaging one on one with a man had brought back memories of companionship and even thoughts of love to her. She knew that 'Bike-Crazy-321' was married as he had mentioned something about his wife and him going to bike shows and she suddenly felt guilty at keeping him away from his wife in the evenings with all their chatting about bikes. She needed her own partner, not someone else's. She slowly stopped chatting to him so much and started to feel lonely again—it was time to do something about that, she felt.

In a moment of loneliness, Elizabeth searched for an online dating website—it was not like she could get out to go proper dating and anyway, she just wanted some companionship—perhaps a digital adventure and nothing more. There were lots of websites, but one caught her eye as it talked about Adventure and re-uniting people who were travellers—she and Teddie had been travellers and so this appealed to her. With confidence that she could just walk away from it all if she didn't like it, she joined the site—'Expats Reunited'—she browsed around the site and caught sight of a handsome older man who listed 'motorbikes' as a hobby—that was good enough for her—so she clicked 'unite' and waited to see what would happen.

The next day she got confirmation that 'Joseph' had accepted her 'unite' request and they were now 'friends'. The website didn't give out direct contact details for two weeks and you could only communicate via the website's in-built chat messenger—so she sent a tentative message and he responded. It felt very natural she thought (but then she had got used to talking to strangers on the internet now) and they quickly struck up a relationship… although she would have no idea where it would lead…

Chapter 9
Brains and Ambition

Billy Gant and Penny Moore had worked all through the night to track down various leads that were taking them on a merry dance right around the world. But they were so full of excitement with the breakthrough they had made, that they didn't notice how tired they were. The boss would be in soon and they were going to make sure they got to her first.

Billy had joined the Cyber Crime Unit before Jane Porter was the Unit Head as he was so into everything to do with computers and the internet, and he couldn't believe the opportunity it would provide him with as a policeman. His hobby had become his job. Billy was super clever when it came to computers, he sort of just got them from when he first used them at primary school. He quickly got bored of the games the other kids were playing and asked the teacher if there was anything else you could do with the laptops they had for the children? The teacher was pleased to be able to show Billy her Raspberry Pi.

The credit card-sized mini-computer that was great for learning to write computer software had been an inspired purchase by the school, with many of the children learning how to use it faster than the teachers. Billy soon learnt how to make it operate a simple robot that the school had bought with it and also managed to create a song machine like a jukebox that the children could choose songs from.

Billy further mastered computers at High School, with little intervention from the teachers, who were woefully behind in their IT skills. They learnt stuff from him. Once he could program a database and had built a few simple Apps, he went onto networking and the security side of things. Meaning that he started to hack systems.

It was a popular activity amongst his generation, as there were lots of high profile hacks going on around the world—celebrity photos being stolen from their private cloud storage; take-over of websites of companies that were thought to be too uncaring about how they made their money; personal details of people involved in tax avoidance schemes… Billy didn't do anything that bad, but he did hack into the school's email system and send an email from Mrs Jones the Geography teacher to Mr Stewart the PE teacher suggesting they meet behind the bikes shed. He got into trouble for that but mainly because Mr Stewart had wasted 30 minutes getting cold waiting for Mrs Jones!

He was a bit of a Mummy's boy and liked being spoilt at home, hence his slightly expanded waistline. He was quite tall and so carried the weight well. He lacked confidence in general and wasn't sporty, so didn't socialise much. His father had left home when he was young and maybe that had made him a little shy—plus his Dad was of Black Caribbean origin and even though mixed-race families were common these days, he had still suffered some racism at school. He had two older brothers, who had lots of confidence, and they looked after him, taking him to watch Norwich play and making sure he could handle himself if needed—plus they taught him how to drink.

As such, his confidence grew a little. But, even so, Billy didn't want to go to Uni. Plus, it was clear that he was ahead with computers and didn't feel he needed to study them more. However, as he lived in Norfolk and didn't fancy the long commute to London, jobs for self-taught computer programmers without degrees were hard to find. So, he joined the Police.

It was a bit of an impulse decision, but he had relatives in the Police and so he had respect for what they did, and it was a good career. He had also heard that they were keen to use technology more and more to solve crimes and this sounded like it might be an opportunity to use his skills. When the Cyber Crime Unit launched, he jumped at it straight away.

Penny wasn't really into computers in the same way Billy was. She had gone to Uni (1st in Psychology from Cambridge) and saw the Police as somewhere she could exercise her interest in the human psyche. She was fascinated by what drove people to behave and act as they did. She had been introduced to Criminal Psychology as one of the modules on her degree course in the 2nd year and had really been interested in it. They looked at cases that had used Psychology to catch the criminal—like Ted Bundy the serial killer and John Wayne Gacy Jnr, the 'clown killer'—these had gripped her, and she wanted more of that to wrap her large brain around.

Penny was into growing her career and she planned (schemed?) her rise to the top. Everyone was surprised when she joined her county Police Force. A 1st in Psychology from Cambridge and she wanted to stay in Norfolk. They understood the police and her desire to get into Criminal Psychology but surely the Met Police would snap her up? Penny knew the Met would take her, but they would also take the top 5% from around the UK and she felt that it would be harder to shine with peers as good as her.

Her Dad had always told her 'If you want to look beautiful, stand next to an ugly person'. Having been brought up in Norfolk, she couldn't quite bring herself to think of Norfolk people as 'ugly', she loved Norfolk and the people around her. However, as with many rural areas, the young talent often left for the bright lights of a big city, leaving the less talented to make the best of it in the countryside—so Penny stayed to give her talents the best opportunity.

Penny was from an upper-middle-class family—part of the Norfolk 'Country Set' as it were, and she had been brought up with Pony Riding, Piano Lessons and Private school. There had been a lot of expectation on Penny from a young age and so far, she had delivered on it—that is until she joined the Police. Her parents saw that as a comedown and initially Penny had absolutely played up to that, rebelling against her parents. However, she actually was fascinated by criminals and the police work, so it became more a labour of love than just something to spite her parents.

She was a little 'horsey' looking but a pretty young girl who had grown into a tall, slim, attractive young woman and who knew how to dress for the occasion and how to behave in every circumstance (private schooling paying off there)—it was all this combined with her top-notch brain, that gave her confidence (sometimes a little too much) and she was determined to make the most of her God-given talents in the pursuit of her career.

So, Penny had conspired to avoid the Met's advances and enrolled on the Norfolk Constabularies new intake 2 years earlier. She was on the fast path plan, of course, and had already been spotted as a potential highflyer. She had learnt about basic policing fast and spent many extra hours that should have been off-duty, volunteering to help with legwork on any investigations that had a slightly 'intellectual' angle to them. But after two years, she was not getting any closer to criminal psychology work—maybe she had underestimated the number of Psychopaths there were in Norfolk—perhaps it was only city air that turned people into Psychos? That hadn't come up in her degree course!

When she saw the request for officers to transfer to the Cyber Crime Unit, she had initially dismissed it. Everything she knew about computers came from the overuse of Instagram, Pinterest and Snapchat with her friends. But then she heard that Jane Porter was going to head up the new unit and had been promoted to Detective Inspector as well—Penny couldn't miss the chance to follow Jane's rising star.

Penny did admire Jane, but it was more the fact that she knew Jane was a big champion for women's progress within the police, especially into senior roles. Penny believed that equal opportunities within the workplace should apply to both women and men, but she wasn't going to worry too much about riding the wave of women being given 'priority' for promotion in order to re-balance the in-equality of the last few decades. So, the day after Jane Porter's new appointment had been announced, Penny put in her unit transfer request. It went through with lightning-fast speed; which Penny took to mean that Jane wanted her talent. It didn't cross her mind that her current boss may have wanted shot of the talented (and she knew it) Miss Moore....

Chapter 10
Family Pressures

Amelia wanted to stay strong for her children and she managed it for the first few months. She got a cousin to arrange the sale of the motorbike business assets. They didn't get much, really just the value of the bikes he had refurbished over the years, along with the stock of spare parts and equipment. The workshop itself was rented and the landlord had been sympathetic but wanted to re-rent it quickly—so they had to sell everything at a reduced price for speed.

She was determined that money would be put aside for Eb and maybe even Su's education, but that meant getting a job to pay for their day to day living. Amelia had worked since she was fourteen of course and wasn't scared of hard labour, but she had to balance that with being available for the children—the same problem single parents the world over have.

What the world doesn't have everywhere are employers who care about the plight of single parents. Nigeria certainly didn't have any laws or benefits in place to help support families in this situation. So, with some help from her wider family and Eb, just turned twelve, sensing he had to step up as the 'man of the house', Amelia took a full-time job in a factory.

Amelia was only around five feet tall and was slightly plump but not really fat. She was not a beauty but made the best of what she had. Although since Dev had died, she didn't really see the point in making herself look nice—she did the basics for the kids, but that was it. She was very house proud, even though their bungalow had seen better days and could cook as good as anyone in the community. Eb and Su would still read with her every night, snuggled up on a second-hand settee—she never wore perfume (another luxury she couldn't afford), but always smelt of fresh baking and that was perfume to Eb and Su—that was the smell of their Mum and they loved her.

The factory-made counterfeit designer clothes. Whilst this didn't sit too well with Amelia's spiritual and moral beliefs, she had to agree with herself to compromise those for the sake of her family—another universal dilemma for many. She 'allowed' her morals to slip even further when it came to 'perks of the job', often leaving with a fake FCUK t-shirt or fake Tommy Hilfiger underpants stuffed into her own underwear—it was the only time in her life that she was glad of the extra weight she had always carried.

The children grew bigger (more fake clothes 'borrowed' from the factory) and ate more and needed more clothes, and that was without the schoolbooks she had to buy for Eb. When he turned 11, she had managed to get him into a half-decent secondary school that was run by a charity—there were no school fees as Eb had taken an exam that showed he had excellent maths and language skills, but she did have to buy all his books and writing materials.

Eb was excited by school and prepared for it by reading any books he could get his hands on. However, he also took his perceived domestic duties responsibly. For Eb, this meant making sure Su did the housework, washing and preparing dinner whilst Mum was at the factory—equality of the sexes not having quite reached the Nigerian working man's culture yet. Despite this gender division, Eb pulled his weight—literally, as he worked from 6 a.m. until 8 a.m. pulling a trolley with market produce (mainly vegetables) from the warehouse to the marketplace for a small local grocer.

Then in the late afternoon, he went back to the market and cleared rubbish with a few other boys of his age. Neither of these 'jobs' earned him enough to make a big contribution financially to his mother, but the free fruit, veg and anything else useful he found at the market at the end of a day, more than made up for it.

Even with the factory job, Eb's jobs, Su helping out around the house and the perks of the job both she and Eb got, Amelia could not make ends meet and pay for schoolbooks. Her wider family tried to help, but they had their own growing children and needs. She refused to touch the children's education fund (ignoring the fact that schoolbooks were part of their education—she thought she should save that for Eb to perhaps go to University) and so decided to get a loan.

Loans in Lagos city at the time were arranged through a local agent but were linked to a larger organisation. That is to say, the local loan shark had the backing (and muscle) of the Lagos Mafia. With many people advising her against it, Amelia went to the 'Bank' (a dingy coffee house at the back of the market). She wasn't scared to go on her own—small she may be, but she knew how to look after herself having grown up in a rough neighbourhood—and she knew or at least recognised many of the young men hanging around outside the coffee house, they were only a few years older than Eb. She felt that although they were here as 'guards', that they would all still be washing the dishes for their Mum after the evening meal—they were just young lads trying to scrap a few pennies together—no reason to be scared of them.

The loan shark, on the other hand, he was a little scarier. Although, again, not very old, about eighteen or nineteen perhaps. He had some older boys around his table in the coffee shop and Amelia did think about leaving when she was sure she caught a flash of the sun off what looked like a metal object under one of the boy's jackets. However, business is business and the loan shark flashed her a big smile and stood, inviting her to take a seat.

He was not exactly the friendliest person in the world, but he wasn't too bad and so they agreed on terms for the loan. Part of this did involve him turning slightly sinister as he explained to her what would happen to her, her family and everyone she loved if she didn't keep up repayments. But then he went back to being the bank manager persona and wished her well. There was a piece of paper that outlined what Amelia had borrowed and what she had to pay each month but not much else—certainly no official contract, but Amelia understood the 'small print' as he had outlined it and swore to herself to make the payments on time.

Who knows, perhaps with a little more economy in her own diet, she could save some more money and pay it off in full within a few months. She took Eb to the local bookshop for some more schoolbooks that afternoon and made herself happy with the knowledge she was supporting her children and losing some of that pesky extra weight around her middle—this loan was a win/win situation!

Chapter 11
Digital Life Meets Real Life

Joseph wasn't her 'boyfriend' and so Elizbeth didn't really know why she hadn't told Philip about him. She convinced herself that her real life and her digital life were separate. She had already slightly re-invented herself on Facebook and Pinterest, so she didn't want to confuse that persona with her slightly older, less active self that Philip came to help every few days.

Philip noticed that Liz was more perky and told him off less than previously. Initially, he just thought she was getting used to him and accepting that he was there to help her because she needed it. She was not 'old', she just had some mobility issues and that was only because she had been in an accident. Once she started being nicer and chatting more openly to her, Philip could see she wasn't old in body or mind. Philip was happily married to Anthony but had always had a bit of an eye for attractive ladies. Not in a sexual way but more admiration for their beauty. He could see now that Liz had been, no, was still a beautiful woman—and that hair, wow.

Elizabeth was making the effort to befriend Philip because she wanted to ground herself in real life. She had been spending a lot of time in the digital world and was a little worried she was losing touch with reality. Philip was her lifeline to the real world and as her digital life developed, she valued her friendship with Philip more and more.

As a child of the late 1990s, Philip had been brought up with technology all around him. As a modern Gay man in the twenty-tens, he was a prolific user of social media and apps—he thought he would find a life partner on Grinder but was disappointed to only find sex (well, disappointed is probably an overstatement as he took full advantage of this discovery but only for a short while!). He eventually found a community of Gay men in Norfolk called 'Gay Outdoor Club' via Facebook and it was on one of their walks at Wells-next-thesea, a lovely seaside town in North Norfolk, that he found Anthony. It wasn't a whirlwind romance but rather a friendship that grew into love. They were both 'out' to their family and friends and had chosen to get married the previous year. Although they decided not to go for the modern Gay trend of adopting a baby, and instead opted for Pugs—3 to be precise—Kylie (Modern gay icon), Judy (Original gay icon), and Paul (as in Hollywood from Bake-off—a new gay icon in the making they thought).

Philip often talked to Anthony about Liz and they liked to discuss what they thought was best for her—she had an interesting background from her travels but was a little closed off and Anthony was convinced Philip was 'good for her', so he encouraged Philip to visit Liz more than his official obligations required—he also liked the compassion Philip showed for Liz and thought it was a charitable thing for him to do.

Elizabeth had never met Anthony but felt like she had—and the dogs—they were Philip's go-to subject for conversation! She didn't mind really—it filled the silence that made up the rest of her time. She had no objection to Gays (although Philip was her only real contact with anyone Gay) and felt that any kind of love in the world was good.

The conversation about her digital life came up one day when she had forgotten to put the iPad in her knitting bag before Philip came into the living room. It was on the poof that he normally sat on next to her to take her blood pressure and he had to lift it and hand it to her.

He decided to take the plunge.

"So how are you finding the World Wide Web then Liz?"

"It's just called 'The Web' these days Philip," she said caught slightly off guard. "And I don't just go on the web—I use Apps as well" recovering slightly and feeling she could boast about her digital capability.

"Well, that's nice—I love apps. What Apps do you use?"

Was she going to get into this with Philip—she hesitated to wonder if she should take the step to blend her physical and digital worlds together—what could be the worst that could happen, she thought? OK.

"Well, at first I only used Facebook, but I kept getting creepy men contacting me and it felt a bit dirty, so I stopped that for a while and switched to using Pinterest, which was much more pleasant—people seemed to like nice things on there. I started 'following' people because that's how it works Philip."

Philip didn't interrupt her to remind her he was a child of the Internet and knew more about it than she ever would, "Who were interested in Motorbikes because I have good memories of Edward and me going out on his motorbikes. Anyway, there are lots of people who like motorbikes, particularly the old fashioned ones that Edward used to own and so I started 'liking' their posts and they then followed me, but I didn't have anything for them to see really, so I decided to dig out some old photos of Edward's motorbikes and took photos of them with my iPad—you can take photos of photos with an iPad, did you know that Philip?" she didn't wait for a reply.

"So, then people could see that I wasn't just following them without any reason and that I had a genuine interest and my own experience with motorbikes. Well, then lots more people started to follow me because some of the bikes Edward had were really rare and people hadn't seen many of them. I got lots of comments and even some questions," she had poured all this out, clearly having not realised how much she had wanted to share her digital adventures with someone 'real'. However, she now paused, not because she didn't have more to say, but because she was wondering if she should say anything about Joseph and her increasingly frequent and long messaging chats with him.

Philip took the opportunity the pause presented to re-balance the conversation into something a bit more two-way, "Well, I know exactly what you mean about Pinterest. Anthony and me just love being involved with all the Pug lovers out there. Everyone is just so friendly like you say and the Pugs are to...die.... for.... yum!" Philip went on and on and couldn't help whipping out his iPhone to show Liz all the pictures of his and Anthony's three pugs and then lots more pictures of pugs in all sorts of costumes and poses on Pinterest.

Elizabeth not only found it exhausting but released she had lost her moment of focus and decided to let it go—revealing Joseph could wait for another day. Anyway, it's not like he was her boyfriend...

Chapter 12
Zeros, Ones and Thoughts

The Cyber Crime Unit had been set up in what had been a conference room at the front of the Norfolk Constabulary Head Quarters just outside Norwich. It was a modern building built in 2000—all glass and shiny metal. Originally hailed as 'seeing Norfolk policing into the next millennium', it was already totally overcrowded, and the conference room was the only space available. The room was about 40 meters square and was laid out with open plan desks, except for Jane Porter's office at one end and a big projector and screen at the other end.

It was at this screen that everyone gathered around daily to give Jane and each other updates on their projects. The dynamic in the room wasn't as exciting as you might think, given the modern work they were doing—Jane put this down to the type of people who liked doing the deep computer work the unit did, but it could certainly do with being a little livelier. The work was serious of course and the computers they had purchased were not your regular PCWorld type—these were meaty machines—Dual Intel Core i9 processors, 128GB RAM, Nvidia RTX graphics cards—they even had an Amazon Alexa installed—it had been insisted on by the team as they claimed criminals were starting to use AI (Artificial Intelligence) to commit crimes—but as far as Jane could see, they were just using it to order their shopping!

There were only six people in the unit when Penny joined and other than Jane Porter, they were all men ranging from eighteen to twenty-six. They were all fairly geeky, both in computer terms and general life terms. The reason Billy stood out to Penny as a potential 'geek buddy' was because he was the only one not wearing head-phones, with his eyes completed glued to the monitor in front of him and who said hello that first morning—it was the most basic form of communication but important for building a relationship.

"Hi, I'm Penny. Is this desk free?" she asked pointing at the desk next to him.

"Sure, help yourself. I'm Billy," he held out his hand.

"Thanks, Billy—I'm Penny. First day in the unit and I am a little apprehensive." She wasn't at all apprehensive (not her style) and was using her psychology knowledge in the most basic way—show someone that they have the power to help you and they will, then they will feel good about it and actual attribute that feeling to you—simple!

"I have only been here a few weeks myself but happy to show you the ropes," he said with sincerity. He was happy to help—nice to have someone around that spoke. The other guys didn't want to talk or go to the canteen together for lunch and having a beer after work was something they just didn't understand. Billy had older brothers and they all worked in manual labour jobs, so a beer after work was more or less the law.

"How about we go and get a coffee now and I can fill you in on what we are trying to do to get the unit established?" he offered.

"That would be great, thanks."

"This was going to be easy," she thought.

They walked to the canteen and Penny bought them a coffee each. Despite sounding very Norfolk and looking a bit like a farmer in a police uniform, she knew that Billy must be clever to have made it into this unit or at least have a special skill they needed.

"What attracted you to this unit then Billy?"

"Well, I know computers like the back of my hand," he subconsciously held it up for her inspection.

"That's great. What Uni did you attend?" she trusted it wouldn't be as good as hers.

"Didn't go to Uni—waste of time and money—taught myself everything I know in my bedroom," puffing his chest out slightly. "It's all just zeros and ones, to be honest."

"Oh, right," she tried not to sound too surprised but did wonder how someone without a degree had got into such a specialist and advanced unit.

"Well, if truth be known, I taught myself a bit too much and nearly went the other way!" he laughed.

Penny didn't understand, "How do you mean?"

Lowering his voice to a conspiratorial level, "Well, I got into hacking, didn't I." Penny looked initially shocked and then a little impressed—maybe she had picked the right Geek!

"I was pretty good at it too—not many systems could keep me out. I mean, just the basic stuff—I can't break into a bank or the Kremlin," he said as if this was obvious. "The thing is, a lot of the criminals we will be trying to catch use hacking of one sort or another and so I decided to turn what I knew against them—so that's why they picked me for the unit."

Penny really didn't know much more about hacking than a layperson would, but she did know that the people behind it often had agendas and that meant her psychology could come into play.

"What about you—you a computer expert then?" Billy questioned.

"Psychology," she said as if it were nothing special.

"How do you mean?" asked Billy slightly puzzled and suddenly wondering if she was in the unit to 'assess' them all.

"That's my speciality. The Psychology of the criminal mind," she paused for dramatic effect.

Billy was impressed. He hadn't met a psychologist before, but he knew you had to be clever to understand it all and he knew it was fast becoming a popular practice to use when trying to track down criminals. It occurred to him that he might have got lucky introducing himself to Penny—he was good at using technology to find criminals, she was good at understanding the criminal mind—those two things together could make them a powerful team. He didn't really know how to suggest this but decided to just wait and see if they developed a close working relationship.

Penny had no such lack of confidence. She had already come to this conclusion and wanted to crack on. "Listen, how about we go back to the office and you show me all the clever tech stuff you have done so far, then I can apply some psychology to your results and we might come up with something together that will impress Jane—how does that sound?"

Billy was used to being a little more tentative with things, but there was something about Penny and he trusted her. "Like I use my hacking skills to find the Zeros and Ones. And you use your psychology to interpret them? Yeah, sounds great!" and with that, they started their partnership.

Chapter 13
Mr JG

Eb loved the school and started to thrive immediately. Teachers could see he had a good aptitude for learning—the proverbial sponge. He turned up early and stayed late. He handed in homework on time and got great marks on his work. His only failing was that he sometimes looked tired and yawned in class, but then they didn't know about his extra work at the market. Eb made up for this by being a star pupil and the school recognised his potential—they felt he could go all the way.

His favourite subject was English—speaking and writing it. Eb knew that English was the language of the business world and if he wanted to be something big in life and become successful, then he needed to have an excellent command of the English language. The teacher for English was an expat Englishman—Eb supposed a gentleman of some distinction—Mr Joseph Grey or JG as he seemed to like to be called.

JG took Eb under his wing within a few days. He could see Eb's potential and knew about his family situation, he wanted to help nurture Eb. Eb found himself liking JG more and more—when he found out that he used to have a Kawasaki Z1 motorbike and loved everything about old bikes, Eb nearly hugged him—they were going to be close friends.

Joseph himself had come to Nigeria on a personal mission. A man of some light spirituality, but some heavy philosophy about the citizens of the world helping each other. He had been a marketing man in the UK for years but had grown disillusioned with getting people to buy frivolous stuff that they didn't need and in a world with so much waste already. With no family to talk of and his old age looming fast (he was actually only fifty-nine at the time), he decided to go somewhere he thought he could help people.

He jacked in his job, sold his beloved BSA Goldstar Clubman motorbike, put his few possessions in storage and bought a ticket to Nigeria. He wasn't completely naïve and so reached out to the Save The Children charity who operated relief work in Nigeria, to see what his approach should be—they hooked him up with a school building charity and he did six months of hard labour until the school was built on the outskirts of Lagos city.

Joseph was a big man—broad shoulders, big hands and six foot four inches—He stopped shaving his square jaw when he moved to Nigeria (hot water was hard to come by on his makeshift home on the building site) and he had developed a white stubble beard, although he kept it short to not let himself totally go. He was strong as well, having spent his spare time in the UK at the gym and doing triathlons. The hot sun in Nigeria has darkened his white skin so that he looked more European than English and overall these multiple changes had made him a handsome older man. Of course, he never saw himself like this and was unaware or perhaps oblivious to the local women that turned their heads when he walked by.

He had planned to go home following the completion of the school, thinking he would have exercised his moral and sociological obligations to the world. But he didn't feel like it, so he just stayed. He had learnt some Hausa (the native language) from his fellow builders and felt he could communicate and that's how he got involved teaching English in the school he helped build—English was the official language of Nigeria these days, but many families still couldn't read or write it. They paid him enough to live on, albeit frugally and he made some friendships in the neighbourhood. His actions of building the school and then continuing to contribute through educating the children who came to the school made him a well-liked and respected member of the community. An outsider still but a nice one.

JG stayed in Nigeria for two reasons—one good and one a bit lame—the good reason was that he could see the benefit that he could bring to the school and pupils like Eb. It was good to be making a difference and not just moaning about the troubles of the world. It was not that he was a 'do-gooder', more that he had taken more from life than he had given, and it seemed time to give something back. The lame reason, and why he was choosing not to give something back in the UK, was because he lacked the confidence to fall in love and was avoiding it by being in Nigeria.

It's not that he couldn't have found love with a Nigerian woman, but they were all taken it seemed and there was no older person dating 'scene' as a result. He had been in love once back in the UK and had lived with that lovely lady for 10 years. They shared an interest in Art and Theatre, eating out and the English countryside, as well as keeping fit. They had never been blessed with children, but they kept themselves occupied with hobbies and it didn't seem to matter.

Until one day it did, and she ran off with a 'younger model' who had the ability to give her a child. Nearly 20 years had not dulled the pain of that loss and so he had reason to avoid love and was doing a good job of it in Nigeria.

Now 64, JG had been in Nigeria for 5 years and had not only helped build and staff the school but had raised more money to have computers and the internet put in the school. He was interested in technology, although not that tech-savvy himself, and he saw the benefits it would bring to this next generation of men and women. He had managed to get a small computer room kitted out with two computers and an internet hub—a slow but reliable connection to the wider world.

Of course, Eb was one of the pupils that benefited most from the computers and using his English skills he was able to communicate with people all over the world. He was also able to look up more and more information, feeding his thirst for knowledge. Being a young inquisitive adolescent, Eb looked at the darker side of the internet as well. That's not to say he spent all day surfing for naked women like most UK teens do when they first get free access. But rather that he started to show an interest in hacking and internet crime—he didn't have a bad bone in his body and would never do anything bad, but it was a mysterious world out there and it intrigued him nonetheless.

JG could see this and knew that blocking access or certain websites or activities would just make them more attractive—forbidden fruit and all that. So, he gave Eb a free hand but spent some time talking to him about the hidden dangers, not just on the internet but in general life. JG trusted Eb to be able to know right from wrong. Eb enjoyed this trust and promised he would never betray it.

Chapter 14
A Long-Forgotten Flutter

Elizabeth had a number of followers and people she followed on Pinterest and Facebook. She had even struck up a few closer relationships with some of them on Messenger, just like she had with Joseph after she met him via the dating website. However, despite her trying to not get obsessed, she was really starting to find Joseph too fascinating and well, yes, attractive. She had never even seen a proper picture of him—just of motorbikes he liked—even his profile picture on the dating website had been a motorbike.

It was just that he was always there for her. When she got fed up with TV or found one of Philip's visits just a little too 'Anthony-pugs-gay…' she could reach out to Joseph and he would chat with her for hours about anything and everything. He wasn't always there it had to be said, but she worked out that he had to sleep and eat. Although she knew he didn't have a family and so his time was his own. Sometimes his responses were a little slow like he was doing something else at the same time as talking to her, but she didn't mind—it felt relaxed like that. She and Teddie had sometimes sat on the settee for the evening and only spoken a few words every hour, but he had been there, just like Joseph was now.

After only a few weeks of getting to know Joseph, he had started to talk about his life in Singapore and how he enjoyed it, but sometimes missed the UK and the old favourites in his life—Marmite; warm beer; Coronation Street etc. Elizabeth saw it as her duty to update him on modern UK society—a lot of this was her parroting out what she heard from Philip, but he seemed very interested and so she continued.

Finally, she plucked up the courage to ask for a picture. Joseph stalled a little saying he didn't have any recent ones, but after about a week, he sent her a picture and she was thrilled. Joseph looked broad and strong. It was hard to tell if he was tall because it was only a head and shoulders shot. He had a gentle white beard that was neatly trimmed, and his skin looked bronzed, overall, he came off looking like a handsome older man.

The background to the picture was of a school sign, but Elizabeth couldn't make it out, so she asked about it. He said this was the school that he worked for. Joseph hadn't mentioned the school in the past and she wondered why. If she was honest with herself, she hadn't even considered he had a job. However, now she had seen his picture and could see he was still relatively young and fit, it made sense that he worked. He played down the work and said it was just some part-time caretaking stuff that he did—nothing special.

When he wasn't telling her about his life or listening to updates about his home country, he was starting to comment on Elizabeth in the pictures and not just the motorbikes. Obviously, he would comment on her gorgeous hair—everyone did—but he would go a little further, "You look radiant in these pictures—I can see the beauty without and within," he once typed.

"That's nice, thank you," she responded, not used to compliments like that these days.

"I mean it," he continued. "It sounds like you have led a lovely life and I am so happy to have become friends with you."

"And me you," she replied. "I have enjoyed chatting with you these last few weeks—I miss having a man my age to chat to."

"Steady on!" he quipped. "You are way older than me."

"By three years, cheeky!" she typed, laughing out loud to the room.

"Does that make me a toy boy?"

"Well, I suppose it would do if were we more than friends…," she was glad he couldn't see her starting to blush.

There was no reply for a moment, and she was left with her heart in her mouth—what was coming over her, she hadn't felt anything like this in years. She hadn't even thought about a new love after Teddie had died, it just hadn't occurred to her. Now, however, she was having feelings for another man—was she able to throw caution to the wind—why shouldn't she. Philip was happy with his gay lover—why couldn't she find fulfilment again with this digital romance that was starting to blossom?

"Anyway, I better be off now," replied Joseph. "I have a busy day ahead. Chat tonight. x." And with that she came crashing back down to earth, replacing what had become a definite heart 'flutter' with a feeling of embarrassment. What had she done wrong? Had she gone too far? He was the one who started it—calling himself her 'Toy-boy'. Elizabeth was confused and felt a mixture of anger and shame. She burst into tears and with desperation not to lose her new love (was it love?), she typed "OK. It was fun joking around tonight—we are funny sometimes. Chat tomorrow. x."

She hoped that trying to play the whole thing down as a joke would rescue the friendship. She had been so stupid but then so had he. He had started being romantic and then realised she was a crippled old woman stuck miles away in the UK and that there was no future. She shouldn't have responded in the way she did. She felt rubbish and got herself up on her sticks and started the going to bed routine—muttering to herself about being a silly old woman.

In bed, she gently sobbed and couldn't bear to replay the evening in her mind. But it would keep replaying… she HAD felt something real—a flutter for sure. And as she went over and over the words he said, she was convinced he had meant them and that he felt something for her as well. She had stopped crying and was convincing herself that she had not misread the situation—a flutter didn't lie. So why did he suddenly stop…. Maybe he was playing hard to get!

Chapter 15
Billy Goes Spiking

Jane had hardly taken her coat off and sat down in her glass ('the doors always open') office when the dynamic duo burst in. Despite both being well-trained officers who were used to being disciplined around senior officers, they stood at the open door looking like a couple of 8-year olds who needed to go to the toilet. They were, however, too well trained to go into their commanding officer's office without an invite.

"Come in Billy and Penny. What can I do for you this bright and early?" she looked them up and down. "Have you two been here all night? You look, erm, slightly dishevelled."

"Yes, Ma'am," they chimed in unison.

"We pulled on a thread just before we were about to go home," Billy said excitedly.

"Yes, and that thread turned out to be a tapestry of intrigue and mystery!" Penny warmed up her story-telling ability.

"Very poetic. Why don't you both sit down and 'unveil' the mystery for me?" Jane was experienced at letting officers work with their own medium. She didn't have a meeting for 20 minutes and she was sure she could be a supportive boss in that short time before calming them down and returning them to the slightly more mundane task of sifting through reported identify thefts in the local area—most of which turned out to be a teenage offspring pinching Mum or Dad's credit card without their knowledge.

"Well, you remember that ex-fireman who reported he had been conned out of several hundred pounds by a supposedly 'new love' he found via the online dating website?" Penny started and Billy was fine to let her lead, this was what she did best.

"Erm, remind me," Jane asked.

"Well, there have been a few of them actually—A fireman, a farmer, a solicitor, a teacher—it seems that people with all-encompassing jobs look to the internet for love," continued Penny. "Anyway, this guy who was about 45 and had stopped being a fireman and realised he had missed out on a relationship, went onto this dating website for people that have been roaming the world and not settled down but want to now."

"Sounds like they are just after a ticket home," mused Jane.

"Well, that's the whole point—they are but are being upfront about it—you pay to bring me home and put me up and we might have a chance of a relationship. I kind of like the honesty and it probably works for some people," explained Penny.

"I long for the old-fashioned way of meeting someone at a local party," Jane tutted.

"Oh, it's much easier via online dating Ma'am—you don't waste time getting off with lots of people you have nothing in common with," replied Penny matter-of-factly.

"That's the fun part!" exclaimed Jane, suddenly blushing and realising she was going a bit off track. "Anyway, so what happened to this fireman chap?"

"It's a standard story—a bit of flirting back and forth through the dating website, then if they hit it off, they make direct contact via email or Facebook etc and the whole thing goes from there. Well, that's what happened with this guy and they agreed she would fly home and live with him. She was in Singapore and so needed a flight home from there. Then this is where the con comes in....

"She says the airline will only allow HER to buy the ticket with HER credit card, rather than him buy the ticket for her, which is what they had agreed. So, he sends her the money and says she has bought the ticket. Of course, she hasn't, she just pockets the money. Normally, at this point, they stop all communication and disappear and that's the man out of pocket and nothing he or we can do about it."

Jane knew all this of course but could tell that there was something different about this one "Right, got all that—so what happened differently in this case?"

"Well, the woman scamming the fireman decided to get more money from him—this is a new thing that we haven't seen before, although some of our colleagues in other counties have reported it happening more and more," replied Penny.

"How did she do that—if she didn't turn up in the UK then the fireman must have smelled a rat?" asked Jane.

"We are not sure exactly how she continued to convince him that she was legit, but she did, and he agreed to send her more money," Penny explained.

"And that's when we found out we could track them down!" interjected Billy with excitement.

Penny let Billy explain how they couldn't get enough information from one financial transaction, but that if a second one was made via the same route, then they could use the similarities to track down the user who was making the request. It was all based around them being able to get a warrant to access a money transfer companies record—one transaction wasn't enough to prove to a judge that fraud was being committed, but two was. In this case, the transactions had passed, and they wouldn't be able to use this case to get a warrant, but now that they knew they were looking for victims who had been scammed twice, they had some hope they could track the scammers down. The best bit was that the two transactions had both used the same username and Billy had tracked down the scammer online via that—they were closing in…

Chapter 16
A Loving Ambush

Amelia was so proud of Eb. He was excelling at school and seemed to have formed a close relationship with one teacher, in particular, a Mr Grey, who sounded very nice. His school reports were showing that he was an enthusiastic and capable learner, with a talent for Maths and English Language. Traditionally, it was the father's duty to talk to the children about education and make sure they were doing their best. Even though she wished Dev was still here to do it, she made sure she talked to Eb about his education regularly.

Over the next few years, she diligently attended his parents evening and any events that the school put on. There were fund-raising fetes and concerts, which she quite liked—it made her feel like she was part of the educational establishment, something she had not actually ever been in her childhood. Eb was particularly fond of acting and had joined the school's drama club—fortunately, this was a lunchtime club and it didn't interfere with his work after school. However, it did mean that Eb never got involved in the various plays the school did each year. Amelia asked him about this.

"You seem to love that lunchtime drama club?" Amelia brought up one mealtime.

"Yes, it's really great—I love playing other characters," Eb replied with enthusiasm. This was nice Amelia thought, as he often was a little withdrawn these days. Nothing more than he was becoming a teenager, she was sure. But it would be nice if he showed more enthusiasm for things.

"And guess who runs the club? … JG!" Eb was positively animated compared to recent weeks.

"You really like Mr Grey, don't you? I like him as well—he has always been a big supporter of yours each parents evening."

"Yeah, JG is the greatest!"

"Does he do the school plays as well?" Amelia asked, already knowing the answer.

"I guess," Eb was back to his lacklustre replies.

"You could always ask for time off work when the plays come around…," again knowing this would cause a negative reaction.

"Mum! You know that my boss would go mad if I asked for time off. Anyway, it's not like we can afford for me to have time off—we need the money!" Eb was in full teenage anger mode now.

"Well, I think we could afford it. I have managed to pay the bills and loan payments and have kept a little aside each week. So, let's see what happens next term, shall we?" motherly calming mode on full power.

"Purfhh!" was the teenager's conclusive remark.

Amelia wasn't any more interfering a mother than any other mother who wanted her child to do well, but unbeknownst to Eb, she was already in regular contact with Mr Grey and this conversation had been staged by her as the opening scene in her and Mr Grey's plan to get Eb on the school stage. Joseph, as she had come to know him, had spoken to her at a parent's evening when Eb was off talking to his mates. He had been keen to try to recruit her in encouraging Eb to take his acting further and the first step is to be in that year's production in Autumn—A traditional folklore play in the traditional Yoruba style. Amelia jumped at his suggestion that they should collude in getting Eb involved and so the plotting began…

It was the spring holidays and nearly the start of the next term when Amelia brought up Eb's acting and his job.

"You know I said we were doing OK with money, Eb?" opened Amelia.

"Did you?" replied Eb uninterestedly.

"Yes. When we were last talking, a few weeks ago, about you giving up your job so that you could concentrate more on your acting with the school and Mr Grey," she reminded him.

"Hhmmm. Funny that JG mentioned a few days ago the new school play he was doing this Autumn—it's like you two are ganging up on me…." Eb could feel an ambush coming.

"Did he?" Amelia tried innocence.

"Mum! What's going on?" Eb didn't like being manipulated.

There was a knock at the door and Su ran to open it. Returning a few seconds later with JG.

"JG! What are you doing here?" Eb realised the answer before he had even finished the question.

"Eb, please welcome our guest in and offer Mr Grey a seat and a drink." Amelia was acting as if they had visitors for dinner every day, which of course they never had before.

"Good evening, Mrs Azikiwe. Hello, Eb and Su," said JG with an air of politeness that Eb was not used to from him.

Amelia quickly decided to confess "Eb, I invited Mr Grey here because he and I both think you are wasting your acting talents and you should join in with the school play—I am sorry, but I knew you wouldn't discuss with me about giving up your job, so I asked him to come and help me convince you."

Su passed round the drinks, a simple fruit mix, and they all sat down. They talked about school, both Eb's achievements and also how Su was doing and JG talked a little about his life in the UK, which fascinated Amelia and Su—Eb had heard much of it before. It wasn't until they had finished the main course and Amelia had brought out a big bowl of fresh fruits that she had got from the market that afternoon, that the subject of Eb giving up his job came up again. Eb had forgotten about it and such was his adoration for JG that he was just enjoying him being at their home.

"So, Eb. I know you enjoy your job, but your mother tells me that she is able to support the family without you doing it anymore," opened JG.

"Well, I feel like I should still bring money into the house—after all, I am the man of the house," Eb replied with no little feeling.

"That's true. Well, perhaps there is a way you could do both…." JG was smiling.

"What do you mean?" Eb asked puzzled.

"I need someone to help design the set and scenery and help me build it—the school give me a small budget to do this and I thought I could pay you to help me?" JG offered.

"Oh, that would be great to work with you on the set and scenery. I have helped my boss at the market with building some stalls and so I know how to use the tools," was Eb's enthusiastic reply. "Although I would kinda miss the market and I don't want to let my boss there down—he has been good to me over the years."

"Mr Lees is an old friend of your Dad and that's how you got the job in the first place. He will be pleased to see you doing something you love. You don't need to worry about that," said his Mum.

"I feel like it might be letting Dad down if I don't work for his old friend," Eb looked conflicted.

"Well, let's you and I both go and see Mr Lees and I am sure we can sort it out," said Amelia putting her hand on his shoulder. "So that's all sorted then—thank you Mr Grey for giving Eb this opportunity."

"Well, I like to see everyone playing to their strengths and it will be great to have a strong male actor for the play," said JG rising to leave. "Thank you for a lovely meal and a pleasant evening. Rehearsals start next Tuesday Eb when school is back from holidays, but your new job starts after school Monday—so don't be late and bring some work clothes as we could get messy!"

"Thanks, JG—I won't let you down," Eb was shaking his hand vigorously as he saw him out of the house.

"I suppose I will have to let you off going behind my back with my teacher Mum, as it turned out to be so great a result—thanks Mum," Eb gently planted a kiss on his Mums cheek and went to his bedroom.

Amelia set about clearing up from the evening's meal and she was happy—her job and money were OK, her children were getting a decent education, her son had a great teacher and was going to be a star actor. For the first time since Dev died, she really felt positive about the future.

Chapter 17
Still Got It

Philip let himself in as normal with the key Elizabeth had given him reluctantly after the first week of his visits. She had initially said he didn't need it as she would always let him in, but it ended up taking her 10 mins to get to the door each time during those first visits and eventually she gave in and told him to get a spare key cut. He got one cut straight away and treated himself to a picture keyring with a picture of his pugs—adorable he thought.

Elizabeth was waiting in a dressing gown as normal for her massage and manipulation. Philip would give her legs and lower back a basic muscle rub with some slightly perfumed oil (the NHS only provided non-perfumed, but Philip had decided to buy his own as it was much nicer to leave a room with flowery smells) and then do some light twisting and stretching of Elizabeth's legs in order to make them more flexible. The treatment did seem to be making some progress, slow but sure. Elizabeth certainly seemed to be standing taller and straighter today, but there was something else he couldn't quite put his finger on.

"Is that a new dressing gown, Liz?" Philip asked whilst starting to set up his massage table.

"What, this old thing?" Elizabeth meowed and fluffed the hems of the silk gown as if she were an actress from the '60s.

"Erm, well it doesn't look old to me—it looks expensive," said Philip a little surprised with this different persona that Elizabeth was projecting.

"My Teddie bought it back for me from China a few years ago as an anniversary present and I thought I would get some use out of it," she said a little more matter-of-factly.

"Well, it suits you Liz—very Asian beauty if I may say so!" Philip was never one to miss out on a flamboyant look.

"Do you really think so? I mean… do I look… 'sexy'?" Elizabeth went from blushing to purring to coy in a matter of seconds. Philip wasn't sure what was going on but went with the flow.

"Of course you do 'daaarrrlling'," he drawled theatrically.

They both laughed and the slightly weird atmosphere seemed to break and return to normal. Liz took the robe off to reveal some of the normal vest top and shorts she wore for these sessions and climbed onto the massage table with Philip supporting her gently.

They didn't speak during the 20 minutes of light massage, but that was sometimes the case. Elizabeth knew that if she kept quiet then Philip would respect the silence, but if she started a conversation then he would be off and there would be no shutting him up. Philip concentrated on the massage, but he pondered this slightly different Elizabeth as he worked. He looked down at her and took her in. Being gay he had never looked at her as a sexual figure and he had gotten used to seeing her in nothing but practically her underwear several times a week for the last year. But, like many men who were a little more in tune with their feminine side, he could admire a woman's body and see the beauty in it. Liz had a great body for her age and considering her lack of mobility. Yes, a few extra curves and bumps but still very trim and definitely sexy. Had she been messing around or was there something deeper worrying her he wondered?

His thought was answered a moment later. As she turned over at the end of the massage to lie on her back for the leg work, she stopped on her side with her arm propped under her chin and one leg slightly crooked above the other—much like a model might do for a lying down photoshoot. Philip felt the atmosphere coming back.

"But seriously Philip. Do you think I am attractive?" Liz asked with a bit more seriousness.

Philip decided to stick with the comedy approach he had 20 mins earlier, "Well, my love, you're not really my department if you know what I mean (giggle). But I know some guys who wouldn't say 'no'!" he replied with a wink.

"No, I'm not joking around Philip. I want your honest opinion." She sat up and grabbed the dressing gown around her. Her lip started to wobble.

"Oh my god, Liz! What's the matter? Sorry, darling, don't get upset. I was only having a laugh. I thought you were just teasing this old gay." He was mortified to have upset her. Philip had grown very fond of Elizabeth and wouldn't do anything to upset her.

Elizabeth wasn't exactly crying, but she was upset. She didn't really know what had come over her and why she was being so silly. Well, except she did. It was that silly conversation with Joseph last night—she had tossed and turned all night worrying about it. She was convinced that it was her—she was old and unattractive, past her prime and Joseph had realised that.

"Let's have a cuppa and a chat," Philip decided that leg stretches could be skipped today, and mental care was to take priority. He was good at supporting people with stress and anxiety—Anthony had said so. Anthony had bought Philip an audiobook course in life coaching and he had tried out his newly learned techniques on Anthony's sister when she came last Christmas and was stressed about cooking the turkey—it seemed to have worked, although it might have been the sherry.

"Thanks, Philip. Sorry, I am being silly," Elizabeth sniffed.

"No, you are not. Something's niggling you and we should talk about it. Come on, sit down and I will get us those biscuits you keep for visitors." He walked over and flicked the kettle on. Elizabeth knew that she would have to come clean about Joseph. She couldn't have an outburst like this in front of Philip, who was becoming a trusted confidant, and then not explain why.

She breathed in deep and let out a slow breath, "Philip, I need to tell you about something, well, someone that I have met online."

Philip almost collapsed into the seat next to her on the sofa and grabbed her hand. He didn't know what she had been going to say, but he wasn't expecting something like this—whatever this was.

He remembered his coaching 'training', "Go on Liz. I'm listening."

Chapter 18
Man-in-the-Middle

Jane picked up the phone and spoke to her PA, "Jeff, please can you postpone my next meeting."

Jane was gripped but needed to concentrate so she didn't lose the thread, "OK, so we have a username for this supposed con person—what can we do with that?"

"Well, in my experience, people are lazy and insecure when it comes to creating usernames and passwords—they don't want to have to remember too many and so they re-use them all the time or a variant of them," Billy had taken up the explaining now that Penny had pitched the story so well.

Jane thought this would not be a good point to agree that usernames and passwords were annoying and that she always used the same ones—anyway, she hadn't told anyone her cat was called Tiddles, so 'T1ddle5#' was probably keeping her safe for now.

Billy continued, "This person had done exactly that and so I set about looking on various social media sites for the same username that they used to make the money transfer. They had used the same username or very similar on Facebook, Twitter, Pinterest, and Instagram."

"OK—I have heard of all of those, although I don't know how to use half of them," Jane said with some disbelief that so many social media sites existed—no wonder people never met each other down the pub anymore, she thought.

"The activity on those social media sites backs up our view that these scammers are operating from Singapore for sure," Billy explained. The catfishing scams they had been tracking all seemed to involve someone in Singapore—so they had reached out to the Singapore Police.

Jane reflected on the time they had spent trying to track down who was behind these Singapore catfishing scams and the hours she had spent talking to

DI Wong, her counterpart in the Singapore Cyber-crime police department. They had not really been that helpful and were in denial that they had a major scamming problem in Singapore.

"OK. So, does that give us new evidence to convince the Singapore Police? We can get this scammer rounded up," Jane was back in control and planning the next steps.

"Erm, not really—we can follow these scammers online via their usernames, but until they do something to give away their details, we don't really have anything solid to go to the Singapore Police with—sorry ma'am."

Penny and Billy had talked about this most of the night after their discovery. It seemed like they had opened up the case, only to hit a brick wall straight away again. It was Billy who suggested something which was a little 'alternative' and Penny had been sceptical about suggesting it at all. Now was crunch time—if they didn't suggest a next step to Jane, the whole discovery would deflate like a balloon and their recent efforts would be wasted—not to mention the chance to impress Jane, which Penny always looked out for.

Penny looked at Billy who nodded and then she said, "There is one possible approach that we could try, but it is a little out there…."

"Try me," invited Jane.

"Well, there is this thing called a 'Man-in-the-middle attack', where a scammer pretends to be someone else that the victim wants to talk to—for example, their bank—but the scammer is really intercepting the victim's communications and using their bank credentials to defraud them and the bank," Penny explained.

"I don't see how that helps us here?" Jane looked puzzled.

Billy expanded, "It's more the principle of a man-in-the-middle attack I thought we could use—we sit between the victim and the scammer and intercept all communications until we find a way of trapping the scammer."

"Right, I think I understand. But I think you have missed one crucial point… the victim doesn't know they are a victim until after they have been scammed, by which point it is too late." Jane felt bad they had missed something so simple.

Penny smiled, "Billy says he can track the scammers to try and pick up when they start on new victims—it's a lot of work and not strictly by the book, but…. Ma'am?"

Jane paused. She hated these situations. Good cops asking if they could bend the rules for the greater good. She looked at Penny and Billy—they had been working well together and the unit needed a result, she needed a result… "OK. Well, the less I know about that the better. Let me know when we have one of the scammers on the hook. Or rather they have their next victim on the hook. Well, you know what I mean… when someone is on the hook and we can catch the person with the rod!"

Chapter 19
A Working Office

The 'Den' as Jem liked to call it was actually an old disused office block, three stories high. It had been abandoned a few years earlier when the business had gone bankrupt. No one knew who owned it, but no one ever came asking, so Jem had decided to try his luck until they did. He and Azi had found it a couple of years back when they were looking for somewhere to live.

They had both finished school officially (unofficially they had hardly attended) and were trying to make their way in the world. They were not averse to some light theft and had been doing that since their late teens, but ever since that incident with the motorbike workshop owner, they had been steering clear of 'earning' money that way.

Jem had learned to play cards and had started to hustle kids and then later adults, winning a lot of money this way. It was a little dangerous as people didn't take kindly to be caught out, but Azi was his muscle and it never really caused any issues. As they built up a reputation of being good at conning people and able to handle themselves, they came to the attention of the local mafia leader.

He decided to give them a chance to work for him as his loan sharks and Jem and Azi took to this like sharks to water. Jem had the gift of the gab and could charm people to take out loans with them and Azi would be his enforcer if payments were not kept up to date. They were a profitable little team for the mafia leader.

Despite this, they still didn't have much money and no real freedom to make any more from the lending business—it was no more than a salaried position for them both. Now you don't give up working for the mafia just like that, but on the plus side they don't tend to check what you do with your spare time and they had a lot of spare time. So, they decide to branch out on their own.

Jem and Azi had both got into the internet in their late teens after stealing a load of computer equipment one night during a raid on a grocery store—they were just after some cash from the till, but had struck lucky when they found the owner of the shop fixed computers on the side and had all sorts in his office at the back—they cleaned him out. They didn't have access to the internet at their homes (Jem and his younger brother Gil were living in a shelter for homeless young men by this point and Azi had left home and moved in with a mate), but soon learned how to tap into the electricity and internet from local businesses and cyber cafes, by hiding in the alleyway round the back. The trouble was that each time they got caught within a few days and had to move on.

Even though their access had been sporadic, sometimes going weeks without being able to use the computers, they had used them and the internet enough to learn what they were capable of. It was no surprise, given their previous activities, that they soon looked at the darker side of the internet and how it could make them money. That is what drove them to find a more permanent office location. It was just lucky that the office they chose was big enough for them to work on one floor and live on another. Jem, Gil and Azi all moved in and set up the house.

To everyone else, this empty office block would be exactly what it was, a run down, dirty, rat-infested mess, but to them, it was their first proper home as adults and a place where they could set up 'business'—they felt like they were making something for themselves.

"This is great! We can use this floor for living and the top floor for working. We will keep the ground floor empty, so it looks like no one is here—put off anyone who comes creeping around," Jem stood in the middle of the five-hundred square foot first floor and panned his arms around as he spoke. "We can have a kitchen at the back there, the beds can go along those sidewalls near the windows and this whole area at the front can be for chilling and playing computer games."

"Where we gonna get beds Jem? We haven't got no money," Gil asked tentatively.

"Where we get everything silly?" laughed Azi. "We nick them. I got my eye on a nice house not far from the café—looks like they would have comfy beds and they hardly ever seem to be at home as far as I can tell—probably those posh foreigners who have another home in their own country—they won't miss them."

"And they have water and electricity over by that cupboard—used to be some sort of office kitchen I reckon—that'll do us no problem," chimed in Jem trying to sound enthusiastic for Gil's sake.

"We can make it well lush Gil—don't worry! Let's go and look at how we are gonna set-up the computers upstairs."

With Gil feeling a little bit better because of Jem and Azi's enthusiasm, they all trooped upstairs to a slightly smaller floor of about three hundred square feet. It had an outside roof area that took up the remaining space from the floor below, which was accessible from a glass door that was still in reasonable working order. There were several old desks from the previous occupants still on this floor and Jem started arranging them straight away, with Azi and Gil joining in as he directed. "Stick those two over there and make sure you are near that electrical socket for the computers. We only need four desks for now."

"Why, who is there apart from us three?" asked Azi surprised.

"You will see in time," replied Jem, mainly because although he knew they needed a woman on the team he hadn't actually found anyone he could ask to join them yet.

"Am I getting a desk then? Does that mean I am part of the team properly?" Gil asked with excitement. Up to this point, he had been very much a runner or lookout or some other small role in their 'work'.

"Of course you are Bro—you are heading up the 'Research Department'," Jem gesticulated with air quotes.

"Wow—thanks Filly!" in his excitement, Gil forgot that Jem had decided to drop his old school nickname and quickly added, "Sorry, I meant Jem."

Jem walked slowly over to Gil and grabbed him by the scruff of the neck and lifted him just off his toes with real menace in his eyes. Gil was scared—this wasn't the first time he had been on the wrong end of Jem's fists for annoying him. "That's 'Managing Director Jem' to you sonny," Jem spat in his face with mock anger and quickly put his brother in a headlock and started ruffling his hair, laughing loudly. It took Gil and Azi a moment to recover, but then they started laughing, perhaps a little bit forced laughing, but then as most employees know, it is always best to keep on the good side of the boss.

Chapter 20
Feminine Intuition

"I honestly don't see what you are so worried about Liz. This Joseph sounds like a great fella and he would be mad not to be crazy for you—I mean look at you!" Philip's voice increased in pitch as he carried on, "You are gorgeous, interesting, got a bit of money and know all about motorbikes—you are a straight man's dream!"

Elizabeth had been crying a little for the last thirty minutes as she had explained to Philip all about Joseph and how they had started their relationship and then got closer and closer, but now she smiled and gave a light laugh, "Oh, Philip, thank you. I feel so relieved to have told you. I am so pleased you think it's OK—I couldn't bear it if you thought I was being a silly old fool."

Philip knew when tea and sympathy were called for and he had played that role for the last half hour. But in truth, he was a bit worried about the situation, but he put that to the back of his mind for talking over with Anthony later—Anthony would know what to do.

"Well, my darling, what we need to do is get you back in the game properly. What pictures have you been sending Joseph, or have you been doing FaceTime?" asked Philip.

"Not FaceTime—I have never done that before and he says that the internet signal is not strong enough for that. We just send pictures and messages via Facebook Messenger—I know how to do that."

"Oh, right. But you have spoken to him on the phone?" Philip queried.

"Erm, no. I didn't really think about it—that would cost a lot of money with him being in Singapore wouldn't it?" she replied honestly.

"Well, you can do internet calls from your phone or iPad now Liz—I can set it up for you. He probably has enough bandwidth to do an audio call," Philip said with confidence.

“Bandwidth? Audio Calls? You really know your stuff, Philip. I thought I was modern with my iPad!” Elizabeth smiled.

“Oh, it’s all the kids talk about these days—I guess I just picked it up. Anyway, give me your iPad and phone and I will make sure you are set up,” Philip had gone into productive mode now and was determined to get Elizabeth sorted.

“All you need to do is press this little phone image in the top right corner of your chat with Joseph,” Philip pointed at the blue phone receiver image, but then he accidentally touched it.

“Oh my god, it’s started calling him!” he practically threw the iPad in the air and then fumbled it onto the settee between them, with the ‘calling Joseph’ flashing on the screen—neither of them could move. They knew it was wrong to just call him out of the blue (even though it was an accident), but it was clear that they also both wanted to see if he would answer.

Of course, he didn’t, which was a bit of an anti-climax for them both. Philip started protesting that it was lucky he hadn’t answered his accidental ring and Elizabeth started saying things about it being too early in the morning for him anyway. Slightly embarrassed and disappointed for them both, Philip got up to make a fresh cuppa. He decided to shift the conversation away from Joseph a bit, “So how are you finding your iPad anyway—easy to use? Does the battery last long enough?”

Elizabeth realised and appreciated his attempt at defusing the previous two minutes, so replied, “Yes, it’s really intuitive and I only have to charge it once every two days. Although the man at the shop said that the battery life would get worse and I might have to charge it every day.” She picked the iPad up and made a show of pointing out that the battery was currently a healthy 87%. At that moment when they were both staring hard at the battery percentage, Facebook Messenger sprang into life on it, announcing that ‘Joseph’ was calling!

Now it was Elizabeth’s turn to fumble holding the iPad, but this time Philip was sturdier and grabbed it. They looked at each other. Then at the iPad. Then at each other. Philip held it out in front of them both, but with the microphone end near Elizabeth. He nodded. She nodded and bravely pressed the flashing ‘answer’ button on the screen. Elizabeth swallowed hard, opened her mouth, closed it, opened it again, got a dig in the ribs from Philip whilst he mouthed “Say ‘Hello’!”

“He… Hello?” Elizabeth whispered.

“Is that you, Lizzie?” spoke the voice on the other end.

“Yes. Is that…. Joseph?” she asked as if expecting a different answer.

“Yes! It’s me Lizzie—I didn’t know you were set up for phone calls on your computer—this is great,” an enthusiastic Joseph replied.

“Well, I have only just worked out how to do it,” she said nervously. Philip gave her the thumbs up.

“I can’t believe we get to talk at last,” Joseph said.

“Yes, it’s lovely. You sound so …. Young,” she replied being honest with her thoughts.

There was a cough from Joseph’s end and he replied in a deeper voice, “Oh, I have a bit of a dry throat first thing in the morning. It will be OK after a cup of tea.”

“Oh, you sound more like I imagined you now,” Elizabeth started to relax.

Philip gave her another thumbs up and slipped off the end of the settee. Elizabeth hardly noticed. She was staring so hard at the screen and leaning into it every time she spoke. Philip decided to let himself out. Clearly whatever this Joseph had been thinking last night when he had ended their chat so abruptly wasn’t bothering him now and it sounded like they were at the start of a good old chat.

As Philip reversed down the small driveway he was buzzing for Elizabeth at her first real conversation with this new man in her life; by the time he got to the end of her cul-de-sac he was wondering why Joseph had been funny last night when he seemed so ‘into’ her today; by the time he drove around the Morrisons roundabout half a mile from Elizabeth’s he was pondering on the young sounding voice he had heard on the call; as he rounded the corner of his own road he was wondering why Joseph would tell Elizabeth the internet signal wasn’t good, Singapore was known for its technology advancement and he knew that Wi-Fi was available everywhere there; As he unpacked his massage table and put it back in the garage he was remembering something Elizabeth had showed him during the thirty minute breakdown to him, some photos that Joseph had sent of him on old motorbikes, the background should have been either England or Singapore, but it had been somewhere much drier and run down; As he unlocked and opened the front door and the pugs rushed to greet him barking enthusiastically, he called out “Babe? I think there is something strange about Liz’s new internet lover—stick the kettle on, I need your advice….”

Chapter 21
Traffic Lights

It took another week for Billy to get a hit off the username he had been tracking. He had actually been tracking several variants of the username, knowing that people were lazy when it came to security and would just change a letter or number of a previously used username or password and think they were safe. But in fact, this scammer was using different names, but with the same ending—so he uncovered several accounts that all seemed to link back to the same profile of his scammer.

It was standard in detective work to create a profile for your suspect and this was no different when it came to cyber detective work. Although you had to be a little more flexible in your profiling. A standard person profile would include things like Height; Sex; Ethnicity; Build, Hair colour; any distinguishing features. Whereas a cyber profile might have these things but might also need things like Avatars; Memes; and of course, usernames—these were the digital footprints that helped Cyber detective work.

From their discovery of the username 'Melanie-Singaporelove1#' as part of the double-dip money trail they had been able to follow, Billy had uncovered a series of usernames which all used the slightly unusual 'Singaporelove' followed by a number and a hash. Initially, he found 'Melanie-Singaporelove2#' and then a '3#' and a '4#'. He had then found it used again but with a different name at the front—'Julia-Singaporelove1#'; 'Evie-Singaporelove1#'; 'KateSingapore love1#'; and 'Tasha-Singaporelove1#'. Again, these new names all had variants with a different number on the end. He did some research to check there wasn't a club or society in Singapore called 'Singapore Love' that lots of girls with the same name happened to belong to, just to be sure. He was certain he had found the multiple usernames that were used by one person to do their scams.

Penny had been away for a week's holiday and Billy excitedly filled her in on her first day back. She understood the significance straight away and opened her mouth to ask if Billy could set up some kind of tracker that could alert them when one of these usernames was being actively used—he was way ahead of her. Billy toggled his computer screen to a black page with a series of traffic lights set up in columns. At the bottom of each column, there was one of the usernames he was tracking.

Billy explained, "If a username is referenced in a post on any of the major social media sites, then the traffic light will turn amber and an email will be sent to you and me with a link to the post so we can follow up and see what the post is about. If the username actively logs into any of the major social media sites, then the light will turn red and an alarm will sound from my computer so we can try and follow actual communications between the scammer and whoever they are trying to scam."

Penny was impressed, but ever wanting more, "What if we are asleep at home or not in the office?"

Billy looked at her as if to say, 'How dumb do you think I am?' but said "Outside of our shift hours, it will send a text to your and my phone. I can always write a rule that applies a rota between you and me if you don't want to be on-call every night?"

Penny enjoyed her beauty sleep, but she wasn't going to miss out on a major catch if it happened, "No, that's fine. I am happy to be called at any hour."

"OK, cool. Right, well the post tracking is really just to give us some background on who is potentially in touch with the scammer, but when the scammer is active, that's when we do the clever stuff," Billy enthused.

"I was going to ask how we are going to be this man-in-the-middle," asked Penny, secretly impressed with what Billy had achieved so far.

"Well, once we know what messaging app they are using and the usernames of both the scammer and the victim, we can instigate a chat with one of them and when they respond (even just to say 'sorry you have the wrong person') we can use the 'netstat' command on the computer to find out their IP addresses and then we can spoof the user accounts so that we can log in as if we are them and start communicating with the scammer ourselves."

Billy really was a whizz when it came to this computer stuff, thought Penny. But it wouldn't do for him to get too big-headed and think it was all down to him. Penny turned the conversation to something a bit more psychological,

"That's really great Billy—well done. But the tricky part is what do we SAY to the scammer to ensure he doesn't think it is not his victim and how are we going to get them to give themselves away?"

"Oh, I hadn't thought that far ahead," replied Billy sheepishly.

"You leave that bit to me, Billy—it's all in the psychology of the individual…," said Penny with confidence.

Chapter 22
Quality Control

Eb graduated high school with a few qualifications, but perhaps not as many as Amelia, or Eb for that matter, had expected. What had started out as an interest in drama with JG, had turned into an obsession and the hours Eb had put into building sets, helping out with scriptwriting, training the younger actors, and playing lead roles himself, had taken their toll on his schoolwork.

However, JG was able to pull a few strings and that combined with the fact that the headteacher didn't know who would play the lead role of Romeo in next year's production of Romeo and Juliet, enabled Eb to be given a place in the sixth form. Amelia was so grateful that JG was invited round for tea—his second visit in 3 years.

"Come in JG. Mum's baked our favourite cakes—butterfly buns—you will love them!" invited Eb, grabbing Joseph's arm and dragging him into the house.

"Hello, Mrs Azikiwe. Hello Su. Are you both well?" Joseph knew the formalities even if Eb had still not learnt them.

Su never really got a look in with Eb around, but she smiled and nodded at Joseph. Su was happy being in the background and watching Eb fly. She had been brought up as a proper Nigerian girl (well she was nearly a Woman at 13 now) and she just wanted to meet a nice man and bake cakes for him, like her Mum. That's not to say that she didn't enjoy herself, but she took most of her enjoyment from watching Eb in school plays or helping her mum bake—She didn't expect too much from life and took pleasure in simple things.

"Please call me Amelia—I feel you are part of our family for all the help you have given us," Amelia gave Joseph a big smile and a warm hug.

He reciprocated both the hug and the informality offering, "Then you must call me Joseph. Something smells great!" he added.

"Well, let me show you what's in the oven," and she led Joseph by the arm into the kitchen area.

Su looked at Eb and raised her eyebrows suggestively.

"What's the matter with you?" he asked puzzled.

Su nodded in the direction of the kitchen and did a charade act of their Mum walking Joseph through to the kitchen holding his arm and ended in kissing all the way up her arm as if Joseph was doing that to their Mum. Eb got the gist.

"Don't be ridiculous. He is just a family friend," snapped Eb, angry with the idea. Su carried on being suggestive and Eb jumped up from the settee landing on her and immediately started pummelling her on the arm—typical brother and sister fight. Joseph and Amelia walked back in, Amelia holding a tray of fresh-smelling buns and Joseph carrying a tray of teacups and a steaming pot of tea. Neither of them blinked at the fight in progress, they were both too familiar with the antics of teenagers.

Eb and Su separated and went back to their respective seats—the power of the smell of mum's baking having worked like magic on them. Eb brooded a little whilst wolfing down a cake so quickly that he burnt his mouth on it. He was looking from JG to his Mum and wondering. His wondering was short-lived as Joseph spoke with laughter "Your mum has just been trying to set me up with one of the women from her factory!"

"Well, a handsome young man like you should have a woman in your life," Amelia teased.

"Handsome—I don't know about that. As for young—I don't feel it so much these days!" he laughed back.

"Well, if you do, then Seema from quality control is VERY keen to meet you," continued Amelia.

"I am sure she is very nice," he replied more seriously, "But I feel I am a confirmed bachelor these days. I keep myself busy and the kids at school mean I never get a minute to myself anyway."

Amelia turned slightly more serious, "You need to prioritise yourself sometimes. You have done so much for the children around here—you deserve a bit of happiness."

"I can't deny that I sometimes get lonely in the late evening and at the weekends, but I am happy the rest of the time and that will have to be enough," he replied with a small amount of sadness in his voice.

Eb was relieved that his Mum wasn't making eyes at his teacher and soon recovered from his initial anxiety. He listened to what JG said and felt some sadness for him also. Then that turned into an idea.

"I can always get you up on one of those dating websites if you like JG," he said with enthusiasm.

Lots of laughter from Joseph and Amelia.

"What? Lots of people in the UK use them—I read it on the internet," continued Eb confused as to why they found it so funny.

"Well, you won't catch me putting up silly pictures of myself on the internet!" laughed Joseph.

"You might get caught out by someone pretending to be someone else—Eb is always talking about people using the internet to hide who they really are," Amelia joined in.

"Knowing my luck, I will probably get paired with Seema from quality control!" another burst of laughter from Joseph and Amelia, which Eb and Su joined in with this time.

The laughter settled down and they moved onto talking about Eb going into sixth form next year and how he would need to balance the schoolwork and the acting commitments a little better. Eb hardly listened, partly because he knew he would always prioritise acting over schoolwork, but partly because he was thinking about how he could help JG to find love via an internet dating site. He was determined to do some research and get it all set up—it could be a surprise and a thank you for all the help JG had given him. As things would turn out, it would certainly be one of those....

Chapter 23
Wagon Wheels and Psychology

Anthony sped down the stairs and went straight to the kitchen. He put the kettle on and then stuck his head around the dining-room door. They always used the dining room for serious discussions.

"KitKat or Wagon Wheel lover?" Anthony asked.

"This calls for a Wagon Wheel babe," replied Philip with no small amount of melodrama. Anthony's head disappeared into the kitchen again. Only to appear 2 minutes later with a small tray covered in a Pug Doggy pattern, containing two mugs (one with a picture of Kylie and Judy, the other with a picture of Paul) and two Wagon Wheels. He put it down gently and placed the mugs onto the two pug patterned coasters that Philip had reached down to the sideboard for moments before the tray arrived—a well-practised drill altogether.

Philip and Anthony had one of those houses that were so camp, you would have thought Miss Marple lived there with her lifelong friend Betty—flock wallpaper; doilies everywhere; anything that could have a pattern of a pug on it, did; and the whole house looked immaculate and smelt of roses. Neither Philip nor Anthony were particularly camp outside of the house and they certainly were not the kind of people that thrust their sexuality down everyone's throat, but in their own little world they liked to let loose and it showed.

"First things first lover.... Is that darling alright? I mean is she hurt or anything?" Anthony asked with genuine concern.

"Well, not physically babe. Emotionally, I think she is in danger!" he replied seriously.

"Danger? Right—tell me everything." Anthony sat a bit more upright and put on his serious listening face.

It was sweet the way they were so into each other and supported each other. Anthony had not once thought that Philip might be worrying about something unnecessary. Philip had concerns and Anthony was there to support him through it. Philip loved him for that.

Philip relayed the sequence and content of the events of the visit to Elizabeth's. Anthony only interrupted to check details, but he always did this—Philip knew he liked to build the complete picture in his mind. Anthony did perhaps ask too much about the specific pattern on the sexy dressing gown but never mind. Once Philip had retold everything from start to finish as it happened, he asked, "So do you see why I am concerned Babe?"

Anthony was a caring partner and he loved Philip unconditionally. He provided a fabulous home for them both and was a great cook. He did the shopping and washing and supported Philip as the breadwinner. Philip loved all these things about Anthony. But sometimes he got jealous and his mind ran to the worst conclusions, "Erm, are you worried she fancies you lover?" he asked tentatively.

Philip's love for Anthony had enabled him to not get too frustrated when these moments arose in their lives "No, babe."

Minor hidden sigh and then a deep breath, "She is being scammed!"

"No!" Anthony gave the appropriate response and then, "What makes you sure?"

"Because I can see that this bloke she has clearly fallen in love with is a dodgy geezer!" Philip got his summary out at last.

Philip took Anthony through his observations, starting back with his confusion at why Liz had tried to initially hide her iPad and that she was 'on the internet'. He re-explained how he had seen the iPad in her knitting bag and knew she was using 'Lizzie-pops' as her username because it had popped up as the Bluetooth connection on his iPhone. He had actually told Anthony that night a few weeks back and they had instantly found her by searching on Facebook—they had nearly sent her a connection request, but decided against it—if she wanted to keep it private, then they would respect that—now they wish they had!

He then updated Anthony on today's happenings—Liz being all funny about if she had 'still got it'; The tearful reveal about her online 'boyfriend'; The fact they had been communicating for weeks but not spoken on the phone yet; Joseph cutting off the text chat sharply the night before; Joseph not answering when they called but then calling back a few minutes later; Joseph's very young sounding voice; Joseph telling Elizabeth the internet signal wasn't good in Singapore; some photos that were not taken in Singapore or England.

Anthony listened intently, only disturbing his focus to dunk his Wagon Wheel in his tea (which in itself interrupted Philip because he hated it when Anthony did that—eww!) or to tell one of the pugs to 'go away! Daddy and Daddy are busy'. At the end of this outpouring, Philip was drained, "So that's it, I think this 'boyfriend' is not the real deal and I am worried our Liz is in trouble," he finished.

"Well, lover, that's quite a leap to make," Anthony was clearly sceptical with Philip's hypothesis.

Philip was disheartened not to have full agreement from the man who was his rock, but at the same time hoped Anthony was right and it was all just his mind overthinking it. Philip folded his arms, sat back and said, "So what do you think it is then?"

Anthony may have kept his and Philip's home as a little bubble of fluffiness, but he was as sharp as a tack when it came to the psychology of life. He had studied Social Biology at Sixth Form and then gone on to do a degree in Sociology and Psychology with his final thesis being entitled, 'The effects of social norms in modern-day Britain on people who are embracing their own psychology to understand how to be different'—he had got a first!

"I'm not saying you are not right lover, but just that we need more evidence before going running to the police."

"You think we should go to the police?" Philip spat in astonishment—he just hadn't thought beyond telling Anthony.

"Well, if what you think turns out to be true, then definitely. It's the right way to protect Liz," replied Anthony with certainty. "But, as I say, we need to do a bit more detective work first I think."

Philip was consoled by the control Anthony was bringing to the situation—like any couple, it felt good to share these concerns and support each other, but more than that Philip knew that Anthony was already thinking of a way to get that evidence.

Chapter 24
Amber, Amber, Amber... Red!

The Amber traffic light for 'Evie-Singapore1#' had been flashing on and off all day. The first time it flashed Billy and Penny leapt over to the separate computer they had set up for monitoring the usernames. That was one of the benefits of working with technology that people didn't really understand, you could ask for special equipment and tell the finance team it was essential, and they would have no way of challenging you.

By the time the amber light had flashed eight times, they were getting a bit more relaxed about it. Turns out that 'Evie' was just being tagged by some 'friends'. Although they did notice a pattern to the type of things she was being tagged in—beekeeping. There was a video on YouTube of some English beekeepers explaining what type of honey the bees produced at different times of the year; and another video on Instagram of some tribesmen in the rainforest climbing trees with no protective clothing and just a lit homemade fire torch to create smoke to pacify some tree-dwelling bees fifty feet up the tree, whose honey they want to get; and various 'likes' of bee and honey related products that some people were promoting via Facebook.

Billy looked smug and said, "I predict that our scammers next victim is going to be a beekeeper!"

"No, shit, Sherlock," replied Penny unimpressed. "So, this is how they prepare for a scam. They must have been 'researching' their victim but haven't yet made contact. I bet they will in the next few days."

"I feel a bit helpless sitting here watching the groundwork being done to set someone up and we don't even know who it is. Worse than that, they don't even know who 'Evie' is yet. Poor schmucks," Billy observed.

"We can't think like that Billy. We have to remain dispassionate. Otherwise, we won't do the right thing when the time comes," Penny parroted their basic training at him.

"I know, I know," he sighed.

Billy busied himself documenting in a spreadsheet every 'hit' of the username—time, description, any comment used and a link to the actual post. He wasn't sure it was a good use of his skills or time, but it made the day go by. Penny went a little deeper and searched through all the connections of 'Evie' that she could find to see if there was a clue to their identity or anything that would give them away.

As made-up profiles went, it had been well prepared. Not lots of friends, but enough. Most of them are in the UK or Singapore. No contact details or specifics for any of the friends. It looked real, but you couldn't tie the users down to reality. Neither of them felt like they had really got anywhere, and it was in a slightly disheartened mood that they left the office for the day.

Billy got them both coffee when he got in the next morning and so Penny had a steaming mug on her desk when she arrived five minutes later—black, no sugar—no-nonsense, just like her. Billy had a double macchiato with whipped cream—he aspired to grander things in life clearly. They settled down to work, which mainly meant repeating the research they did the day before and waiting for something to happen. Then something did happen—the red light flashed vigorously on the monitoring computer screen at the end of the desk! But it wasn't on 'EvieSingapore1#', it was on 'MelanieSingapore1#'. Billy and Penny were confused at first—surely the next step was for the scammer to log in as 'Evie' to start contacting the 'Beekeeper'.

Then Penny had a thought, "Billy, can you do a past scan of posts where 'Melanie' has been tagged?"

"Yes, of course. I just have to run my search manually and look in the past—no problem. How will that help?" he asked.

"Just give it a go—I have a hunch," Penny didn't want to reveal too much in case she was wrong—always protecting her brand!

Billy got his search script up and changed some data to search in the past and ran it. Ten seconds later over forty results of posts where 'Melanie' had been tagged appeared.

"I knew it. Don't know why we didn't think of this before," Penny was annoyed with herself. "Oh, right… We were only looking forward, and of course, we know that the scammer has been doing this with these usernames for a while," Billy caught up.

"So, we thought 'Evie' was the one to watch, but she is in the early stages of prepping for a victim. 'Melanie' has been being prepped for a while—the last two weeks by the looks of these posts," Penny continued.

Happy that a new part of the jigsaw had been placed in the puzzle, they turned their attention back to the present.

"So, what have they logged into and what are they doing Billy?" eagerness coming through in Penny's voice.

"Let's have a look-see," Billy stuck his tongue out the corner of his mouth as he always did when taping away at his computer—it was his way of concentrating. "Erm, right. 'Melanie' has logged onto Facebook and is using the Facebook Messenger app."

"Who is she talking to?" Penny urged.

"Hang on. I just need to... Right. Got it... someone with the username 'Lonelygoatherder1987'," he smiled with pride at having got there.

"Sounds like another farmer to me," Penny suggested. "So how do we get in the middle of them?" Penny wanted to crack on.

"I need to do some IP tracking and see if I can lock them down to unique internet addresses—then I can spoof them," tongue stuck firmly out. "Oh, so we can't just do it now?" Penny looked deflated.

"The impossible I can do straight away, Miracles take a little longer," Billy quipped but didn't stop tapping away. Ten minutes later he was ready. "Shall we tell Jane so she can see how it works?"

"God no! We need to test this out ourselves to make sure it works and also, so we don't look like idiots," snapped Penny.

"It'll work—don't you worry," Billy knew what he was doing. "OK—here we go.... See those two windows? Well one is 'Melanie's' Messenger app and the other is goat-mans."

"Goat-man is typing!" Penny almost squealed.

"Great—time to test out my delay code... come on, come on... hit send... there," Billy punched his keyboard and cheered himself.

"Nothing happened," exclaimed Penny. "It doesn't work!"

"Look more closely," Billy indicated 'Melanie's' messenger window—there was nothing on it.

"There is nothing on it," Penny was confused.

"Exactly! I have stopped goat-man's message from getting through. He has 'sent' it, but it hasn't 'arrived'," Billy said with an air of triumph.

"Oh, right—that's great! So how long can you delay it for?" Penny was back at excited again.

"As long as we like. And what's more, I have nearly got the third window feature working," Billy stated.

"And that's how we join in the game—right?" the full solution revealed itself to Penny.

"Yup. Best let that message go through now or they will get suspicious," Billy pressed a button and the message appeared in 'Melanie's' window. "I should have it done by the end of the day and then it's over to you, Penny."

Penny couldn't believe how they had moved on since yesterday and now she was 'on' this was her big moment—playing the go-between in a game of fabricated love, where only one party knew the truth—she almost felt nervous. Almost.

Chapter 25
The Business Model

Gil had worked hard with his brother and Azi. The office was starting to look good. Well, not good but not a complete dump. They had blocked up the broken windows and managed to get the water and electricity working by tapping into two supplies from an office block just down the road—it had been dangerous work in the middle of the night, but at least they wouldn't have to pay for the services. The desks and chairs were all in place and they had even managed to section off a corner of the top floor with a curtain they found as Jem's 'office'.

Getting internet access was more tricky and so they opted for using some extenders to bounce the internet signal of the school one mile away—they already knew how to access the school's internet as the school hadn't changed its Wi-Fi code since installing it a few years earlier and the extenders could be run off car batteries and hidden along the route—it wasn't the most reliable network, but it was free and fast. Their office was ready to go.

Jem and Azi had been talking a lot about the computers and what kind of business they were going to run with them. They had already tried some small-scale hacking, but neither of them was clever enough to do too much of the techie stuff—they knew how to use the computers and social media etc but couldn't really do anything more than that—they were just basic computer users.

They had read on the internet about a great scam where you called people pretending they had won a prize and asked them for their email address so you could email them details—in the email, you sent there was a backdoor virus that would allow you to control their computer—you would call them again and ask them to log in to their online banking service via their computer and check if the money had landed—when they went to log in, you would use the control you had over their computer to see what they typed in as the username and password for the account—then you could use that to access their account and clean them out—perfect!

The only problem was that Jem and Azi didn't have the skills to write a backdoor virus and so they had to look for something simpler. They found something quite quickly and set to work getting it set up. The basic premise was to befriend a man or woman and get close enough to them that they would send you money for some reason.

There had been some scams of this kind that had got attention—the one where you befriend someone and then ask for help with medical bills (so you choose people who are charitable); the one where you befriend someone and then say you are being persecuted by your unjust government and need money to flee the regime (so you choose someone with strong humanitarian views); the one where you befriend someone and then ask for help with your child's education costs (so you choose someone with views of education being a right for everyone).

They felt that these versions of the scam were too well publicised, and people wouldn't fall for these as a result. They needed something that people didn't talk about so much—so even if lots of people got scammed, they might not publicise it and so they could keep doing it to more people. The answer was, of course, love. Lots of people wanted to be loved and often didn't talk about bad love experiences—particularly the British, they thought. They would need a dating website to lure people in, but that was easy to set up—well within Jem and Azi's technical capabilities. They decided to bring Gil up to speed.

"Gil!" Jem called from his corner office.

Gil came running, "Yes, Jem? Erm, boss."

"Azi and I have decided on our business strategy and wanted to communicate it to the staff," Jem stated in what he thought was a big boss style.

"What staff? … Oh, you mean me. Hahahaha," laughed Gil.

"Alright, alright. It might just be us three today, but soon there will be loads of us," snapped Jem.

"Of course. Sorry, Jem," Gil looked at the floor.

"Right. Well. What we are gonna do is set up a dating website for British people and lure in people who are desperate for love—then con them out of money. It's good hey?" Jem gave the pitch.

Gil knew not to challenge his brother too much, but he also wanted to understand the idea fully. "So, who are they going to date?"

"Us you idiot! … Well, us pretending to be someone else of course," Jem was enjoying showing how clever he was to his brother.

"Oh, right, so we set up false profiles on this site and they contact us for a date, and we respond. What happens when they want to go on an actual date with us?" asked Gil trying to unpick the whole idea so he could understand it.

"We won't of course. We just string them along until they give us money—we can send pictures and messages of love to keep them going," Jem was slightly annoyed by the questions now.

"OK. So, we have made them fall in love with a virtual person. How do we get money out of them?" Gil couldn't help looking confused as he asked.

"Well, we spin them some story about needing money for the rent or shopping or something," Jem was making it up now.

"Why would these people want to send money to these online dates who they had never even met—that's not going to work," Gil voiced what he was thinking, forgetting he shouldn't challenge Jem.

"Look, do you want to fucking work here or not you little shit!" Jem burst.

Azi was used to this scenario—Big brother taking it out on little brother because he hadn't got all the answers. He tried to help calm things down, "Hang on Jem—Gil might have a point—surely the person needs an incentive to give us money?"

Gil jumped on this rescue mission, "Yes, that's all I meant—we need to think of an incentive…. Actually… I might have one."

Jem huffed, but Azi had done the trick and Jem's interest in what Gil might have come up with (where he hadn't) made him calm down, "Go on then."

Gil expanded, "Well, what if we made the whole dating theme about UK people who were somewhere else in the world and wanted to come home. Like they had been travelling for a while but were ready to settle down and wanted someone in the UK to do it with."

Azi questioned, "So how does that make it more attractive to send money?"

"Well, if they send money for them to travel home, then they get to see the person they have fallen in love with—that's a great incentive isn't it?" Gil sought approval.

"You might just have something there you little shit," Jem trying to make his previous comments light-hearted.

Azi ran with the idea, "OK—this is great—a sort of dating service that finds travellers who have run out of money and want to come home to love—we need a name.... 'Travel-onlove'? ... 'Bring me, home lover'? ..."

"Well, you remember that English teacher guy from school—you know the do-gooder that built the school and then stayed to help teach English to us all."

Jem missed the irony that if it wasn't for JG teaching them proper English, they would not be able to run a scam on the UK, "Well, he always referred to himself as an ExPat—something to do with not being a UK patriot because he left I think—so how about we call it 'ExPats Reunited'!" Jem said more as a statement than a question.

"Perfect!" shouted Azi and Gil in unison—they knew when to agree with the boss.

"Right—good meeting—now get on with it. I want this site up and running within a couple of days and our first victims on the hook by the end of the week." The CEO of 'ExPats Reunited' declare in his first order of business.

Chapter 26
Baiting the Trap

"Sooooo, how was your chat with Joseph—are you all loved up again?" Philip asked as soon as he was through the door. Anthony had told him to do nothing to put Elizabeth off this relationship and to actively encourage it—that was the key to the plan, the con-man mustn't suspect they were onto him.

"Oh, don't be silly—we are not lovesick teenagers…," she left that hanging whilst slightly blushing, clearly indicating she was enjoying being a lovesick teenager.

"Have you spoken to him many times since I was last here?" Philip was hoping the answer was yes.

"Well, there was last Wednesday as you know and then…. What's today? Saturday? Erm, five times—so not much," Elizabeth replied avoiding eye contact.

"Not much! That's five times in four days—you must have it bad," Philip was gently mocking, and Elizabeth was clearly loving it.

"He is just so caring and interested—we talk for ages," she explained.

"Well, I think it's lovely that you have someone to share time with—other than me of course—I could get a bit jealous!" Philip laughed.

"Ha-ha—you would marry your pugs before choosing me, Philip!" Elizabeth quipped.

Philip's face suddenly turned serious, "Has he mentioned marriage then?"

"No, silly. It was just a turn of phrase," she laughed again at what she took to be Philips wish she would get married.

Philip did an internal 'phew' and then decided to get on with the massage to allow him time to work his way up to the plan he and Anthony had concocted. Elizabeth followed suit and climbed slowly onto the massage table, removing her robe—Philip noted she was back to soft white towelling and not the silky-sexy one.

After a little while, Philip started his soft approach, "Anthony and I went to Singapore a few years back—it's a really lovely place."

"Oh, right, that's nice," Elizabeth was relaxing into the massage and not really paying full attention—Philip often rambled on about nothing much when he was massaging her.

Philip carried on as Anthony had scripted it, "We went to the Palace of Light just outside the city—it was beautiful. Thousands of candles are lit by hand every day for the Buddhists who go there to meditate. The tourists are allowed to walk around the outside but not to enter the palace."

"That sounds lovely—I wonder who lights and puts out all the candles—I wouldn't want that job," murmured Elizabeth.

Normally Philip would have ignored that she wasn't really listening properly, but he wanted to make sure she had got this piece of info, "Yes, that's why it's called the Palace of Light I guess—candles, candles, candles."

The massage finished; Elizabeth turned onto her back for leg manipulation. Philip started the normal cycle of pushing and stretching, turning and bending to help the legs flexibility. After a minute he went onto the next step of the plan, "The reason Anthony and I loved Singapore so much was the way they embraced homosexuality and all things different—they are a very tolerant society and welcomed us with open arms."

Elizabeth was used to Philip talking about his and Anthony's experience of homophobia and generally felt sorry for them as they seemed to come across it so much in the world. She was surprised to hear the opposite for once, "Really, you do surprise me. I would have thought they would have been very conservative about that and the whole gay culture would have been underground in somewhere like that—just shows how much times have changed."

Philip was pleased with the interaction he was getting from Liz and didn't want to push it too far, but Anthony had said they needed to cover as broad a spectrum of topics as they could to give the best chance of a result.

They talked about other things for a while and then when they were sitting down for their regular after therapy cup of tea he decide to go for the last bit of information in the plan. This time one based on Joseph personally rather than a location-based one. "Joseph is such a lovely name don't you think?"

Elizabeth was getting a little fed up with the talk all about Joseph and Singapore—Joseph was her friend and had nothing to do with Philip really. However, she knew that Philip enjoyed imagining things about other people and their lives—probably because he led quite a boring life she thought—so she humoured him, "Yes, I suppose it is—nice and gentle sounding."

This played right into Philips hand's, "Well, you would think that, but apparently it means 'mighty one of Egypt'—I guess because he went to Egypt and became Pharos's right-hand man, which meant he had to be pretty tough with people."

"You seem very well-informed Philip—I didn't know you had such hidden depths," laughed Elizabeth.

"Erm, well I had an uncle who was called Joseph and he never stopped going on about how great he was and how he ruled over us all," Philip quickly improvised to make it sound more innocent.

"Palaces of candles; Singapore culture; and knowledge of Egyptian history—you are surprising me today Philip—I wonder what you will educate me on when you next visit—Flower arranging perhaps?" Elizabeth teased.

It was a cheap shot, not all gay men were good at flower arranging. Obviously, Philip was, but that's not the point he thought. Anyway, he didn't care—his mission had been a success. He had been worried by her lack-lustre responses during the massage that Liz hadn't picked up the data he was trying to land in her brain, but then she had summarised all three points for him just as he was getting ready to leave—it was like she was showing how clever she had been to listen properly. Philip left happy and wondered how long it would take for the next part of the plan to come to light.

No sooner had Philip gone and Elizabeth was on the iPad and opening messenger—she had so far been very impressed by Joseph's knowledge of so many things—he was clearly a well-educated man—but she wanted to show that she knew stuff as well. She typed "Hello, Joseph—are you up yet? Fancy a chat? x."

A few minutes passed, which was normal, and a ping came back "Good morning my lovely—how are you today? How was 'chatty Philip'?"

"I am great—leg feeling better after Philip's visit. You want to talk?" she typed back eagerly.

"Give me a minute and I will call you. x," he typed.

“OK—well don’t be long ‘oh mighty one of Egypt’—hahaha,” Elizabeth thought she was being clever and witty.

The person typing at the other end was confused, but went along with it “OK, ‘oh happy one of England’.”

Elizabeth was disappointed that her little witticism had gone over Joseph’s head—her name meant ‘God is bountiful’, nothing to do with being happy. Maybe Joseph didn’t know the meaning of his name or hers, she thought. Although quickly thought after that ‘But everyone knows the meaning of their own name’. She was left pondering that whilst waiting for the incoming call icon to flash on her messenger app.

Chapter 27
Two Is Company; Three Is a Crowd

Penny was struggling, not that she was going to admit that to anyone. Billy had finished the app so that they could pause and even change messages between two people having a chat. Penny had been trying to ease her way into the middle of Melanie and 'Goat-mans' conversation. Her first attempt had been very light.

M: *Hi Gorgeous!*

Penny paused the message for 4 seconds, which was as long as she dared for the first go. GM: *and hello to you my favourite lover of sheep and goats! How are you doing today—still too humid out there?*

M: *It's not too bad today. Bit muggy.*

M(P): *It's not very bad today. Bit sweaty.*

Changing two words in her first message interruption seemed brave to Penny.

GM: *Well I hope you don't sweat too much and have to have a shower.*

Penny didn't pause or change the response as she was too taken back that he had used her word 'sweat' in the reply. She so easily could have been caught out—what if he had said '*Why are you sweaty*?' or '*That will be because it's muggy*', both of which would have been a confusing response for Melanie.

Penny waited for the conversation to move on a bit before trying again.

GM: *The animals are getting restless with the heat here. I have given them fresh straw every day to try to keep them dry and cool, but they soon mess it up* M: *Poor things.*

Penny took her chance. She paused the response from Melanie and added '*Tell me more about them*', then un-paused it. Penny waited nervously for a reply. Which came less than 10 seconds later.

GM: *They are the same as I told you before—20 goats and 40 sheep—just hotter than before!*

Penny worried that Melanie would question what he meant by responding '*as I told you before*', but she need not have done.

M: *Bless their little hooves—kiss them for me and take one for yourself. x.*

It occurred to Penny that Melanie, well actually the scammer, might be messaging more than one person at once and this might distract them a little from the details of the messages—Melanie's replies had been very generic so far—this could really help.

Penny reported back to Billy—she wouldn't let him look over her shoulder whilst she was doing it, saying it put her off—he seemed pleased, but pointed out that we wanted to get information out of the scammer, not the victim and so we needed them to engage more with the messages not less. A few hours later Penny got another chance.

GM: *hey, me again. Do you know you were saying you were homesick? Well, how about coming back for a visit—I would love to meet properly and show you around the farm—the animals would love to meet you. x.*

M: *That's a great idea. I will start saving my pennies straight away, and in a few months, I might have enough. I would love to see the animals. X.*

GM: Oh, I didn't realise it would take that long. I know you said you didn't have much money.

Penny paused that one and added '*How much will a ticket cost?*' before releasing. She held her breath.

M: *Yeah, well I have to pay my bills and that takes most of the money, but I can save about £25 a month. A ticket will cost £600 and that's just one way!*

It had worked—Penny had got some information from the scammer that the victim hadn't asked for and neither of them was any the wiser. Whilst she was celebrating Goat-man replied.

GM: *Well why don't I help you out with that. You can stay with me for as long as you like, and you don't need to worry about the return back for now.... Or ever x.*

Penny realised that despite the interception working technically she was not doing anything to help the victim—in fact, it felt like her asking about the ticket cost had brought his offer of payment forward quicker than it might have otherwise—she was helping the scammer—aarrgggh!

She didn't bother reporting back to Billy for fear of him questioning her psychology credentials but left for the night. Half an hour later she was curled up on her sofa with a large glass of wine, feeling sorry for herself. She didn't really have any close friends. She could have done with a friend to have been there to listen to her moaning and then tell her it was all going to be alright. 'Blooming friends' thought Penny 'Who needs them?'.... then in answer to her thoughts she said out loud "Everyone!" and immediately jumped up from her sofa and ran to get her car keys.

Fortunately, Penny had only taken a sip of her large glass of wine. It wouldn't do for her to get caught drink driving or speeding for that matter, she thought as she slowed down. She got to the office in just under 25 mins (a personal best, but then the rush hour traffic was going the opposite way mostly) and saw Billy just tidying his desk to leave for the day. She wasn't sure her idea was going to work and should have tried it out before revealing it to Billy, but her ego got the better of her.

"Billy, don't go yet, I want to show you something!" Billy wanted to go home, not because it had been a hard day, more because it had been a boring day and he wanted to do something more exciting (which probably entailed playing on his games console for most of the evening). However, Penny sounded excited and that was what he was after—he crossed over to the message interruption computer.

"I have been studying the psychology of the scammer and think I know a way for them to reveal themselves some more," Penny announced once they were both sitting at the computer.

Billy was used to this kind of thing from Penny by now—always making sure you knew her psychology degree made her special—he said nothing and waited for her to expand. Penny paused for a response, didn't get one and so carried on regardless, "Anyway, the thing is that they are humans just like everyone else—right?" Billy nodded.

"And everybody needs somebody—right" she went on.

"As pointed out by the Blues Brothers, yes," Billy tried to be funny.

Penny ignored his quip, "So the scammer must have friends."

“Right… and?” Billy was thinking Battle Wars 3 would have definitely been more exciting than this so far.

“If we can get the scammer to tell us something about their friends, then we can get closer to who they really are!” a conclusive smile spreading across her face.

Billy was sceptical, but knew that anything was worth a try, “Go on then.”

Disappointed with his lack of enthusiasm and clear scepticism for her genius idea, Penny turned to face the computer and logged on, eager to prove to Billy that once more psychology was the superior science of the day…. Then they sat and looked at the screen for a good 45 minutes until it blinked Red on ‘Tasha’…. “Right!” Penny jumped upright in her chair, “Here we go….”

Chapter 28
Setting up Shop

Azi and Gil looked at the website they had cobbled together. It was basic, to say the least. They had spent the first day trying to work out where best to 'host' the website—they didn't want to use an internet hosting provider in Nigeria as it might be easy to trace it back to them. So, they chose one in China whose website was in English as well as Chinese.

They were not too sure what they were after but guessed they would need all the security options they were offered—partly to make the site look real, but partly to protect themselves they thought. They bought the package that gave them a domain name, meaning they could have www.expats-reunited.com and as many emails addresses for @expats-reunited.com as they wanted.

They also chose a website package that said it would help build the website. Azi had done some basic websites from scratch before using HTML but had never done anything that would have a 'catalogue' of people for dating. Plus, the website builder that came with the package offered some good design templates—neither Azi nor Gil was very creative and so welcomed whatever the templates could provide.

It turned out that there was a catalogue module they could use. The system said it was used for creating online shops that sold products, but they worked out that this is kind of what they were doing (well, pretending to do). The module was set up so they could enter information in fields called—Title; Product Desc(short); Product Desc(long); Product features(a list); Price; Availability. It also had the option for uploading up to 5 pictures and a video for each product. They quickly re-purposed these fields for their purposes and found they could even change the field labels, so it didn't look weird. Having set-up, the module, they then could enter the data—they started with Azi's favourite name first:

Old Label	New Label	Data
Product Title:	Looking For:	Love
Product Desc(short):	Name:	Melanie
Product Desc(long):	Profile:	I am a fun-loving and free-spirited lady who has travelled the world but is now ready to bring my spirit home to the UK. I want to share fun, home and life with a kind and generous man who will hold me on long winter nights. X
Product Features:	Features:	Height—5'8" Ethnicity—White British Hair—Long and Dark Shape—Slim, but with curves Other—Non-smoker; no children; loves cats
Price:	Star rating:	*****
Availability:	Horoscope:	Libra

They were both really pleased with their work and started to fill up the system with several other profiles—all women. It was only when they came across the part of the module that suggested they had enough 'products' that they should consider putting them in categories that they considered the opposite sex. So, they set about creating a load of male profiles as well, along a similar vein as the female profiles.

They then experimented further with the categories and although the main two were 'Men' and 'Women', they had subcategories of 'Coming Home' and 'Come travel with me'—that was the basis of the site, to attract people to either have an adventure with a travelling Expat or to meet Expats who wanted to end their travelling days and settle down—either way, they would have to meet and there would be the cost of a plane ticket to scam out of the victim.

Other modules they activated were 'Registration' to allow people to join the site—that had a basic link to a PayPal payment module, and they used that to collect the one-off membership fee of forty-nine ninety-nine. They didn't intend to make a fortune from the joining fee but felt it was important to have some kind of cost as people never believed things that were free could be real.

The next key bit of the website was how to connect these people. Azi had been researching other dating websites and it seems that in order to protect clients and build trust, they didn't release direct contact details for at least a couple of weeks or longer if the client chose. So, they decided they needed a 121-chat service within the website. Fortunately, there was a module for this as well and they got it working within an hour.

Gil sat on his computer and registered on the website as a client and Azi logged in as 'Melanie' on his computer. Gil requested to 'connect' with 'Melanie' and Azi could then see his details in the chat service. Normally, there would need to be some kind of 'reject' and 'accept' feature between individuals who had asked to 'connect', but they couldn't work out how to do that and anyway there were no individuals on the website side—there was just Azi and Gil, so they would just 'accept' everything by default and their clients would be none the wiser.

"Go on then, chat to me—sorry, 'Melanie'," prompted Azi.

"Oh, OK. Erm…. What shall I say?" asked Gil.

"Anything you idiot—we are only testing it!" laughed Azi.

G: Hello, Azi.

M(A): Hi, this is Melanie (not Azi!)—how are you today sexy?

G: I am fine thank you. Hi, are you Melanie?

M(A): Come on, get into it you little shit—we are meant to be pretending to work this properly—we need to practice!

G: Yes, sorry, Azi.

G: I mean Melanie.

G: Do you want to meet and have sex with me?

Azi burst out laughing, "You old smoothie Gil—you know how to chat a lady up don't you—hahaha!"

Gil sulked "Well, I don't know what to say do I—I have never had a girlfriend."

Just then Jem walked over, curious about the laughing he heard. "What's going on here then lads? I'm not paying you to mess around."

"You're not paying us at all, last I looked," smirked Azi. He could get away with this as his old friend and because no one else was around.

Jem ignored this quip, "So come on, what's so funny?"

"Gil was trying to 'chat me up'—here, take a look," offered Azi.

"Oh, dear. Poor little Gil—not had much experience with the ladies have you boy," teased Jem.

"Well, it's not my fault—I have to hang around with you two all the time and it puts them off!" Gil replied bravely.

Jem was fortunately in a good mood and could see that the guys had made good progress. "I tell you what.... It's been a good few days and I have made some good money from my loans work—let's go out ... a company party to celebrate and get Gil some experience with women!"

"Great idea," cheered Azi.

Gil wasn't so sure. He had literally no experience with girls and didn't really get on very well with alcohol. He also knew that Azi and Jem were unstable when they got drunk. However, he didn't like to go against his brother and so with as much enthusiasm as he could raise, he said, "Sounds like a good idea—thanks!"

"Cool—basic training begins tonight then!" Jem shouted with a wolf howl added for good measure.

Chapter 29
Test Questions

Joseph called a minute or so later as he said he would. He was so reliable, Elizabeth thought.

"How are you today my sweet one?" he cooed.

She loved the way he called her special little names. "I am very well thanking you. Philip has just left, and he was very chatty today—all about Singapore actually."

"Oh, right. That's nice.... Anyway, how is your leg doing? Getting better with the exercise I hope—you are keeping it up, are you?"

Joseph never seemed to like talking about himself or his life in Singapore in any great detail, which Elizabeth always thought was a shame. She always filled the gaps with the minutia of her life and Joseph seemed to enjoy listening to that. Well, not this time she thought, it was time for her to stop being selfish and let him talk.

"Yes, yes. I'm fine. Anyway, Philip was talking about this great place just outside the city called 'The Palace of Light'—it sounded great. Have you ever been there?" she asked excited to know something about Singapore to be able to talk to him about.

"Erm, yes. Yes, I have been there—a fabulous place. I am sure you would love it. A great big palace that anyone can go in and it is lit up by some really impressive lighting designs. It's mainly for tourists though, so I haven't been for a long time," Philip explained.

"Oh. I'm not sure we are talking about the same place—the Palace of Light—is that what the place you have been to is called?"

"I think so," replied Joseph, suddenly sounding less confident.

"With everything lit by candles and only Buddhists are allowed into the Palace—tourists can walk around the outside and gardens—is that the place you have been?" she asked confused.

A second or two passed.

"Oh! The Palace of Light—out near the hills. Right, I know where you mean now. No, actually, I have never been—it is meant to be very pretty with all the candles and Buddhists," his confidence returning.

"Ah, that explains it—your place didn't sound like this place. So, what is the place you went to?" she asked.

"Sorry, what place?"

"The place you thought I meant—with lighting designs for tourists."

"Oh, right. Yes, sorry. That's called .... The Light Castle—similar sort of thing, they like lights in Singapore."

Elizabeth thought he sounded distracted—she concluded that maybe visiting places like that by himself reminded him how lonely he was and how much he missed home. She decided to change the subject.

"Philip and his husband Anthony are getting a new pug soon—I don't really like dogs much—do you?"

"Did you say 'Husband'?" Joseph sounded shocked.

"Yes, you know Philip is gay—I told you."

"Erm, yes. Yes, you did. I forgot, I guess. I only think about you really."

"Oh, that's sweet of you. Yes, I told you he was gay, and he has a husband called Anthony—you remember I told you they have three pug dogs that they are crazy about!"

"And they got married? Is that legal?"

"My you have been out of touch—don't they get the news over there!" Elizabeth quipped.

"I think I must have missed when that became legal—we don't allow that sort of thing over here."

"Really? Philip said when he went to Singapore, they were very tolerant and welcomed him and Anthony with open arms."

"Erm, well some hotels are run by foreign companies and they have more relaxed rules I think—so they must have been at one of those."

Joseph was definitely having an off day—Elizabeth sensed she was making him uncomfortable talking about things in Singapore. She decided to make more of an effort to focus on the UK as he was clearly homesick.

"Anyway, it doesn't matter. When are we going to arrange for you to come back to the UK—I am desperate to meet you!"

"Oh. Yes of course—I am desperate to meet you too!" Joseph snapped back into positive—confirming to Elizabeth that he was homesick.

"Great. We haven't really talked about if you are coming for a visit or... erm.... More permanently?"

"Well, I guess that really depends on how long I am welcome for...," Joseph had gone into full sweetness mode now.

Elizabeth had no doubt of her feelings for Joseph and she would love to have him in her life permanently and close by. However, she knew that neighbours and friends would be shocked if she suddenly had a man living with her that none of them had ever heard of. Plus, she hadn't met him yet—he might pick his toenails on the sofa or snore! She didn't want to put him off—she still couldn't quite believe he was so interested in her given her circumstances—but didn't want to jump in too deep straight away.

"I think it would be lovely if you came for as long a visit as possible. There is a very nice bed and breakfast around the corner from me, I am sure they would be happy to take a long booking." She waited to see how this went down.

"That's perfect then! Let's start thinking about dates and I can book my flight. I hope they are not too much money for a round trip."

Elizabeth thought he had taken her direction of a 'visit' very well, but then wondered if the point about the cost of a return flight was a suggestion that maybe it shouldn't be returned. She decided to dive a bit deeper in, despite her initial reservations.

"Why not just book one way for now—it's cheaper and you don't know when you will go back.... If ever!" She gave a little laugh on this last point and he laughed back with her. "True, true. Those English winters may keep me in the UK!"

She was so pleased he was back to his normal self and had cheered up. She would be careful to not question him too much about Singapore again and try and focus on his return to the UK—to sweep her off her feet... perhaps.

Chapter 30
Another Failure

'Tasha' had appeared amber a few times earlier in the week and so it wasn't a total surprise that it was her and not 'Melanie' that appeared to be coming online to chat with a victim. It was a good job that Billy was there because just like with 'Melanie' he had to do some quick tracking of IP addresses and usernames etc to be able to set up the message interrupter to work for a new scammer and victim—he sorted it quickly and he and Penny were able to see that 'Tasha' was talking to 'BobTheBuilder#38'. A fiddle or two more and he told Penny, with a slightly sarcastic tone she thought, that she was good to start the message interruption.

T: *Hi Tony. Thanks for accepting my connection request on 'Expats Reunited'—I hope you didn't think I was being rude waiting two weeks before replying. I just wanted to be able to talk privately on Messenger rather than through the website—I don't trust that they don't look at our messages.*

Penny saw an opportunity and paused the message before 'BobTheBuilder#38' or Tony as he appeared to be called, could see it. She quickly changed it.

T(P): *Hi Tony. Thanks for accepting my connection request on 'Expats Reunited'—I waited for two weeks because I thought you might fancy my friend Melanie instead. It's OK if you do, just let me know you would like to talk to her, and I will set that up as she is my friend.*

BTB: *Hi Tasha. Thanks for getting in touch. I really liked your profile on the website and would like to get to know you better. I like the sound of your friend Melanie also—can I talk to her as well?*

Penny and Billy were transfixed—the response from 'Tony' could be interpreted in different ways—how was 'Tasha' going to take it they wondered?

T: *Who is Melanie? Is she someone else on the site? What makes you think she is my friend?* Penny paused that one without hesitation. She was acting on her impulses now and deleted the entire message and put a new one in its place.

T(P): *Have you looked at Melanie's profile on the website? Don't connect with her via the website if you haven't already—I can put you in direct contact and then you don't have to pay the website for the referral.*

Penny wasn't totally sure where she was going with this but just wanted to try and see if she could make a link between 'Melanie' and 'Tasha', being fairly certain already that they were the same person.

BTB: *OK—so can you give me Melanie's direct contact details then—her email and messenger username, please? You and I can talk some more later as well because I have to pop out to sort out a customer who has a plumbing issue.*

Tony seemed to be taking this in his stride and Penny didn't feel that his messages needed editing—he was following her lead unwittingly and that was fine by her.

T: *I don't know who Melanie is and why you are interested in her not me—I am blocking you now—goodbye.*

That was the end of that. Penny let the message go through to Tony and he gave one final confused 'WTF!' before it all went dead and that relationship was over.

Penny was deflated—it was harder than she thought it would be to get information about friends or anything that might give some clues about the scammer. Billy could see she needed picking up and convinced her to go to the pub with him (his computer game could wait a few hours). In the pub Penny kept going over the chat conversation as if looking for something that wasn't there—she kept asking Billy if she had got the psychology wrong.

He didn't know of course and felt bad for being sceptical earlier—at one point he had thought it was going to work and they could make the scammer slip up. After two large gin and tonics, Penny started confessing that she didn't really know what she had been doing and was a fraud. Billy knew when the drink was talking and that she would regret this tomorrow—he made a promise to himself to not bring it up in the office—Penny was becoming his friend after all and they needed to look out for each other.

What Penny and Billy didn't know is that they were the cause of an urgent 'staff meeting' in a small scammer's office in Lagos City. Had they been fly's on the wall, they would have heard worrying questions being asked such as, 'How did this guy know about Melanie—I haven't linked her in with him at all!' and 'His answers seemed to ignore my questions—like he thought the conversation with me was going well—it's like I was messaging with someone different'.

Unaware of these far away concerns, Penny and Billy carried on drowning their sorrows. As is often the case when even more drinks are consumed, they passed the point of sorrow and started to round the corner into blind optimism.

"I reckon the scammer knew we were onto them and were testing what we knew!" Penny announced a little too loudly.

Billy continued in his supporting role, "Well, exactly! You had them on the ropes Pen—no doubt about it."

"I know! Don't call me 'Pen' I am not a pig.... [snigger].... Well, I am actually and so are you—hahaha," they both fell about laughing.

Eventually, they ran out of laughter puff, "Right Pennnny. Tomorrow we are gonna get Melasha and Tania and prove they are the same person—I promise you!"

"But they are not the same people—you said it wrong Billy-boy... [snigger]," giggled Penny.

Billy hadn't realised the alcohol had made him muddle the names up and was starting to get his offended face on, "What have I done wrong now... Miss Perfect!"

For once Penny didn't take the high ground, perhaps because she was tiddly or perhaps because she had grown fond of Billy, "No, silly," she cooed, "I mean you took half of Tasha and half of Melanie and made them into each other—it's funny!"

"Is it? Good," Billy regained his composure, such as it was. "Hang on, isn't that the point though… they are each other!"

"Well exactly. Exactly! … I knew we would get there eventually…. You are a clever boy Billy… [snigger]," Penny dissolved into laughter at her own perceived funniness.

"Not as clever as you Pen… Pig… Pennnny… [hic]…. It's cos of that there psychothing… psychobabble… [hic]…. PSY-CHO-LO-GY!" Billy had stood triumphantly as he grasped the word, but then collapsed onto the seat.

"Pah! … Psycho-bollocks more like," concluded Penny in a moment of clarity before she too collapsed in an alcoholic haze.

Chapter 31
Basic Training

Gil didn't really know what to wear. It wasn't as if he had lots of choices, even though Jem had stolen them a variety of clothes over the years. He went for some dark blue jeans, trainers and a T-shirt with a drawing of the Eiffel Tower on it—his logic was that Paris was the city of romance.

Eb didn't really know what to wear. Well, he did because he had no choice—it was his church trousers and shirt or nothing. He couldn't wear his school clothes even though he didn't wear his uniform as a sixth former because if someone from the sixth form was there, then he would never live it down.

Azi and Jem were already drinking some beers they had pinched and brought back to the office. Jem handed one to Gil. Gil wasn't a big drinker as they had never wasted money on alcohol in the past, but he had tried one or two beers before. He didn't like the idea of getting drunk and losing his inhibitions—you never knew where it would lead, and he didn't like the lack of control.

Eb had told his Mum that he was going out with friends and would be back late. He was eighteen now and could do what he liked, although that didn't stop his mum from worrying about him. He knew that he was going to have some alcohol tonight but told himself he would only have one drink and carry it around all night to look like he was drinking all the time. That way he wouldn't get drunk and lose his inhibitions—you never knew where it would lead, and he didn't like the lack of control.

Gil, Jem and Azi walked into town, with Jem and Azi making lots of whistles and whoops to girls who they met on the way, regardless if they knew them or not—the girls didn't seem to mind, Gil noticed. There was only one club in town that was worth going to—it was the only one with music, drinks and the all-important bouncers, suggesting this was such a great club that they might not let you in or better still would throw you out if you didn't meet the standards. Gil had never been inside but had heard stories from Azi and Jem. The stories included rooms out the back where everyone seemed to be crawling all over each other with little or no clothes on—Gil didn't understand what the point of that was.

Eb quietly walked the back streets into town. He had arranged to meet his fellow sixth formers round the corner from the club. It was one of the boys eighteenth birthday and he had been invited along—he had initially said no, but JG had encouraged him to go and make friends. When he got to the allotted meeting place, there were about twenty lads there and he didn't know any of them really, other than some of their names.

They agreed to approach the club in batches of five so that they didn't look like a rowdy gang intent on havoc. He was assigned to his group and they set off towards the club. He had walked past this club during the day many times and always thought it looked like a dusty, run-down, town hall—now it looked like something out of the movies he had seen about Las Vegas, all lights and noises and what he took to be glamour.

Jem and Azi had been to the club many times or more accurately, had been thrown out of it many times. Gil knew this and had thought (hoped) they probably wouldn't even get in. He should have realised that the reason they always got allowed back in was because of money—a swift movement of the hand from Jem to the bouncer and a big smile appeared on the bouncers face and the way was open. They walked in and the noise was unbearably loud, Gil thought.

The area beyond the front door was like magic—it opened out into a dance floor with a bar around the outer edge, but the overall room was much bigger than the outside of the building could possibly hold. The sound and lights and moving bodies were both entrancing and repellent to Gil. He was exhilarated and scared at the same time.

The group that Eb was with had been to the club a couple of times before apparently and they knew there would be a wait. Eb stood in the queue with them and waited. He didn't talk to any of them, but they seemed OK with that—they were hugely enjoying themselves and they hadn't even got into the club yet. Eb nearly left and went home, but his curiosity got the better of him and he went in, following the others like a sheep when the bouncer let them in.

He couldn't believe his ears and eyes—he didn't know there were so many young people living around here and how they could all fit into what looked like a small building from outside. He just stood there gazing around the whole place, taking it all in. When he snapped out of the trance, he realised that his group had gone further in and he had lost them. He was in the most noisy, light flashing, body pulsating environment he could ever have imagined, and he was by himself.

Azi and Jem seemed to know everyone as they moved through the throng on the way to the bar. They didn't introduce Gil, as he followed them through. At the bar, Jem ordered three beers and Gil prepared himself to pretend to drink more than he was. You couldn't really hear anything anyone was saying, but they clinked their bottles together and shouted 'cheers'. Then Jem leaned into Gil's ear and said, "OK bruv—let's get you laid."

Gil hoped he had heard wrong, but he followed Jem with Azi behind him—there was no escape route.

Eb was really out of his comfort zone and decided that he would hide behind his acting abilities. He pushed his chest out and with a confidence that he didn't really feel, he moved onto the dance floor. The only dancing he had ever done was with his Mum and Su in their house and he didn't see anyone here dancing like that. He started to writhe as best he could because that's what others were doing.

He bumped into a small group of girls and they screamed in mock horror. Then one of them grabbed him and pulled him into the middle of them. He was scared but kept his act going and smiled and kept writhing. After a few minutes of this ('what was the point?' he kept thinking as they were doing it) the girl who had grabbed him mouthed something and pointed at the bar, then pulled him by the wrist towards it.

Jem and Azi took Gil to a corner of the club, where they were a group of girls lounging on sofas. Jem leaned in and kissed one of them long and hard—Gil was a bit taken aback, he had never seen this girl before and didn't know that Jem had a girlfriend. Jem appeared to whisper something into her ear, and she got up and came across to Gil. She grabbed Gil by the lapels and pulled him close to her so that he could feel the curves of her body against his.

Before Gil knew which way was up, she had clamped her mouth on his and appeared to be trying to extract one of his teeth with her tongue. It took Gil a moment to recover his senses and he pushed her away violently. Everyone laughed, including the girl and Jem and Azi. Then she came in for a second attempt, but Gil wasn't going to be laughed at again and anyway she tasted of stale beer and cigarettes. With Jem and Azi calling half-heartedly after him, he sprinted across the dance floor and headed for the exit.

Eb was clearly expected to buy this girl a drink and he just had enough money for two drinks—he had been planning on spending that on two drinks for himself that he had decided would be his limit. She had a beer and so did he. Despite the strange surroundings and being completely out of his depth with this girl, he was actually looking forward to tasting his first beer. He watched as the girl drank deeply from the bottle and was just raising his to his lips when she lunged at him and put her lips where he had been about to put his bottle. He flinched, dropped his bottle, followed it to the floor with his eyes and then lifted his head up sharply only to headbutt the girl on the chin.

She screamed (not that anyone heard with all the noise) and blood started to form at the edge of her mouth. She started swearing at him and he tried to apologise and offered her a napkin from the bar, but she started hitting him and he decided that it was best to leave, which he did quickly, leaving blood and tears behind him.

Outside the air was suddenly clean and it felt like coming out of being suffocated. The noise from the music still rang in the ear and even though the visit had been brief, there was a certain smell that lingered on the clothes. Panting slightly, exhausted from the encounter, a place of rest was needed.

Eb and Gil found a quiet side alley one street away from the club. They didn't notice each other, perhaps their senses still reeling from their club experiences. Anyone onlooking would have seen two mirror images leaning hard against the wall trying to catch their breath and stop themselves from being sick. Eventually, their breathing slowed and they both looked up to see where they were. This is when they noticed each other.

"Oh, hello. Sorry, I didn't realise this alley was taken," Eb offered in the hope this person was friendly and seeking refuge like himself.

"No, it's my fault—I think you must have been her first," Gil was apologetic.

"To be honest, there could have been ten of us and I am not sure I would have noticed."

"Too much to drink?"

"Ha! No. Quite the opposite—I didn't get a sip of the two drinks I paid for."

Gil noticed for the first time that he was still holding the bottle of beer Jem had given him.

"Want a swig of this?" Gil held out the bottle to Eb.

Eb moved a couple of steps closer and hesitated for a second before taking the bottle and having a big swig.

"Looked like you needed that!"

"I did. It's my first ever beer and I think it might be my last," Eb laughed.

"Sounds like your night has gone as well as mine!"

They both laughed and then fell into a companionable silence. They shared the beer in sips until it was gone. Then Eb reached out his hand and introduced himself. It was the polite thing to do and Gil did likewise. However, although it had taken him a minute in the darkness of the alley, Gil had recognised Eb and he needed no introduction whatsoever.

Chapter 32
Dropping the Bomb

Philip had phoned the previous evening and asked Elizabeth if she had spoken to Joseph at all in the last few days. She had and said so, then he asked if it was alright for him and Anthony to pop round the next day to talk to her about some concerns they had. She asked, 'what concerns?', but Philip said it was better to talk in person. Philip sounded so sincere and concerned that she decided to agree. She was fairly certain it was about Joseph and just them thinking she was a vulnerable old lady who needed someone else to look out for her—well she wasn't, and she didn't was her view of the world.

Elizabeth had met Anthony before and liked him, although found him a little too earnest in his opinions on, well everything. They breezed in like they visited all the time, which of course Philip did, but this was different. Having slept on it, she was ready to defend Joseph to the hilt. However, the wind was taken out of her sails by them not talking about Joseph.

"So how have you been Liz? How is our boy doing with getting you back to full fighting fitness?" Anthony enquired earnestly.

"Oh yes, very good progress—isn't that right Philip?" she replied honestly.

"Excellent—my best patient by far."

"And Philip tells me that you and he are going to start venturing out for small walks and maybe even some lunch somewhere—how exciting," Anthony was visibly excited, and it was all he could do to stop himself clapping his hands together quickly.

"Well, we don't want to overdo things, but maybe," she replied.

"More than maybe Liz! We are doing it—we are going to walk around the cul-de-sac and back next week if it kills us," Philip mocked a strict headmaster look.

Anthony offered to make tea and Philip used the opportunity to check with Liz that she had been doing her exercises and was feeling positive about the walkout next week. When Anthony returned with the drinks, Elizabeth had forgotten they had arranged this visit for anything more than a friendly chat.

"So, Liz… Anthony and I do want to talk to you about something…."

Elizabeth locked her body back into defence mode and was ready for attack.

"And we want you to know that we truly hope that our fears are unfounded and that this comes from much love for you…," added Anthony.

"Oh god, they are going full out with this," thought Elizabeth. She decided to get on the front foot, "It's Joseph isn't it?"

"Yes, Liz. Yes, it is," they both looked saddened.

"You think I am going too fast and giving my heart away too quickly don't you? I am a grown woman you know. I do know what love is and how to control myself!," anger rose in her as she spoke.

"No, Liz. No, that's not the problem. We know you can control yourself and you can give your heart to whoever you want—you should know we of anyone would never stand in the way of true love however quickly it came," Anthony was quick to reassure her.

"It's more about who you have actually fallen in love with… we are not sure it is 'Joseph'," Philip dropped the bombshell.

"I don't understand—how could it be anyone else? Explain yourselves!" she snapped.

"We think that 'Joseph' is actually a scammer pretending to be 'Joseph' in order to scam you out of money," Philip let the bomb explode.

Elizabeth reeled—she physically collapsed backwards into her chair, requiring its full support. She was not sure what they were going to say, but it was certainly not that. She couldn't even process it—'what did they mean 'scammer' and what was there to 'scam'?' flashed through her dazed mind.

"I…. I don't… understand. … What do you mean?" she stammered.

"Oh, Liz. I knew this would throw you for six—we are so sorry." Philip grabbed her hand with genuine compassion.

Anthony tried to steer them through, "We know it's a shock, but the important thing is that you know now, and we can help you deal with it." He had gone to the next stage too fast. Elizabeth snatched her hand away from Philip, sat up straight and with a sharpness and clarity that took the pair of them back she said, "What EXACTLY is it that you pair THINK you know. All I have heard is that you think someone isn't what they claim to be. Ignoring the fact that none of us really are and that Joseph may well have embellished his achievements or good looks a little to favour himself with me, what EVIDENCE do you have to support this crazy theory?"

She paused for breath and the silence hung in the air. "Well exactly, nothing as I thought. Are you two so jealous of a little bit of happiness I might have that you would try and ruin it for me—that's just petty and you should be ashamed!"

It was Philip and Anthony's turn to reel—they knew Liz would not like the news, but to suggest that they had made it up and were lying to her, well that hurt. Philip actually stormed off into the kitchen, apparently in rage but actually because he didn't want Liz to see how her words had hurt him and brought him to tears. Perhaps because he wasn't so involved personally with Liz or perhaps because he was the rock to Philips love, Anthony remained calm and responded.

"Now Liz. Sorry, Elizabeth," he thought full diplomacy was required, "You know Philip and I care deeply about you and would never do anything to hurt you. If you stop and think for a moment, you will come to the obvious conclusion that we must have a reason for making these accusations against 'Joseph' and that we have some 'evidence' as you say to back them up."

Elizabeth puffed out her chest, ready for another blast. Then Anthony's words must have found their way through because she deflated her chest, sat back a bit, looked thoughtful for a moment and then called to Philip, "Philip. Philip, please come back in here. Anthony is right, I know you would not do me harm on purpose."

Philip slunk back in, teary-eyed. "I can't deny that what you have said does hurt me, but I know you must have your reasons for saying it. We are friends and I want to understand what's behind all this," she patted the poof next to her, indicating Philip should come and sit close. Philip took her hand again and managed a smile.

"Now. Let's start again. Please take me through, step by step, why you think *my boyfriend* is not who he says he is."

Philip and Anthony glanced at each other—it was only for a moment, but the message that passed between them was clear—This woman was not for turning!

Chapter 33
A Nudge in the Right Direction

Jane noticed that Penny and Billy were not at their desks by 9 a.m. as normal. She assumed they had been working during the night on their scammer tracking system, so she wasn't worried. She was a little more worried an hour later when they both traipsed in looking worse for wear. She decided to drop by their desks and see how they were progressing.

"Morning you pair. Good night was it?" Jane smirked.

"Yes, Ma'am," snapped Billy a little too officiously.

"A little too good," admitted Penny, realising they had been rumbled.

Jane decided to be generous, "Well, policing is a hard job—if you can't let your hair down every now and then, what's the point?"

This perked Billy and Penny up a little and Penny offered to update Jane on their progress, such as it was. They explained how the first attempt had ended in Penny effectively encouraging the victim to offer to buy the scammer a ticket and how the second attempt had ended at the end of the victim/scammer relationship. They both looked defeated and Jane knew that a pep talk was needed.

"So, listen you two, it sounds to me like you are forgetting what you HAVE achieved. You know how to find a scammer based on having tracked down some usernames, you know what their process of grooming a victim is via common interest websites and posts, you have created a way to monitor the chat conversations between a victim and scammer and you can even interrupt those conversations and inject yourselves in the middle—I mean most people would give their right arm to have achieved that!"

They both looked a little sheepish, but also pleased to have such praise from the boss.

“I suppose that’s true,” offered Penny, “But we haven’t actually made a difference yet.”

“Pah—if you want to make it in the world of police detecting then you need to set your expectations lower than that! Detective work is slow and painful—you need high levels of resilience. Part of that is celebrating small victories—so last night was not you drowning your sorrows, but a celebration of progress.”

Having completed the pep talk, Jane decided to stay and help them out a bit. “Right, let the dog see the rabbit.”

“Sorry, Ma’am?” Billy looked non-plus.

“I want to help you—show me what it is that you are coming unstuck with.”

“Oh, right. Well, basically we need to find a way of being the victim more successfully,” Penny explained. She then showed Jane transcripts of the two chat sessions they had intercepted. Jane took a moment or two to follow the flow, having to work out when the scammer was the scammer and when it was really Penny pretending to be the scammer and vice-versa for the victim and Penny.

“OK—got that. So, let’s brainstorm this together….” Jane knew what she thought they should do but wanted them to come up with the idea rather than her just tell them. “What is the key risk?”

“That either the scammer or the victim finds out that we have been manipulating their responses,” Penny replied with confidence.

“And what will happen if one of them does?”

Billy wanted to be part of this, “Well, they will think something is wrong and abandon the chat.”

“So, who is that a problem for?”

“Well, the scammer will lose the opportunity to scam—so that’s lost business for them. And the victim will….” Penny paused. “Erm, well they will….”

“Lose the opportunity to be scammed?” Jane said with a sarcastic eyebrow raise.

“When you put it like that, I guess not.”

“But they would be upset of course because they will be left confused and disappointed,” Jane offered generously.

“I would be,” chimed in Billy.

“OK—so we don’t care about the scammer’s feelings or loss of business. But we do care about the victim’s feelings—how could we help with that?” Jane asked the pair who were clearly not following her lead very well.

"Perhaps after the relationship has ended, we could contact the victim and tell them?" offered Billy.

Penny replied to him "No, because that would be too late to avoid them feeling bad and also, we don't want the relationship to end until we have enough evidence to catch the scammer."

"Go on…," encouraged Jane.

"So…. Perhaps we could tell them before the relationship ends?" Penny tentatively offered.

"Great thinking! So how best could we do that?" Jane was happy they were getting there.

Billy is still keen to add something, "We tell them before the scammer chats with them!"

"OK. This is brilliant—you two are on fire," 'eventually' she thought.

Penny took back control, "Billy, you can use your pre-messaging search thingy to identify potential victims and their usernames—right?"

"Yup."

"And we can then contact them, telling them who we are, what we are doing and asking them to help us 'trick' the scammer—in effect, they become part of our team," Penny was getting into her stride now.

"What if they don't want to get involved?" asked Billy.

"Well, they will have been warned, which is better than nothing and we move onto the next potential victim until someone wants to play ball—right Ma'am?"

"Right. So, what you gonna get these victims to do for you?" teasing the next step out of her staff.

"We could give them a script—some questions designed to extract information out of the scammer."

"And we could also have a separate chat going on with the victim to advise them what to say based on the responses they get from the scammer," Billy was getting up to speed.

"OK. So, what info do we want to get from the scammers?" Jane felt they were nearly there.

"Ideally their real name and location!" Billy replied flippantly.

Jane ignored the flippancy, "And if we can't get that…?"

"Details of their friends or other people they work with. Anything about their surroundings that might give away their location. Anything about their operation. Ideally some means of tracking where the money goes." A light bulb flashed above Penny's head, "Perhaps we could get them to use a payment service that we control so that we could trace the money to them!"

Jane rose and put her hands on both their shoulders, "My work here is done…."

Chapter 34
The First Punter

Gil had been ribbed severely by Jem and Azi for a few days following the nightclub incident and he had tried to not let it show. It did annoy him that they had put him in that situation, but he was comforted by the fact that he had found a fellow 'socially shy' person in Eb. They had agreed to meet for coffee two days after their first encounter and had hit it off right from the start. Eb moaned about how his mum and teacher were pushing him to 'get out more' and mix with 'new people', but he just wanted to focus on his acting, which was both his mask from the real world and his release of all his emotions that remained hidden the rest of the time.

Gil had been worried about meeting for coffee—accidentally meeting the boy (well he was a man now really) whose father you had been involved in accidentally killing, was one thing and could have happened sooner than it did given they used to go to the same school and live in the same area, but agreeing to meet for coffee and possibly becoming friends, he had mixed feelings about that.

What made Gil turn up for that first coffee was a mix of loneliness and some idea that he could make up for the death of Eb's father. He didn't tell Jem or Azi that he had met Eb—they would go ballistic at him. Jem and Azi had looked after Gil all his life and he owed them for that, but they never really let him mix with people his own age or, as the nightclub incident proved, allow him to do things his own way—his secret meetings with Eb gave him the ability to progress something for him and at his own speed.

Eventually, the teasing fell away and they all focussed on the work at hand—the dating website scam. Azi and Gil had worked tirelessly to get the website working smoothly and had informed Jem they were ready for their first attempt to con someone. They all then realised that they had to let people know about the website and attract them to use it—no point having done all that work if no one found the website. Jem was reluctant to register their details with Google and Facebook in case it got linked back to them, but eventually conceded they needed to advertise to get the punters in. Gil had worked on the online advert and was pleased with the result.

'Looking for Love? Got a welcoming home to offer? We can match you with a world travelled, modern-day adventurer who is ready to settle down. Expats re-united—bringing love back home to stay!'

He nearly got carried away and created an advert to attract the travellers who wanted to go home, but then he realised that bit was made up and there were no expats who wanted to be re-united—it was just their scammer personas!

Much against Jem's principles, they paid to place the adverts on Google and Facebook, targeting a UK audience, then sat back and hoped it would work. Whilst they were waiting, they created the expats profiles on the website, changing each one just enough to make them sound different. They used pictures that they found on the internet, mainly from porn sites in the hope that people who wanted to find love would not be frequent users of porn sites and recognised the expats false pictures.

Pictures were the easy part—making up names and descriptions for each profile was proving challenging. Then Azi had the idea to plagiarise… they went to match.com, signed up and trawled the profiles, copying and pasting straight from that website to theirs, only changing one of two details as they did it. Gil thought this was wrong to start, then Azi pointed out to him that their whole business was not what you would call 'right' and so Gil complied.

Like any new business, they were keen to get their first 'customer' and they didn't have to wait long. A man signed up called Gerald. He was from the Cotswolds, which meant nothing to Azi and Gil, and he enjoyed fishing and fine dining as his 'interests'. He appeared to be a solicitor and according to his profile submission had 'made a tidy sum over the years' running his own business.

Whilst the website allowed people to register, look at profiles and ask to be 're-united' with anyone they liked the look/sound of, all without Azi or Gil having to do anything, they also had the ability to watch where on the website a user was visiting—what profiles, how long they lingered on a profile etc. Initially, they were just interested, but soon realised they could use this to discover more about the visitor and use that to build their trust later. They discovered that hobbies were a real connection point for punters—they started to visit various well-known hobby websites and like posts and comment on pictures etc using the same usernames as their fake profiles—this meant that they could state their hobbies in their fake profiles and it would attract people more—the past likes and comments enhancing the illusion they were real people with real interests.

They were really pleased and let out a team cheer between them when Gerald selected a profile to 're-unite' with—it was a woman called 'Evie' (Blonde, 5'9", Slim with curves, likes baking and long walks). This cheer brought Jem over from his corner and he joined in the monitoring of Gerald. They were slightly surprised when Gerald then also selected two other profiles to 're-unite' with—it hadn't occurred to them that this would happen, but they reasoned it was a good way to do it from Gerald's point of view—keeping his options open they guessed.

They decided it was best to wait twenty-four hours before responding to make it more authentic. The next day they replied by accepting the 're-unite' request for each one Gerald had sent—they accepted as 'Evie' at 10 a.m., then waited two hours until they accepted as 'Melanie', then 3 hours until they accepted as 'Tasha', congratulating themselves on being clever to space out the replies to maintain the charade they were different people.

Almost as soon as 'Evie' had accepted the request, Gerald sent 'her' a message via the 121messenger module they had built into the website:

G: Hi Evie! Thanks for accepting my 're-unite' request. It's great to be connected. Your profile sounds brilliant and you look stunning in your picture. I guess you liked my profile, and hopefully, I don't look too bad in the picture I used [laughing emoji]! I would really like to chat and get to know you better. I look forward to hearing from you soon. X.

Waiting a little while before responding, the three of them concocted a reply:

E: Hi Gerald! You are a sweetie—I am so glad you like my picture. We seem to have a few things in common and I would love to get to know you more. I will try and be on here at about 4 p.m. this afternoon so that we can do an instant chat—chat soon! X

It was obvious but funny to see Gerald send the first 121 messages to the other two women—they were identical to the one to Evie but with the name changed. They couldn't send their same message back of course and had to come up with two different replies—they realised that they were going to have their work cut out if they got lots of customers and they all selected multiple profiles!

Chapter 35
The Honeypot

Phillip and Anthony slowly took Liz through their initial suspicions—the way 'Joseph' had started flirting and then stopped; the young voice; the bad internet signal in modern Singapore; and the background to the photos he had sent her. Naturally, she had answers to every one of these.

"We are not young anymore and neither of us had 'flirted' with anyone for years—he was just out of practice and spooked himself. He soon recovered the next day and has been very flirty ever since. As to the young voice, well that is just ridiculous—you can't say he is a fraud because he has a young-sounding voice!"

"But what about the internet and the pictures Liz?" persisted Philip.

"Some people have bad reception where they live even in this country—you know that. I can never talk to my Aunt Lil unless she goes into the next village as her village has awful mobile reception and she lives just outside Manchester!" she paused from breath.

"As for the pictures—I know you two have been to Singapore, but you can't know every little bit of the landscape—they were pictures taken years ago and he could have been anywhere—he didn't say they were pictures taken whilst in Singapore you know," she concluded her defence.

The men looked at each other and pressed on.

"OK. We knew you might say something like that—to be honest, we came up with similar possible explanations ourselves," Anthony said.

"Well, there you go then," she snapped.

"But…," continued Philip, "Do you remember last week I was talking to you about our visit to Singapore?"

"Yes…," Elizabeth replied suddenly feeling that something was not right.

"Well actually, we never have been to Singapore and I fed you some false information about it—hoping, no, knowing that you would not miss the opportunity to show off to 'Joseph' your new knowledge—sorry!"

"Well, I never. That's very sneaky Philip—how dare you!"

"We dare because we care," interjected Anthony. She glared at him.

Philip continued, "So did you talk to 'Joseph' about 'The Palace of Light'?"

"Yes, we did. He knew all about it."

"Did he really?" Philip wondered if their trap had gone wrong.

"Well, we were talking at cross purposes to start with—I was telling him about your place, and he thought I was talking about another place called—what was it? … 'The Light Castle', that's it—very similar apparently," she said with some satisfaction.

Anthony got out their iPad and went to a Google Search page—he held it so that Liz could see and typed 'The Palace of Light Singapore'—it came back with no results that were about somewhere in Singapore with that name. He then searched for 'The Light Castle Singapore', and again no result was found.

Elizabeth was taken aback, "What does that mean? Why can't Google find either of them?"

"That's simple… neither of them exists. We made them up to see how well 'Joseph' knew Singapore."

Elizabeth didn't know what to say and so Philip pressed their advantage, "Did you also talk to him about our trip out there?"

"Well, sort of…. He seemed to be annoyed talking about Singapore and so I changed the subject to the new pug you are getting. I then talked a little bit about you two and he realised I was saying you had got married—he then said something about gays not being welcome where he was and I challenged that saying that you had been welcomed with open arms when you went to Singapore—now I think about it, he did then backtrack and say that some hotels are more friendly towards gay people than the country in general so that makes sense with your experience."

She was clinging to hope that it all made sense and their trick questions hadn't worked.

"Ah, but it is well known that Singapore is NOT at all sympathetic to gay people and that we would have to have kept it a total secret—so he got that wrong as well," finished Philip.

“Well, he did initially say gay people were not welcomed—so he sort of got that right,” she was clutching at straws a little and knew it.

Anthony took over from Philip, “Well, if that is not enough to convince you… did you tell him you knew the meaning of his name?”

Elizabeth realised she had really been suckered into taking this false information and they had relied on her wanting to impress Joseph, which of course she did and had fallen straight in with what they had planned with these tricks.

“Well, I did try and make a joke about him being ‘the mighty one of Egypt’, but he didn’t seem to bite and I got the distinct impression he didn’t know that’s what his name meant, which I admit I thought was strange at the time—are you telling me that was a trick as well?”

Anthony held up the iPad once again and there on the screen was the true meaning of the name Joseph—*‘The name Joseph is a boy’s name of Hebrew origin meaning ‘Jehovah increases’.*

Elizabeth couldn’t help a small gasp, “It doesn’t even mean what you told me it meant!”

With this final piece of misinformation revealed and the false responses that Joseph had given being laid out in front of her, Elizabeth had no option but to concede. Her initial reaction was to break down in tears, then a bit more denial, with some going over the facts again, then final acceptance and then… anger!

“Right, well. No one makes a fool out of Elizabeth Gresham! How are we going to get this so-called ‘Joseph’ and make him pay for his crimes?”

Anthony left Phillip consoling Liz and went to make them all a cuppa to calm their nerves. He was glad for Liz and also for Phillip, who had been worried sick about telling Liz, that they had got to the same conclusion. He and Phillip had argued about the next bit and had not yet reached an agreement as they thought convincing Liz that ‘Joseph’ was some kind of scammer would take more than one trip. The fact that they had convinced her so quickly just underpinned in his mind how susceptible she was to a persuasive person, which is what had got her into this mess in the first place. He would have to push Phillip a bit now, whilst they had momentum.

“I put extra sugar in it for the shock Liz,” Anthony placed the cuppa beside her.

“Thank you, Anthony.”

"I think we should try to breathe a little now Liz and think about the way forward another day—you have had a lot to take in today," Phillip spoke soothingly.

"But what happens when he contacts me later today—he will you know—we speak every day." She started sobbing again as she said this, realising that it had all been false.

"Well, Phillip and I have been thinking about this and I think we have a plan."

"No, Anthony—I am not sure that's the right thing for Liz—she has been through enough," rebuked Phillip.

"What? What is the plan and why don't you like it Phillip?" she asked.

"Anthony thinks we should get the police involved."

"I agree!" Elizabeth was regaining her composure and the fight was coming back.

"Hang on, you haven't heard it all yet… go on then Anthony…. Explain your idea," Phillip conceded.

"OK—well we tell the Police, but we get you to keep communicating with 'Joseph' so that he doesn't think he has been rumbled. That way we can help the police track him down."

"Oh. I am not sure if I could do that—I don't ever want to speak to that horrid man again!"

"We understand that which is why we think you should pretend to have a bad cold and not speak to him, but just do online chat," expanded Anthony.

"I am not sure I could even do that and remain civil, let alone be romantic with him."

"But that's the point, you won't have to—me, Phillip and the police will be the ones messaging him—you can just help by directing us with how you say things to him."

"Hhhmmmm. I'm not sure. Can't we just stop communicating with him and give the police all the details we have about him?"

"We don't have any really though—do we—he is just your online boyfriend that says he lives in Singapore—we don't have an address, a phone number or anything—we need to 'keep him on the line' whilst the police work out how to track him down." Anthony was treading carefully, but getting the point across to help Liz make up her mind.

"I think I know what you mean—I am to be the bait that distracts him, whilst the police go around the back to nab him," she was getting into it a bit now.

"Funny enough," chimed in Phillip, "it's a well-known technique called 'The Honeypot trap'—so you will be getting your own back by scamming him."

Elizabeth had gone through a range of emotions in the last hour, but now she had a new one welling up—revenge—and it was starting to feel better than the other emotions….

Chapter 36
The Average Person

Initially excited by the idea 'they' had come up with during the brainstorm with Jane, Penny and Billy were fasting losing the will to live again. Yes, Billy's pre-messaging search was turning up potential victims all over the place, but they started to realise that was part of the problem—they were not necessarily in Norfolk and this made it difficult to engage with them. You couldn't just phone or email someone and tell them they were about to be scammed and could they help you prevent that—they were likely to think you were part of the scam! There was the added complication that if they tried to work with a victim outside their jurisdiction, they might get their hands slapped.

They did find several possible candidates in Norfolk and decided the best approach was to just turn up on their doorstep. Again, this was harder than it sounded, yes the police could use their special privileges to find out where people live based on no more than their name, but often they didn't have that really, Farmer John'; 'Barrythechat'; 'SexySarah78'; and 'Suecrosswordqueen1#' were not exactly full names. The way they got around it in the end was to actually become a type of scammer themselves—Billy would track a username and see where it appeared on Instagram, Facebook, Twitter etc and then would join the same communities and try to connect with them by showing they were interested in the same things.

Once they had connected on one of the social media platforms, they could message them and offer to send them some material through the post about whatever the thing was they were interested in. A complicated approach, but more successful than it might be thought, mainly on the basis that people will connect with anyone on social media who shows them the slightest bit of interest—in itself a huge problem, thought Billy.

At the end of three weeks of chasing people around and trying to establish a real connection with them to get their full name, they had a list of ten people in Norfolk who they thought were about to be scammed or had already started to be scammed—all without these people knowing, which was slightly ironic.

Penny and Billy booked an update session with Jane before going out to try and convince the potential victims to help—partly because they wanted her to sign-off on the work they had done and the approach they were taking, but partly because they were quite nervous about this next step and needed some advice.

"So, today is the day you start knocking on doors then is it?" Jane knew what they had come to talk about. She gestured for them to take seats in front of her desk.

"Yes. We have practised what we are going to say and feel confident that we will be able to convince them to let us help them not get scammed," Penny said with confidence.

"What we can't work out," Billy cut to the chase, "is if we should wear a uniform or not?"

"Ah. On the one hand, you think it might frighten them and put them on the back-foot, and on the other hand, you think they will take you more seriously than if you go in civvies. Yes, tough one...." Jane rubbed her chin in the way people do when they want to show they are thinking about your question.

"I think uniform will make them pay attention to us," Penny cast her vote.

"I think it will make us come across as less empathetic," Billy cast his.

Jane took a moment to think about how these two colleagues had rubbed off on each other—Billy had been the straightforward, no-nonsense copper and Penny the 'I've got a degree in psychology' new breed of police-persons that thought everything could be solved with thinking. Now Penny wanted to use the old fashion uniform 'police brand' and Billy was banging on about Empathy—maybe these two were the perfect team or maybe they needed some time apart—she wasn't sure.

"I think you are both right," Jane said without explaining further. "Who is first on your list?"

"A Mr Paul Underwood. Fifty-five years of age. Local accountant, who is interested in sports cars—that's how we found him—it's one of the topics the scammers' target," Penny trotted out efficiently.

"OK—well I suggest that Billy goes in uniform and you wear plain clothes then Penny."

Before she could stop herself, Penny blurted out "But I was the one who thought the uniform was the best approach."

"So you were. However, and I am surprised you didn't apply your psychology here Penny… a man will take a man in uniform seriously immediately and then open up to a woman not in uniform over a cup of tea. Vice-versa for women. In my humble experience…." She threw the last bit in to see if they would contradict her. They didn't. Politically correct it wasn't but spot on in the main—the boss knew her people techniques alright.

"You can swap around when the potential victim is a woman—it will be good for you to practice your in-the-field interviewing techniques together. Good luck!" That was all the advice they were getting evidently and they both trouped out.

"How are we meant to keep swapping from uniform to non-uniform and back again—I'm not superman you know. I can't just go into a phone box!" Billy wasn't very happy.

Penny wasn't pleased with the arrangement either, but knew it was the right way to do it and so was more pragmatic, "We can just change in the back of the car or go to a petrol station and use the toilets or something—it's not like anyone is going to object if one of us is in uniform."

"S'pose," Billy could be a real teenager sometimes. He traipsed off to the men's locker room to put on his uniform.

Penny went to the women's locker room to pick hers up and apply a bit of lipstick—no point in looking shabby, she reasoned with herself.

The first address was just outside Norwich on a small housing estate that was recently built. They found the address easily and Billy parked the car and they both got out and approached the front door. They had decided not to go in a squad car for fear of making the neighbours talk, but they underestimated the local estate 'curtain twitchers'—they were not halfway up the path before at least two curtains visibly twitched. It was dark because they had decided to go around 7 p.m. as most people were in at that hour, but Billy's fluorescent strips on his uniform were enough to get the neighbours excited. Billy rang the doorbell.

"Oh gosh, officer. It's not my son is it?" Mr Underwood went white as a sheet as he feared the worst. This was a common event whenever police knocked on someone's door who were not expecting them—Penny and Billy had covered it in basic training.

"No need to panic sir. We are just here on a routine enquiry. We are not aware of any accidents or danger to you or your loved ones. May we come in please?" Billy hadn't said that since his first few weeks on the beat a year or more ago, but he pitched it right and Mr Underwood visibly relaxed.

"Well, thank goodness for that," deep exhaling, "a routine enquiry you say—well I hope I can help you officer and … erm…. Miss?" he opened the door to allow them both in.

"Constable Penny—I'm not in uniform," she said somewhat pointlessly.

"Oh right. Please come in. Can I get you a cup of tea or coffee?" Mr Underwood wanted to know what this routine enquiry was, but he knew his hosting duties and particularly for servants of the public.

"Yes, please," replied Billy enthusiastically. Penny glared at him—she wanted to get on with it. Mr Underwood led them into the lounge, asked how they took it and promised to be back in a minute.

"Why did you say yes? He was only being polite. Anyway, we might only be here for a minute," Penny moaned at Billy as soon as Mr Underwood was out of earshot. Billy didn't respond and they sat in silence, looking around the room. It was a perfectly normal lounge—brown three-seater settee and a matching armchair, both with those modern oversized cushions; a part glass/part wood coffee table, a little more dated but standard; a TV in one corner mounted on the wall with all the modern-day set-top boxes and DVD players wired into it; and a few pictures and a lamp.

"Billy went off into a bit of a daydream and would have been surprised to hear that he and Penny were having the same thought as they took in the very average, normal surroundings of Mr Underwood's home…. 'How can someone so normal, living in such a normal place, become a victim of a scammer on the internet, hidden thousands of miles away in some hell-hole?'"

The answer, as they would find out, was nothing to do with what you saw in a victim's outside world, but everything to do with what was going on in their mind—where there is no such thing as 'average'.

Chapter 37
Coming of Age

Amelia woke with a start. She often did when she had been dreaming or more likely having a nightmare about Dev. It was coming up to the anniversary of Dev's death and even though seven years had passed, she still thought of him every day. He had meant the world to her and the children—she didn't really know how she had survived all this time without him. She carried him in her heart and that seemed to just about get her through.

That and the children—both of them. As she settled from her sharp wake-up, she thought about that a little more—both of them. It was the way in Nigeria that boys and men were the focus for progress and success, with the girls and women being a supporting act. Amelia had liked it this way. It was certainly the way her parents' marriage had worked and that is how she and Dev set out in their life together.

Recently, however, having in effect been the main provider and in charge of the family, she had started to wonder if this was an old-fashioned view and that women should have a better place in society. Perhaps 'better' was not the word she thought, as they were not badly treated in general—perhaps 'equal' was the word. Although she quickly dismissed this from her mind, knowing equality of the sexes in her country was a long way off. She settled on 'fairly' as the mid-ground word.

That led her to think if she had followed her own thoughts when it came to her children.

Since Dev had died, she and many of her extended family had consistently told Eb that he 'was the man of the house' now and must behave like it. A tear warmed her cheek in the early morning air as she realised how unfair that had been on Eb as a young boy—he should not have had that burden put on him so young. However, she was proud of how he had risen to the task over the years and was a man, in most ways, now. He was being well educated, had good manners and a great work ethic. He had even talked of a friend outside of the sixth form who he was growing fond of and met for coffee a couple of times a week—this was a real sign of maturity, she thought. Then she thought of Su. She always thought of Su second—it was not that she loved her any less, far from it, but first-born children and particularly boys always had priority—that's just how it was.

Su had also struggled with the loss of her daddy—she had been so young that she didn't really know him, but it was more whilst she was growing up that she missed having that father figure around the house. Eb had been a good brother, but their relationship was typical of siblings. Amelia had lost count of the number of times she had been called into school to listen to Su's bad behaviour or to apologise to another parent for how Su had treated their child.

There were certainly a few grey hairs on Amelia's head that Su was directly responsible for. Not that it made up for the loss of a father or a mother who poured most of her energy into her son's success, but Amelia made sure that at least once a year she would focus solely on Su—on her birthday.

This year Su was turning fourteen and that's the age of becoming a woman in Nigeria. Amelia knew that she wouldn't want a party with girlfriends like in previous years—she would want to go 'out' with her friends. This didn't mean anything as serious as a nightclub, but she would expect a meal out somewhere with friends. The trouble is, that cost a lot of money. As Amelia got dressed in her small bedroom and went through her getting up routine, she tried to think how she could give her daughter the kind of 'coming of age' treat that she deserved. She had some money put aside for a present for Su, but she couldn't afford to pay for a meal out as well as a present.

Amelia moved into the kitchen and started preparing food for the meal that evening, so she wouldn't have too much to do when she got home from work. She wondered if she could go back to the loan shark and ask for a month's breathing room on her repayments—she had been on time every month since taking it out, so surely, she deserved some support with this. She determined she would ask them—she had a week before Su's birthday. She dug out the 'contract' she had with them and found the phone number on the back. They didn't have a phone at home, but there was a public phone on the way to work, so she hurriedly finished her preparations, popped her coat on and left for work.

The phone rang three times and then was answered gruffly, "Yeah?"

“Oh, hello. Is it possible to speak to Mr J. Adeyemi please?” Amelia put on her best voice.

“Who wants him?” Azi replied although Amelia had no idea who the voice belonged to.

“This is Mrs Azikiwe I took out a loan some time back and I wanted to ask him if I could have a break from payments for one month. It’s my daughter’s coming of age birthday you see, and I want to treat her to a party—you know how these things are,” she spoke quickly to get it all out.

“Ha! Well, I can’t see him agreeing to that, but I will pass you a message on,” Azi laughed.

“Oh. OK. Well, thank you. How will I hear from him please?”

“We know how to contact you—don’t worry,” and Azi cut her off.

There was nothing more likely to make her worry than the last sentence this gruff man said. She put the phone down and stood wondering if she had done the right thing. She didn’t notice the queue behind her waiting to use the phone until someone shouted at her to get a move on. She snapped back to reality and rushed off in the direction of the factory.

When she got to work and joined the part of the production line she worked on, she told her co-workers about what the gruff man on the phone had said and asked what they thought. They didn’t hold their opinions back—ranging from a simple ‘they mean they have your address and will write to you to let you know their decision’ to ‘I wouldn’t walk home by yourself tonight if I were you!’ Normally a problem shared is a problem halved, but thanks to the opinions of her workmates Amelia felt quite scared by the time it was time to go home.

The journey home was normal, apart from her nervously looking over her shoulder all the time and she was just starting to relax as she got the key out to unlock her front door when she realised it was slightly ajar. She froze and then had an instinct to run, but Su would be home soon and she needed to know what was going on with her home. She slowly pushed the door open and tip-toed in.

“Good evening, Mrs Azikiwe—I hear you want to change our arrangement. So, I thought I would provide good customer service and drop round to ‘discuss’ it with you.” Jem was pleased to be out of the office and dealing with another one of his business ‘interests’, although this particular client had some personal history, which made it a little more challenging for him.

Chapter 38
Google Me

It had been two days since Philip and Anthony's visit. Elizabeth had driven herself almost mad going back over all the conversations she had with 'Joseph'—literally in most cases because she had all the messaging history stored on her iPad. No matter how hard she looked, she couldn't see how she could have seen that he was not for real—there were just no indicators that he wasn't completely the person he was pretending to be. She wrote down what she knew to get it clear in her mind.

- Joseph White
- 64 years old
- Tall and broad
- White stubble beard
- Handsome with tanned skin
- Lives in Singapore
- Works at a school doing Caretaking work
- Interested in old motorbikes
- Likes Marmite, Warm beer and Coronation Street
- Kind, thoughtful and a bit cheeky
- Has a young voice

The last point about his young voice was the only thing that was even vaguely weird about him and plenty of people sounded different from their age. She decided to take a look at the photos he had sent—mostly of him with old motorbikes. Most of the pictures were a slightly younger-looking man than the one of him in front of the school he worked at ('did he actually work at a school?') and also mostly in the UK judging by the backgrounds. She couldn't find any picture with Singapore landmarks in the background, but then she didn't really know what modern-day Singapore was like so that was not conclusive. 'Maybe he isn't even in Singapore' she thought but couldn't think of anything in the information she had that would disprove that.

She was feeling totally despondent when Philip came in for her therapy—he was his normal cheery self and it was as if the other day hadn't happened at all. However, that was just his bedside manner—as soon as he had put all his gear down, he came across and went into full drama mode.

"So, my lovely, how have you been holding up?" he stroked her hand.

To Philip's surprise, she said "Well, I am going crazy trying to unpick that bastard's web of lies and just not getting anywhere!"

"Oh. Right… well I suppose that's better than crying yourself to sleep."

"Why would I be crying myself to sleep?" Elizabeth snapped in reply.

"Well, you know… under the circumstances…." Philip wasn't sure what to say.

"Philip—I may have behaved a bit like a lovesick puppy for the last few weeks and I apologise for that. However, please remember that I am a strong woman who has been the innocent victim of a criminal mastermind. I am not to blame, and I don't wish to feel like a victim—so please stop talking to me like one!" Elizabeth could have been running for parliament with that speech.

"Sorry, my love. I just don't know how you do it—I would be so distraught. You are so brave," Philip replied with genuine feeling and a desire to not annoy her more.

Elizabeth knew she had overreacted, but it was the only way she could hide that she really was distraught. She was heartbroken. She felt like a victim. She still had moments where she thought 'Joseph' was the real deal and this was all a bad dream. But she had to remain strong and not give in to the weakness she felt tugging at her constantly. She decided to tell Philip about her investigations. They had agreed not to go to the police for a few days. Elizabeth was keeping 'Joseph' at bay by telling him she had the flu and would be in bed sleeping for 4-5 days, so not to worry. She had hated even sending that one message to him now she knew he wasn't her Joseph, but it had to be done to buy some time.

Having reviewed her list of facts they knew about 'Joseph' and re-looking at the photos, Philip had to agree that it didn't look dodgy on the surface. They needed something to prove that this made-up person wasn't real, but he just sounded and looked so real. Philip had an idea.

"Have you tried Google image search?"

"No—what is that?" Elizabeth asked.

"Well, I haven't really used it, but apparently you can search for things using an image."

"How will that help?"

"You have some pictures of 'Joseph'—so let's use them to search for him."

"I don't understand—how can we find him with a picture of him—anyway, he doesn't exist?" Elizabeth reasoned.

"Well, that person in that picture must actually exist—perhaps finding something about him online will give us a clue to who the scammer is," Philip was losing confidence in his idea as he spoke. "Here, let's use a picture of me to see how it works."

Philip picked up the iPad and gave it to Liz to take his picture—he sat with his back to a cream wall without any pictures or furniture to make it as plain a picture as possible. Liz took it and then Philip sat next to her to upload the picture to Google Images. They were both surprised when instantly twenty results sprang up on the page. Many of them were of men who had a reasonable resemblance to Philip, but three of them were pictures of Philip with links to related websites.

The first one was to his own Physiotherapy website that he used to advertise his service—he had put up a nice smiley picture on the front page as Anthony said it made people feel he was open and approachable; the second was to a Pugs fandom blog, where Philip had registered to be able to comment on cute pictures of Pugs (he squealed with delight at this one, but Elizabeth remained calm); and the third one was a dating website—Philip was shocked at this because he hadn't used that website for seven years (before he met Anthony), although he couldn't help being flattered that Google thought he looked the same today as he had seven years ago!

"Well, that works then!" Philip was chuffed his idea had proven good.

"So, shall we try it on 'Joseph' then?" Liz asked tentatively.

"Let's go for one of those pictures with a motorbike—I read that the more detail in a picture, the more likely you are to get good results—context or something."

"OK. I have them all stored on the iPad from when he sent them to me… right, how about this one?" 'Joseph' was sitting astride a Kawasaki motorbike and looked about forty years old.

She uploaded the photo, and they waited anxiously for a result. They got plenty of pictures and links to websites about the Kawasaki motorbike, but none of the men sitting on them looked remotely like 'Joseph'. They were bitterly disappointed.

"Try the one of how he looks today," suggested Philip.

"The one in front of the Singapore school he works in. OK…."

The photo was uploaded, Elizabeth clicked 'submit' and again they waited. This time they were both surprised to see the first result was the exact same picture of 'Joseph' and it had a link to a website. It was a link to an Online Newspaper called 'Lagos weekly' and the summary info under the link read "Mr Joseph Grey, one of the founders of building the school and now a well-liked teacher by the grateful children of Lagos."

Philip couldn't contain himself, jumping up and walking fast around the small room, "Oh my god! Oh my god! Oh my god!" he kept saying.

Elizabeth was equally moved but controlled her emotions—she needed them for the next click….

Chapter 39
Help Us to Help You

"Thanks for the tea, Mr Underwood," Penny was in charm mode.

"That's fine—least I can do for our boys-in-blue. Oh. Sorry—girls, oops I mean women as well," he fumbled his words trying to be calm. "Please call me Paul—it's not like you are arresting me or anything," he added with a nervous laugh.

Penny and Billy had also been taught in their initial training that this was an expected reaction from the public—a 'guilty without reason' reaction they called it. Despite rating high on the 'most trusted people in society' across the UK, the Police managed to scare everyone into admitting guilt they didn't have without evening saying anything. It was annoying, but they had got used to it quickly.

What Penny couldn't get used to was the sexism, "It's OK, we don't arrest people for misogyny… yet." She gave a broad smile that anyone paying attention would have realised meant 'but I would if I could you bigoted little man'. It was a pet hate of Penny's, but funnily enough not of all women in the Police—most seemed to think of themselves as sex-less when in uniform and therefore somehow equal. Penny was a bit more of a glamour-puss and wanted to 'own' that and still be an effective Police officer, which seemed fair enough to her.

Billy knew about Penny's feelings towards equality and cringed as soon as Paul Underwood had made the error, but he didn't feel that Penny's response did her any favours. It was a complex issue for a young, male Police officer and Billy did his best to steer clear of it—he found that thinking of the women in the Police as sex-less was the best way to do that.

They had agreed that Penny would do most of the talking, but Billy could see that she was annoyed already and that wasn't the way to start this conversation, so he took the initiative, "Paul. I'm Billy and this is Penny. We work in the cyber-crimes unit of Norfolk Constabulary."

"Ooh, that's sounds interesting. I use the internet a lot. Erm, mainly for research for my work." Paul was still a little nervous and overtalking a little.

"That's good—you will understand the dangers of the internet then. That's what we want to talk to you about," explained Billy.

"Oh yes, I know all about those—we did a course at work. A very nice man and woman came in for the morning and tried to scare us with talk of viruses, hackers, scammers. I mean I am sure everything they said was true, but no one is interested enough in the work we do that they would 'attack' us—so I am not sure it wasn't a little melodramatic." Paul was almost talking to himself. They could see it would be hard to keep him on the topic.

Penny had re-focussed and took back the discussion, giving Billy a little nod to show that she was 'back in the room' and would proceed as they had discussed. Billy was perfectly happy with that and sat back to drink his tea.

"Well, that's great, Paul—you are clearly up to speed on these things. However, in our experience, it is those that least expect it that often get caught out."

"Well, yes, that's true as well. There was this time when I," Paul began.

Penny cut him off—this was going to take forever if they were not careful and he was just their first potential victim. "The thing is Paul," Paul stopped talking and clearly wasn't offended at being interrupted—something that happens to him a lot thought Penny.

"The thing is—we think someone might be targeting you."

"Me? But I am nobody. I am an accountant—you can't get much more boring than that. Why would anyone be interested in me," Paul was fast going into panic mode.

"Well, I understand that," Penny replied, not bothering to contradict that he was a boring accountant, "but as I said, in our experience, everyone has something that interests people with bad intentions."

"What do you mean bad intentions? Does someone want to kill me? Oh my god—I need to go into protective care!"

This was not going well Billy thought, but let Penny carry on as she was the expert in human emotions.

"Sorry, Paul. I didn't mean to scare you—no, nothing like that. Please calm down and let me explain," Penny knew she had got the approach wrong and wanted to get back on track quickly. "We are talking about people trying to scam you for money—not even large amounts of money."

Paul immediately calmed down and for a moment Penny thought he was going to faint or something as he had suddenly relaxed. "Oh, well that's not a problem then," Paul simply stated.

"Sorry, why is that not a problem," Penny was confused.

"I am an accountant. Boring it may be, but I am good at it and no one will ever be able to pull the wool over my eyes when it comes to money," Paul said confidently.

"Ah. I see. I am sure that's true and we were not saying you had been scammed, but that someone might be targeting you to try and scam you."

Penny continued, "We think that someone has been following your interest in sports cars and is using that as a way to gain confidence with you and become an online friend."

"That's rubbish," dismissed Paul, "I am not an idiot—I don't just accept friend requests from anyone you know."

Billy piped up, "Well, you accepted me as a friend two weeks ago after I commented on two of your posts on Facebook."

He should have put that across a little more professionally, but he was getting annoyed at this man's attitude to them helping him.

"What do you mean?"

"Dave 'Porsche' Edwards," Billy made air quotes, "Ring any bells?"

"That was you? I thought you ran a Porsche enthusiast club in Kent—that's what you said!" Paul looked embarrassed and was looking to blame something else, "Anyway, why did you trick me—just to prove I was gullible?"

"No, not at all. We needed to find out your address details and so I tricked you into connecting with me because you thought we shared an interest—sorry, but it was the only way we could contact you. I guess it does also highlight how easy it is to trick people online." Billy was seeing it from Paul's side a bit now.

"Well, I think that is underhand." Paul was not shaping up to be the helpful individual they needed.

"I have not connected with anyone new recently and no one has contacted me for anything—apart from you guys—so it looks like you are on a wild goose chase!" he folded his arms and it didn't take Penny's degree in Psychology to know this meant the meeting was over.

Penny sighed. "OK. Well, it's good that you haven't been approached by anyone and hopefully now that we have raised your awareness of the potential threat, you can be on the lookout for this sort of thing. If you do think you are being approached, then please get in contact with us and we can help you tackle the scammers."

Penny and Billy stood to leave. As they got to the door Billy turned around and held out a business card with their contact details on—Paul took it in silence. After he had shut the door, he threw the card onto the table in the hall and said to no one, "I know how to contact you 'DaveporscheEdwards'—ha!"

Penny and Billy collapsed into their seats in the car. They could feel the twitchers looking at them and wondering why they hadn't arrested Mr Underwood—it didn't help. They agreed to drive to the local MacDonald's and get a coffee. Billy went in to get the coffee, knowing his uniform would mean they would be free—some said this was an abuse of power, Billy just saw it as a perk of the job.

"Well, that didn't go very well," Penny sighed.

"I thought you did really well with someone who was.... well, a bit of an arse really," Billy was trying to be supportive, but he agreed it didn't go well.

He tried to be upbeat, "At least we learnt something from it."

"Did we—what?" Penny snapped.

Billy tried to think of something to back up his statement, "Well... we learnt that people think they are better at spotting frauds than they actually are—I mean I tricked him into giving us his address easily."

Penny understood that Billy was trying to make things better and for once she decided to follow his lead, "You are right—we did learn some things. We learnt that telling people they might be being scammed leads to them dismissing it... What we need is someone who IS being scammed—then they won't have any choice but to believe us and help."

"Right! So, who is next on the list?"

"Mr G. Madford—a pharmacist, 49. His interest is Cricket apparently—you will have to help me with that one Billy, I know nothing about Cricket."

As it happened, they didn't really need to know anything about Cricket or the interests of any of the other people on their list—they spent every evening that week calling on the people and got a mixed set of responses.

Mr G. Madford took them very seriously and admitted he had recently made a connection with someone called 'Melanie' who seemed as interested in Cricket as he was. He hadn't got very far in his relationship with 'her' but she had suggested they could meet up at the Cricket World cup in Australia in a few months. What Penny and Billy told him had an immediate effect and he said he would break off contact straight away, but he wouldn't help the police bait the scammer. Their approach must be getting better but still no result.

The next person was different again—they knew they were being set up for a scam and were already stringing the scammer along, but just for fun—a bit like when the phone rings and the person on the other end says, "Our records show us that you were recently in a car crash…," and you reply saying "Yes, I was and my legs are still broken—are you going to help me?" just to see how they react at thinking they have found someone who is taken in by their scam.

He refused to help the police saying, "You will only balls it up and they will disappear back into the ether where they came from—at least my way I mess with their heads a bit!"

Throughout the week they talked to several people who believed them and as a result would break contact with the scammer, but no one wanted to help them. People were grateful for the heads up but thought very much on a 'no harm done' basis. Penny and Billy were fast coming to the conclusion that people were very selfish and were losing faith in finding anyone who would help them…. Then Philip called.

Chapter 40
Diversity in the Workplace

Obviously, Azi and Gil had added male personas to the website as well as female ones—it needed to look right after all. They were a little surprised however when the punter's ratio of women to men was about three to one—this didn't fit with Nigerian culture and it took them a while to get their heads around it. However, it did mean that they could be more themselves, as it were when interacting with these women—they didn't have to think like a woman, which had been proving to be quite difficult with the men who had applied.

Their first customer, Gerald, had taught them a lot about how best to handle the 'relationships' between punters and the personas they had created. The first thing they learnt was that it was too blooming difficult to manage more than one persona relationship per punter. As a result of this discovery, they quickly learnt how to close relationships when a punter was trying to build more than one. 'Melanie' and 'Tasha' quickly became very particular people with high expectations of what a relationship meant. It was quite fun to do this and see the punter recoil.

M: "Hi Gerald—How are you doing today Gorgeous?"

G: "Great thanks Mel—how about you?"

M: "I am planning our wedding—I was thinking of a marquee in your back garden with about two hundred guests. I want Robbie Williams to sing and one hundred white doves to be released—what do you think?"

G: "That sounds lovely, but I am not really ready for marriage yet—we have only chatted on here a few times."

M: "But I thought you loved me?"

G: "Well, now love is a big word."

M: "You are making me cry now Gerald—I can't believe you don't love me and don't want to give me a big wedding."

G: "Mel—There is someone at my door—I will message you later—sorry."

Azi and Gil would then take bets between them on how long it would be before the punter logged back into the website and hit the 'un-unite' button on the personas profile. Normally Azi won with something below two hours. Gil believed in chivalry a bit more and normally went for a day.

Azi and Gil were OK at searching the internet for typical romantic phrases women might say to men, but they were fast running out and sometimes forgot what they had already said to a male punter. This wasn't the case with the female punters because it seemed like more of a natural conversation to them.

It was Gil who came up with the answer, "Can't you talk to one of those women at the club and get them to tell you some stuff to say—they seemed very skilled in the art of.... Erm... romance."

"Great idea Gil! And I know just which one can help," Azi leapt up and went over to talk to Jem.

Gil was happy that Azi liked his idea and went back to messaging some more punters. Azi sat with Jem for about ten minutes and then they both said they were going out and that "Gil was in charge" with a laugh. They returned about 45 minutes later and Gil was about to ask if they had brought him anything to eat when he realised it was not just the two of them. They had a woman with them. It was the one that had forced a kiss on Gil at the club that night—he immediately went bright red.

He hadn't heard her talk that night and was surprised how posh she sounded when she spoke, "Have you been standing too close to the sun my lovely."

She walked straight up to Gil and grabbed him by the chin. He thought he was in for another 'attack', but she just laughed as she turned his face from side to side and then stood back. She was dressed in nearly the same gear as she had been wearing at the club and her hair was tied up into big bunches—in the daylight, she didn't look very attractive, Gil found himself surprised to be thinking that.

"Gloria is going to be working with us from now on Bro," announced Jem. "She is going to cover the 'man' part of the operation."

Gil suppressed the temptation to say, "Well, she has got more balls than me," and just kind of gargled his understanding of what Jem had said instead.

Azi spoke up, "It's what you said Gil—we needed someone who understands what a woman would say to a man in a romantic situation—what better than a real woman!"

This time Gil suppressed a laugh—he wasn't sure that Gloria had any idea about romance and couldn't see any man who was looking for love enjoying a conversation with her—but he managed to turn it into a smile.

"Oh, isn't he sweet—doesn't know what to say. Well, we will change all that boy—I am going to teach you how to suck men dry!" Gloria did some kind of hand and mouth action as she said this, but Gil had no idea what she meant and so just carried on smiling. "Right, where is my desk then boys?" she was keen to get to work.

Once seated, Gil kept taking sneak looks at Gloria—it was like a car crash, he didn't want to look but it kept drawing him in. He observed that she was about thirty (so older than Jem and Azi), slightly overweight, dressed like she was about to go clubbing and not all her skin was fully covered—he could see the curve of her left breast under the t-shirt arm-hole and despite it being the most naked female flesh he had seen, he was not turned on at all. Her face was heavily made up with bright eyeshadow and thick orange lipstick. Her best feature by far was her hair—black, thick and curly, even tied up in bunches it cascaded down the sides of her face in curls. Gil understood where women were in modern Nigerian culture, they could work but were still considered beneath men in the workplace—Gil had never agreed with this, some of the girls he had sat next to at school had been much cleverer than him and sharp as nails—he had long thought they deserved the same opportunities as men. He made the decision there and then, that despite her advances to him in the nightclub and the humiliation she had put him through (that was more down to Jem and Azi than Gloria he decided), he was going to welcome her as part of the team and try and make it a nice place to work for everyone.

Gloria had not really stopped to think when Jem and Azi came and found her at the club and offered her the opportunity to work with them. They didn't say it was full time and so she might have to carry on with some work at the nightclub, but basically, she saw it as a way out. She was treated like a piece of meat there, not just by men like Jem and Azi, but also by the owner, who was a nasty man that liked to 'dip his hand into the profits' as it were and she didn't like him abusing her like that—their offer of work sounded like the life raft she had been waiting for and she grabbed it with both hands. Like many young people in Lagos who fell outside normal society, she had been brought up by loving parents, even wealthy ones by Lagos standards—but she was full of spirit and wanted adventure and they quashed those things out of her until they built up a head of steam and exploded out resulting in her running away from home. She could read and write but hadn't completed her education and was having to use her body to make ends meet—it wasn't what she or her parents had dreamed of for her.

"Right, well let's get to work then—who shall we tackle first?" she asked.

Azi sat down next to her and leaned across for the mouse, brushing her breasts with his elbow—she gave a cheeky laugh and Gil thought 'this is going to be a long day'.

"Why don't we give you Gerald. He started off with three of our girls and we whittled him down to one—Evie—because it was too hard to juggle three conversations. We have been keeping him going, but we seem to be running out of conversation and think we might lose him," Azi explained as if he were talking about a common office issue.

Gloria quickly read back through the messages between Gerald and 'Evie' and occasionally laughed, Gil wasn't sure what at.

"Well, it looks like I arrived just in time," Gloria puffed out her not inconsiderable chest and started typing.

Chapter 41
Fiction vs Fact

Elizabeth clicked and was taken through to the 'Lagos News' website and the article—"British man helping Lagos education." She and Philip read the full article.

'Mr Joseph Grey (64), one of the founders of building the school and now a well-liked teacher by the grateful children of Lagos, agreed to give a rare interview about his time in Nigeria and his love for the children and the work he has done in the last three years. Our lead reporter 'Lucy Beck' asked the questions:

Lucy: Joseph—what made you decide to come to Lagos in the first place?

Joseph: Well Lucy, I had led a fairly boring life as a Marketing Executive and was becoming disillusioned with the way the citizens of the world were not helping each other—so I decided to put my thoughts into action.

Lucy: You actually quit your job and moved here—that was a big action to take, wasn't it?

Joseph: I don't have any family, I have made enough money to retire—there was only the local motorbike club that was keeping me in the UK.

Lucy: Some of the children were telling me that Motorbikes are a passion of yours—do you have one now?

Joseph: Yes, but only a little Honda to get me around Lagos. But when I was in the UK, I had a BSA Goldstar Clubman bike—I loved that bike—it was my pride and joy.

Elizabeth thought all the circumstances of this Joseph were the same as her 'Joseph', and the motorbike was the exact one he had described to her—in a lot of detail—there was no way this wasn't the same man that had been talking to her for the last few weeks. She read on eagerly.

Lucy: Talking of pride, you must be proud of the achievement of having built the school for the community here?

Joseph: I didn't build it single-handed—there were lots of us. I am proud of what we achieved as a community.

Lucy: And once you had helped build it you then decided to stay and become a teacher—what inspired that?

Joseph: Once I had been here for several months, I found it difficult to think of anything to go back to the UK for and I could see the value staying would bring to the community and me.

Lucy: well that's certainly true. We spoke to several of the school mothers to see what they thought of your contribution. Everyone was really grateful for the work and commitment you had put into better education and life for their children.

Joseph: that's really great to hear—the Mum's are very supportive and want better lives for their children.

Lucy: Some of the Mum's would like to be even more supportive—are you aware that there is a bit of local competition amongst the single mothers to see which of them can 'hook you' first?

Joseph: Ha-ha! I don't know about that—I'm not looking for love—I enjoy my work and that's what I focus on.

Lucy: Well that's a shame for those women out there—I can confirm to our readers that Joseph is very handsome and a gentleman. Is there anything else you would like to share with our readers Joseph?

Joseph: Just to let everyone know that we are doing another school play this year—Drama is becoming a new passion of mine—and we need lots of support for costumes, props and help building the sets, please.

Lucy: Well thank you for sharing those insights with us Joseph and good luck with the school plays and fighting the mums off!

Philip and Elizabeth finished reading the article together and looked at each other speechless.

Then they read it again.

"I can't believe it Philip—that's my Joseph!" exclaimed Elizabeth.

"Well, it certainly seems to be him—but he is in Nigeria—not Singapore!"

They were both confused, but then Philip was first to remember that there was no 'Joseph' anyway and so it couldn't be him.

"But we know it is a scammer and he doesn't sound like a scammer from that interview," Philip stated.

Now it was Elizabeth's turn to apply logic, "But surely that's the point—the scammer can take anyone and pretend to be them—I assumed they would make up a character, but I guess there is no reason they couldn't base it on a real person?"

"But it seems so far apart—a scammer in Singapore using the character of a man in Nigeria? I mean what's the link?"

"Maybe it's this newspaper article—there is a lot of information in there—they could have just decided to use that to create the character," Elizabeth couldn't believe she was starting to think about the inner workings of the scammer's brain.

"Let's have a look at that list of facts you created and see if we can match them against the article facts—that might tell us if they used the article to create this character," suggested Philip.

Elizabeth opened up the notepad app on her iPad where she had written the original list and created a column alongside it. They then stepped through each fact and tried to see similarities or differences between what they knew of her 'Joseph' and the Joseph in the article.

Elizabeth's facts	**Newspaperarticle facts**
• Joseph White	• Joseph Grey
• 64 years old	• 64 years old
• Tall and broad	• Tall and broad (same photo)
• White stubble beard	• White stubble beard (same photo)
• Handsome with tanned skin	• Handsome with tanned skin (same photo)
• Lives in Singapore	• Lives in Lagos, Nigeria
• Works at a school doing Caretaking work	• Works at a school as a teacher of English and Drama
• Interested in old motorbikes	• Interested in old motorbikes—same make and model

• Likes Marmite, Warm beer and Coronation Street	• No information
• Kind, thoughtful and a bit cheeky	• Sounded kind and thoughtful. • Didn't come across as cheeky
• Has a young voice	• Clearly is not young

So, the key differences were location, he wasn't cheeky and he wasn't as young as he sounded. They both thought about this and then Philip came to a conclusion.

"The scammer has used this article and the picture to create this character. They are in Singapore and wanted to take the profile from someone in a different country so that no one would find the real Joseph if they looked for him in Singapore. The reason that your 'Joseph' comes across as cheeky and sounds young is because he is—it's the scammer's personality coming through—they are using the real Joseph's details but letting part of themselves come through."

Elizabeth was still reeling from having found the 'real' Joseph—it had been a turbulent few days—she had gone from falling in love; to discovering her new love didn't exist and she was being scammed; to finding out her new love DID exist but wasn't actually aware of her and wasn't her new love—it was enough to make anyone a little unstable.

"Oh, Philip—I'm just so confused now—I don't know what to do or think," she whimpered.

Philip could see the trauma she was going through and decided that enough was enough—"It's OK my darling. I will look after this for you—I am going to contact the police and share with them everything we have—let them deal with it. You have been through too much."

"Yes, please. As far as I am concerned, I don't ever want to set eyes on this man again—whoever he is," she said with the last bit of strength she had. However, at the back of her heart, she felt a mourning pain start to build…

Chapter 42
Prank Caller

Billy took the call from Philip and nearly dismissed it as one of their fellow officers pranking them because they knew that their mission was failing. He started looking around the room to see if he could see any colleagues cowering in a corner making the furtive phone call—he, therefore, missed some of what Philip said.

"So, Elizabeth thinks that 'Joseph' is a real person, but that the scammer is pretending to be him and making her fall in love with her to scam her in some way—do you understand?" Philip certainly sounded convincing to Billy, but also a little bit of a caricature which only increased Billy's belief that this was a prank. Then Philip said something that caught Billy's attention.

"It all started when he showed interest in her pictures of old motorbikes."

This was the way that many of the victims had first been approached—by the scammer showing interest in a hobby. Billy and Penny had not talked with their colleagues about the details of how the scammers operated and so Billy wondered how they would know this—he decided that maybe this was not a prank call.

"Sorry, could you just say that again please?" asked Billy.

"Which bit?" Philip questioned.

"Erm, look, I am really sorry, but I thought you were a prank caller and wasn't really listening fully. Something you just said made me realise you are not and so I would be grateful if you could run me through the whole thing again please—sorry," Billy thought honesty would be the best approach. It wasn't....

"Well, of all the cheek. As if I would prank call about something so serious—I want to speak to your superior!"

Billy squirmed in his chair—he now thought this might be a real lead, the kind they needed for a breakthrough and he didn't want to hand it over to his boss just yet—he knew enough about protecting his career to realise that. So, he had another go.

"Sorry, sir. I am really am. I didn't mean to offend you, and in fact, this sounds like the kind of breakthrough we may have been waiting for in a case that my colleague and I are pursuing. It would be really helpful if you could just tell me the basics again. Truly sorry to mess you about."

Billy used his most simpering voice he could muster and hoped it would do the trick. Philip was fiery, but also liked an apology—he didn't often get them—so he decided to relent, "OK. But please listen this time. It's about my friend and it's very serious."

"Of course, sir. Sorry. Please continue."

Philip ran Billy through his story again and Billy scribbled lots of notes. In the end, he was convinced they had 'a live one' and wanted to progress things straight away.

"That's really great sir—thank you—my colleague and I would love to come and interview you and Mrs Gresham first thing tomorrow if that is OK?"

"Well, there is no need to sound so excited about my friend's misfortune," Philip was getting tetchy again.

"No, of course not, sir. We take these things very seriously. It's just as I said, we have been waiting for a breakthrough for some time. No offence intended," Billy spoke with genuine remorse.

"None taken."

Then why did you kick up a fuss, thought Billy—this guy was going to be a handful he knew. "Anyway, we were going to help more and be involved, but my friend has decided it is too much stress—so if you give me an email address, I will just send over everything we know and then you can take it from there please."

"Oh, are you sure your friend won't talk to us—we really need to hear it from her to make sure we understand everything."

"You really are not very good at this are you young man—that's the third time you have insulted me. I know all there is to know about this sad state of affairs and will put it in an email—you can do what you will with it."

Billy gave the email address that he and Penny had access to for this project and Philip signed off huffily.

Billy rushed to the toilet—excitement and nerves had that effect on his bladder—and then went off in search of Penny. He found her in the canteen sitting talking to Jane Porter, their boss. He nearly didn't go over to them as he thought it must be something private or he would be involved, but he knew they would want to know.

"Ma'am," Billy slid up to their table.

"Is it important Billy—Penny and I are having a private chat," Jane looked at him with an eyebrow raised.

"Sorry, Ma'am, Penny. I think you will think of it as important, yes," he was rigid with excitement.

"I don't mind if you don't mind Jane?" Penny offered.

Since when were they on first name terms thought Billy? Blooming Penny, he would have to watch her persistence in wanting to climb the greasy pole—she would leave him behind without blinking and he didn't like that. He wasn't over ambitious but didn't want to be at the bottom of the ladder if he could help it—a comfortable place halfway up would suit him. He knew Penny was his ticket to getting there sooner.

"Sit down then Billy and tell us all...," Jane slid one space over on the chairs to make room.

Billy relayed the phone call, leaving out anything that made him look too stupid, and finished by saying that they could expect an email.

"An email? That's not good enough—we need to speak to this woman Billy—you know that!" Penny forgot herself for a moment and raised her voice. A few people in the canteen turned and looked, so Jane stepped in.

"Thank you, Penny—let's try to keep this collaborative, shall we? Billy—I am sure you tried to get an interview?"

"Yes, Ma'am. I asked several times, stressing the importance of us getting a first-hand account. Unfortunately...."

Billy hesitated checking his next words didn't paint him in too bad a light, "The gentleman seemed to think that his knowledge and the email he would send should be sufficient. Also, he said that his friend had been through enough."

Penny was about to carry on stressing at Billy, but Jane held up a hand and put the other on her temple and rubbed—a gesticulation that stopped Penny saying anything further as the boss was obviously 'thinking', which is exactly what Jane had intended to happen so she actually could think!

"Billy, did we log the telephone number that this man called from?"

"Yes, Ma'am. Standard procedure," he didn't mean it to sound so flippant.

Jane ignored the tone and said "Great. Let's use that to find the address and go and visit."

"But Ma'am," Penny had gone back to the formal mode in her surprise at this blatant suggestion by a senior officer that they break the rules, "That's against the rules—if anyone finds out or if they lodge a complaint…."

"Well then, let's make sure they don't—we need to be convincing about the urgency and importance and the role this woman could play."

Penny and Billy were looking puzzled about how to do that, which only made up Jane's mind on what she had been thinking, "I think you guys need a bit of experience on your side—I could do with getting out of the office for a few hours anyway." And with that, whilst trying to suppress their annoyance that the big boss was wading in, Billy and Penny were both excited and nervous that they were moving things forward—they rose to go back to their office, with Billy taking another quick trip to the little boy's room.

Chapter 43
Personal Service

Jem had known at that first meeting in the café when Amelia had come for one of the loans he arranged on behalf of his 'associates', who she was. In fact, and he would never tell anyone this, he had only agreed to a loan for her because of his guilt—she had not met the normal criteria for a loan (desperate and not really able to afford it—so his associates could lay claim to people's assets!). She was far too safe a bet for a loan and had proven that over the last several years by keeping up her repayments—not good for business as far as his associates were concerned. Whilst he often thought of the raid that night and how wrong it had gone—ending in Dev dying—he had never really talked to anyone about it.

Partly because the less people who knew the more unlikely the police would ever find out it was his gang and partly because he tried to block it from his mind. Despite his wayward life, he had never intended to cause that sort of damage to anyone's life. Especially not to take away a husband and father from a family—he of all people knew the impact of not having parents left. He had let Amelia have the loan, giving the normal level of threatening customer service as he did with everyone (so as not to raise suspicion) thinking that he was in some way making amends for the harm he had done to her and her family.

It turns out that it didn't feel like that—in fact, he resented having her in his life again as it made him think about the incident that night more and more. So, over the time Amelia had the loan, Jem ignored her and left her alone—hoping no one would notice she was just a person paying off a loan.

Now, here he was in her house, which in itself made him feel the weight of responsibility again—would the family have prospered better if he hadn't killed Dev?—having to deal with the fact she wanted to break the terms of the loan. He had got used to sending Azi to deal with their loan clients—he was very effective at driving home the terms and conditions—but Azi had insisted that Jem should deal with Amelia directly. Turns out that Azi hadn't missed the favour Jem had shown her and didn't want to get in the way of whatever that was.

"Erm, yes. That's right," Amelia was shaking on the inside but successfully not showing on the outside what she was feeling.

"Did you find the door open? I must check that lock again."

Jem decided to play along with her little game that he hadn't just broken in by picking the lock, "Yes, the door was slightly open, and I called to see if anyone was at home. I thought I had better stay until someone got here in case you got broken into…," he sneered.

"Well, that's very kind of you…. Mr…. sorry, I have forgotten your name since we last met?" This wasn't true—Amelia knew his name and had heard it starting to spread around the community as evil.

"Mr J. Adeyemi—at your service," he tried to maintain his sinister version of customer service.

"I understand that you want to 'pause' your payment for a month—is that right?"

"Yes. It is my daughter's coming of age, and I wanted to be able to get her a nice present and take her out with some friends for a meal, as is the custom—I just can't quite afford to do both and as I have been a good customer for you over the last few years…."

"Ha-ha—you think you have been a good customer do you?" again he sneered. "Well, you don't really fit the definition of a good customer in the loans business, but I can see why you wouldn't understand that," he added as she looked puzzled.

"But I have paid each month and on time?"

"Yes, yes. That's true. Never mind. OK—so here is the thing. We are not a bank you know. We don't really have the same attitude towards our customers as they do. Also, you have to consider that if I let you have a break, then everyone would ask for a break in payments and where would we be then?" He actually sounded like a businessman when explaining this.

"Oh, I see. So, does that mean you are saying 'no'?" she asked crestfallen at the thought of not being able to treat her daughter.

Jem was just about to dash her hopes of ever getting the terms of her loan changed when Su got home from school.

"Hi, Mum," she called in the normal way from the front door. She drew breath again to start telling Amelia all about the scores she had got in her Maths tests and how none of the other girls had done as well as her when she noticed the visitor.

"Oh. Sorry, I didn't realise you had company."

"Hello, darling. Did you have a good day at school?" Amelia wasn't going to let this vile man upset her family home.

"Yes. Is this the man from the restaurant we are having my party at—has he come to arrange the details?" Su was suddenly very animated as she jumped to completely the wrong conclusion.

"Erm, not exactly. He .... Umm.... He is here to talk to me about money." Amelia didn't lie to her children and they both knew she had taken out a loan some time back. She didn't really want to let her daughter down in front of this man and so she wasn't sure what to say next—opening and closing her mouth several times in an attempt to find the right words.

Then Jem, for the second time ever and for the same woman who forced these feelings in him the last time, showed someone else some favour. "Hello, Su. I am talking to your Mum about the party and she is right that we are just sorting the money out. We have agreed how it will be paid for and it's all going to be OK," he couldn't believe what he was saying as he said it.

It was like someone else had taken control of his mouth and he was standing five feet away watching them make him say this. In truth, the feelings he was having were guilt and remorse and his subconscious was trying to make amends in some small way for the loss of this poor girl's father. Su jumped up from the arm of the sofa where she had perched next to her Mum and threw her arms around Jem, thanking him enthusiastically. Amelia was both delighted and horrified—on the one hand, something in Su had made this horrible man have some compassion, but on the other hand, Su was hugging someone that she had hoped she would never meet.

Su ran off to her room and Jem turned to Amelia, "You must have caught me on a good day. But you don't get to skip a month and add it on the end, you have to spread the payment for that month over the next 3 months—that's the deal, take it or leave it."

"Well, I suppose I will have to take it now that you have told my daughter she is getting her party," Amelia tried to remain composed but couldn't help showing her frustration with her voice raised and agitated. It was this that caught Eb's ear just as he walked in the front door—he was immediately on the attack.

"Mum! Is everything OK? Who is this man—is he hurting you?" he walked over to his Mum quickly and stood between her and Jem.

"Ha-ha—the big man of the house—protector of the women—willing to fight to protect what is his! I could do with someone like you in my company."

Amelia stood and this time it was she who stood between Jem and her son—she pointed at the door and said, "We have concluded our business and my son will never work for you—so please leave."

"Alright, alright. I'm going. But remember lady, if you don't meet those terms, then you and your son will end up having to pay for it one way or another!" and with that Jem slammed out of the house.

Chapter 44
Not a Victim

Elizabeth got up normal time and went about her normal routine. Well, except that she would normally look at her iPad as soon as she had made her morning tea and read any messages that 'Joseph' had sent whilst she was asleep. Anthony had come up with a way to avoid her having to communicate with 'Joseph' for a few days—he had sent a message saying that she had got a bad case of the flu and was going to be offline for a few days to recover. 'Joseph' had answered saying "OK—get better soon my love x," but otherwise had accepted this slightly feeble excuse without question.

What wasn't normal was the knock at her door at 9 a.m. Philip wasn't due today and no one else came calling unannounced. She pulled her dressing gown around her tightly and put the chain on the door before gingerly opening it. She immediately gasped when she saw one policeman, one policewoman and a lady standing on the doorstep and slammed the door shut. She didn't know why she did that but didn't have time to work it out before Billy called out.

"Mrs Gresham. It's the police—may we come in and talk to you please?"

Elizabeth couldn't think what they wanted, but she also couldn't ignore them. She breathed deeply, took the chain off the door and opened it, mustering a smile as she did so, "Good morning officer. How may I help you?"

Billy re-worded his request "Hello, Mrs Gresham. We are here today to ask you some questions about a phone call we received from a friend of yours—Mr Philip Edwards? May we come in please?"

"Yes, of course. Please do. You will have to excuse me for not being dressed—I am slightly invalid and sometimes have a slow start first thing."

Jane Porter stepped into the house and said kindly, "That's alright. We all like a slow start sometimes" followed by "I am Detective Chief Inspector Jane

Porter and this is Constables Billy Jones and Penny Green" indicating the two uniformed individuals.

Elizabeth showed them through to the lounge and offered them a drink. Billy was on the cusp of asking for a coffee when Penny glared at him and he thought better of it. Jane Porter started off, "As constable Jones just said, we received a phone call from Mr Edwards, informing us that you had been the victim of a scammer. I head up the Norfolk Cyber Crime Unit and I thought we would like to find out more about that—what can you tell us, please Mr's Gresham?"

"Please, call me Elizabeth" offered Elizabeth, and then, "I thought Philip said you didn't need to speak to me?"

"No, it was Mr Edwards who suggested that we didn't need to speak to you—we told him we did and that's why we are here."

"Oh, well do you mind if I go and get dressed quickly—it somehow seems wrong to talk about these things in my nightclothes," Elizabeth asked, not sure about what she was entitled to do at that moment.

"Yes, of course," replied Jane Porter.

"Could we just have a look at your computer that you used to communicate with this… person, please? That will save time, whilst you get dressed," asked Penny thinking quickly. Elizabeth wasn't sure what to do but didn't feel she could refuse the police and so handed over her iPad and then went to the bedroom.

As soon as she was out of earshot, she phoned Philip on her landline in the bedroom, "Hello? Philip. Oh, it's you, Anthony. I have the police here asking questions about 'you know who'! I thought Philip said they didn't want to investigate further!"

Anthony called for Philip who was in another room and he put the phone on speaker, "Philip is here now Liz—you are on speakerphone so we can both hear you. What did you say the police wanted?"

"I don't know! They just turned up before I was even dressed and started saying that Philip had said I didn't want to speak to them…."

Following his phone call with Billy, he had not been impressed with the police and had decided they wouldn't be any help. He had been going to tell Liz that the police couldn't help and then just tell her to cut all communication with 'Joseph' and forget about the whole thing—he and Anthony discussed it when he got home and agreed that was the best way forward. Now here they were being more active than he had imagined. He knew he had not given the police Liz's details, so they must have traced the phone call, but he hadn't thought the police would track them down like this. He decided to see where they could go with it—"It's OK Liz—just tell them what you know and remember that we all want this 'Joseph' to get his comeuppance!"

"OK—if you say so—I hope I can answer their questions," she replied nervously.

"Call us later when they have gone, and we can talk it through—good luck, Liz!"

Whilst Elizabeth was in the bedroom changing, Billy had made good use of having her iPad. He had quickly discovered all the messages between her and this 'Joseph' and had copied them onto a USB stick, as well as all the pictures and her login details that she had conveniently written down in a notepad. He also popped a bit of spyware onto the iPad so that they could directly track any communications she did across the internet—strictly speaking, they needed to tell her they were doing that, but somehow Billy forgot to mention it when she came back out.

"Sorry about that. All dressed now. Are you sure I can't get you a drink?" Elizabeth had put on her best smile to try to appear confident, although she felt anything but.

Jane Porter smiled and with a kind, but firmer tone said, "Thank you, but we must crack on—lots to do I am afraid."

"Of course. So how may I help you?"

Jane Porter nodded to Penny and Penny started, "Well, when Mr Edwards called, he mentioned that you had met a man online and started a relationship with him."

"That makes it sound a bit sordid when you say it like that. We shared a mutual interest in old motorbikes and met through an online dating service. We hit it off and then decided to keep in touch and chatted online quite often."

Elizabeth was defensive but not sure why. Penny was about to apologise for making a mistake (that she knew wasn't a mistake) when Jane Porter jumped in, "We understand that this may be awkward and even embarrassing for you, but trust us, you are not the only lonely woman to get taken in by scum like this—we just need you to suppress those feelings and help us catch them." It was a ballsy move and it took Penny and Billy aback to hear their boss talk to someone like that.

Elizabeth wasn't sure how to respond to this frankness—on the one hand, this woman was completely right and she should do everything she could to help bring this scammer to justice, but on the other hand, she didn't like the idea of unleashing this aggressive woman and her team onto the person she had shared so much with over the last few months—it was at this moment that Elizabeth realised she felt sorry for the scammer. She wasn't a stupid woman and she knew that everyone would think this was a classic case of 'Stockholm syndrome', but it wasn't like that—she didn't like or admire her scammer, she just felt that they must have their reasons for doing something like this and she wondered if punishment was the right thing—surely there was room for compassion, she thought.

"Mrs Gresham?" Penny tried to break into Elizabeth's silent thoughts that she had been in for a good minute. Elizabeth decided, "Sorry, I was just thinking that your boss is right and I have been a silly old woman."

She tried to sound as those she meant it, "I will do everything I can to help you capture this person." The team took her through some questions to help them understand everything they could about the scammer and then explained they would use their technology to intercept the messages between Elizabeth and the scammer, with a view to finding out information about them that would hopefully lead to them being arrested. Elizabeth paid enough attention to make her seem interested in helping them, but the rest of her mind was occupied with a new mission—she was going to help the scammer—she didn't know what this meant or how she would do it, but having made that decision she suddenly felt less of a victim.

Chapter 45
Big Brother Is Watching You

They left Elizabeth's house with lots of information, full access to her iPad and between them a real buzz that they had made a breakthrough in their pursuit of scammers. Jane decided to treat them to a celebratory fry-up. "What's it to be then Billy—full English?"

"Yes, please Ma'am—white toast please and a latte," Billy wasn't shy in making the most of this rare treat.

"Just a slice of wholemeal toast and a green tea for me please," Penny really wanted to order the full English but didn't want to give the impression of being a glutton like Billy. "Great—and a full English with black coffee for me please," Jane told the waitress and then turned to the team, "so that went well—good work guys."

"I didn't think she was going to be helpful at first," said Penny, "but then she seemed to decide to be and it all opened up from there" although she had her own reservations about Mrs Gresham's commitment.

"And I got full monitoring on her iPad—so we can track her every move," Billy revealed for the first time.

"But we didn't get the right warrant to do that Billy!" said Penny in shock, "Ma'am, we need to go straight back and remove it and hope she doesn't sue."

"Sorry, Penny—what did you say? For that matter, I didn't hear what Billy said.... I must be going deaf...." Jane winked and enjoyed the horrified look on Penny's face and the joyfully conspiratorial look on Billy's face.

Taking that as official approval, Billy got his laptop out, moved the sauce bottles aside and opened it on the table in the café. He clicked a few buttons and a window popped up on the screen with a picture of an old motorbike on it. "That's her background picture on the iPad—she is not using it at the moment, but as soon as she does anything I will get notified." He beamed, pleased at his work.

They all sat staring at the motorbike picture willing for something to happen, but then their drinks arrived and broke the spell.

"Right, well if anything happens, I am sure you will let us know," Jane picked up her coffee and slurped noisily.

Their breakfasts arrived and Billy and Jane tucked in vigorously, Penny nibbling at her toast in what she considered a more sophisticated way.

"Ma'am," Penny wanted to get back onto the more comfortable ground, "Mrs Gresham agreed to us using the message interrupt software, so I think that should be our focus. Wait until she gets a message from the scammer and then takes control of the conversation as we discussed."

"Yup, sure," Jane managed to say with a mouthful. Billy raised his eyes to the heavens in an exaggerated way, making sure Penny saw that he thought she was being too prissy about his monitoring approach.

Ignoring him, Penny continued, "I was thinking that we, acting as Mrs Gresham, in the chat message should focus on trying to get the scammer to reveal something about his surroundings or even his friends—anything we might be able to use as a reference point to try and identify where they are."

"Sure, sounds good Penny. We may have to be quite persistent—they are probably very protective of giving out too much 'real' information."

"Well, I thought about that. I wondered if we could achieve it by giving away some secrets of Mrs Gresham and therefore encouraging them to tell secrets—it's a well-known psychological technique." Psychology Penny was back.

"Good idea. What did you have in mind?" Jane was curious.

"Erm, perhaps she could say that she is different than she has led him to believe so far—her height, build, hair colour etc and then perhaps her age and finish with confessing she has used a false name. Often the person opposite you in the conversation will mimic you—so we could get key info about him."

"It seems like a long shot, but I understand the theory behind it—let's give it a go."

They got back to the office about thirty minutes later and Billy got a notification just as they sat at their desks—he quickly logged on and Penny looked over his shoulder. They saw Elizabeth open her Messenger app on the iPad and start typing to her scammer 'Joseph'.

E: Hi Joseph. I'm better now! It was a horrible flu, but it's gone now, and I feel well enough to chat again—hope you missed me!

Penny and Billy were a little surprised at this message and so soon after they had told her they would be 'sitting in-between' the messages and able to change them in order to try and trip the scammer up. But they decided to let it run a little.

J: My Darling—so glad you are better, and I missed you a lot of course. It must have been terrible being sick all by yourself. I thought about you a lot.

E: aww, thank you, my love. It wasn't too bad because my friend Philip kept popping in and checking on me.

Elizabeth didn't often mention Philip before—she had referred to him as her physio but not said he was a friend—she had decided to play along with 'Joseph' as before, but something in her subconscious had made her say about Philip being her 'friend', perhaps so that 'Joseph' didn't think she was totally on her own and totally vulnerable. Whatever the reason, she was pleased with his reaction.

J: I didn't realise Philip was that close a friend to look after you when you were ill—I thought he just did your physio? Should I be jealous?

E: No silly. He is just my Physio and he is a kind friend—that's all. Nothing for you to worry about.

J: Phew—I thought I had competition there!

Penny and Billy couldn't see why Elizabeth was having this chat with 'Joseph' as she had clearly understood he was a scammer and yet here, she was having a pleasant, almost flirty conversation with him. They also couldn't see an opportunity to intercept and change messages to their advantage. They decided to message Elizabeth.

P: Hi Mrs Gresham. It's Penny from the police here, who you spoke to this morning. Our system had alerted us to a chat session you are having with the scammer and we have been following your messages. Nothing for us to intercept yet, but we thought we would let you know we are on the lookout for an appropriate point where we can take over the conversation and see if we can get some information out of him.

Elizabeth saw a notification pop up on her screen from 'The Police' and was initially shocked, then she looked at it and remembered what they had said. It didn't matter to her what they were doing as long as she got the chance to carry out her plan. So, she played along.

E: Hi Penny. Thanks for your visit this morning. I feel so safe having you watching over my shoulder. I just thought I should try and keep up the façade of the relationship so that you get every opportunity to help.

P: Well that's very brave of you—thank you. We will try our best. Keep chatting to him and we will find a way in.

Penny and Billy were really pleased with themselves. At last, they had a cooperative victim, who was in an active relationship with a scammer—they just had to bide their time and they would get a break, they were sure.

Chapter 46
Bad Day at Work

Eb knew about the loan and when Amelia explained what Jem had been doing there and that he had just overheard her being strict with Jem, he understood and calmed down. He didn't like the fact this man had something over them, and he knew his mum would struggle to pay a month spread over the next three months, but he also knew what it meant to his Mum to celebrate Su's coming of age properly—so he was supportive if only to keep his Mum's spirits up.

Amelia, on the other hand, didn't really think she had been left in much of a better position. She desperately wanted to give Su a nice present and now she didn't even have the chance to choose between a present or a party—the party was happening because Jem had told Su it was. Amelia had always been sensible with the money they had and had always paid the loan payments on time—she was not going to mess that up now. It would be hard to pay the month back over the next three months, but she would do it she told herself. As to a present, she would just have to use the perks of her job to sort that one out, she thought.

The next day she went into the factory like normal, except that this time she had a bigger bag than her normal handbag. It was actually Eb's school rucksack that she had borrowed from him—she told him she had to pick up Su's present from the shops and could do with the rucksack to carry it home. The factory did lots of fake designer products, although most of them were clothes. Amelia—and all the women who worked there—regularly stuffed a t-shirt or some shorts down her trousers but never something larger for fear of discovery.

Occasionally the supervisors would hold an inspection at the end of the shift to check for employees pinching stuff, but the supervisors were nearly as lowly paid as the workers and pinched just as much stuff, so no one had ever actually been caught and prosecuted by the factory. Amelia was banking on this today more than ever.

There was a 'Prada' handbag that her production line had been working on for the last few weeks—she thought it was a bit garish but knew that Su would love it. It was quite chunky and that's why she needed the rucksack. She waited until afternoon tea break when they were allowed to go to their lockers and get snacks, they had brought with them.

She let a few of the women go first and waited until the supervisors turned to go and have their break, then she swiftly lifted one of the 'Prada' bags off the finishing station she sat next to and casually carried it as if it were her own handbag—hiding in plain sight, as it were. She got to the locker room, opened her locker and slipped the bag straight into Eb's rucksack, then closed the locker. She was happy no one had seen her, and she grabbed a biscuit and tea, returning to her point in the production line less than five minutes later.

The rest of the shift went fine but was a little slow in her mind, which was constantly distracted thinking about the 'Prada' bag she had pinched. The end of shift whistle blew, and she quickly got up and almost ran to the locker room. Maybe they had seen her at break time or maybe it was the sweat pouring down her brow as she queued to leave the factory—whatever it was, the supervisors on the door asked her to step to one side for an inspection. Although she was nervous, she felt sure they would turn a blind eye as they always did. What she didn't know, was that there was a new supervisor, who had only been there a week and it was this person that she was ushered over to for them to inspect her bag.

"Hello, Mrs?" asked the supervisor.

"Azikiwe. Amelia Azikiwe. You must be new here—everyone knows me," Amelia replied trying to remain light and airy.

"Well, I don't," the supervisor indicated that Amelia should put her rucksack on the table and open it. She did so, maintaining her smile.

"And what, may I ask, is this?" The new supervisors hauled the 'Prada' bag out of the rucksack and held it high for others to see.

Amelia wasn't sure how to respond, "Erm, well it's for my daughter—it's her coming of age birthday next week."

"That doesn't explain why it is in your bag—did you buy it before you came to work and if so, then please show me the receipt."

Amelia looked around at the other supervisors who she knew well and would have turned that blind eye she so desperately needed. They looked at the ground and shuffled their feet—they didn't want to be involved.

"Well—I am waiting for your explanation!" the new supervisor barked.

"Erm, well. It's kind of what we do around here—like the occasional perk of the job—everyone does it every now and then. I thought no one would miss one little bag," squeaked Amelia.

She could tell it was the wrong answer as soon as she said it. The new supervisor called over two of the longer-term supervisors and asked them if they were aware of this practice. They of course had to deny it, which only made Amelia's story look even worse. The new supervisor was obviously keen to make her mark and she loudly announced that she would have to take Amelia to the manager's office. Amelia's colleagues all looked on in horror as they realised this so easily could have been them many times over the last few months and years.

Amelia was marched to the shift manager's office, and the new supervisor explained the offence that had taken place. The manager was clearly embarrassed for Amelia—he knew that minor theft was part of the job and was happy to turn a blind eye as long as no one took advantage too much, but he wasn't sure the factory owners would feel the same way and he knew he wouldn't be able to bury this with this new supervisor being so officious about her responsibilities.

"Oh. Well, Amelia, this is very disappointing," the manager talked to her in a stern voice but tried to convey compassion in his face.

"We will have to think about some kind of punishment for this—perhaps some unpaid overtime."

"I am sorry sir, it shouldn't have happened. I don't know what came over me and it won't happen again. Of course, I will do whatever you see as a fit punishment and be grateful sir."

Amelia played the game but was starting to feel relieved that she was going to keep her job. "Sir. I am afraid it's more serious than some free overtime," the new supervisor chipped in with some force, "The rules of the factory clearly state that theft will result in instant dismissal—so I must ask you to perform that duty now."

The manager didn't know what to do—he had only recently been promoted from supervisor to shift manager and didn't want to get it wrong and risk being reported to senior management. He looked at Amelia, hoping she would see the regret and apology in his eyes and said, "I am sorry Amelia, but that is correct—I forgot—it is my duty to inform you that as you have been caught in the act of stealing from the factory, you must be dismissed with immediate effect. Please collect your belongings and leave." He winced as he spoke the words and grimaced at the new supervisors, vowing to get his own back on her one day.

Amelia had seen the regret in the manager's eyes, but it meant nothing to her if he couldn't do anything to help her. She was reeling from the last 5 minutes since the whistle blew for shift end and now she felt like the bottom had fallen out of her world—she had the shame of being caught stealing, had lost her job and the income that came with it, wasn't going to be able to pay the normal loan payments let alone the one month spread over three and worst of all, she still hadn't managed to get a decent present for Su's birthday—it had not been a good day for Amelia.

Chapter 47
Tricking the Police

"Babe—we need to get round to Liz's straight away—the police have gone now, but she has gone mad!" Shrieked Philip up the stairs to Anthony as soon as he had put the phone down from Elizabeth.

"What? What are you talking about? I thought we told her to just cooperate?"

"Well, we did and that's what I thought we agreed with Liz .... but that's not all... she says she has agreed to let them monitor her messages with 'Joseph' and they might even intercept some of them and change them in the hope they can trick him into giving away some information about himself so they can catch him—are they even allowed to do that babe?"

"I don't know—I guess they can if she has agreed to it." Anthony had calmed down enough from this news to wonder what the urgency of a visit was, "So why do we need to go round now lover? Is she upset about the police? I would have thought she would be glad in a way—I know you wanted to hand the whole thing over to them anyway."

"Oh, babe—I haven't told you the crazy bit yet.... She isn't going to help the police... she is just making them think she is cooperating with them."

Philip paused to build up for the worst bit, "What she is really going to do is try and help the scammer!"

"Sorry, what? What does that mean? And why would she want to help someone who tried to rip her off?" Anthony looked confused but started to get his coat and shoes on as did Philip—this called for a visit to Elizabeth.

Elizabeth was not surprised when Philip rang the doorbell and let himself in. She knew that the phone call she had with him half an hour earlier would result in a Philip-Anthony Spanish Inquisition.

"Come in boys—sit down and make yourself at home." She was extra cheery. Since making her decision to help the scammer she had felt like this—like she had a purpose. Philip and Anthony were either going to have to get on board or shut up.

"So, Liz. Darling. What's all this I hear about the police and you helping the scammer?" Anthony opened.

"Yes, that's right. The Police are trying to catch him, and they want me to be their bait. But I have had an epiphany… this scammer needs help. The Police can do whatever they like, but I am not going to let them just lock up this person—I am sure they need help and I am going to give it to them!" Elizabeth spoke with confidence and conviction.

Philip was in disarray and didn't know what to think or say—he just kept pacing the room, rubbing his forehead. It was Anthony that recovered quickest.

"Sod the Police darling—you and I never liked the idea of going to them in the first place," he glanced at Philip and raised his eyes in mock frustration, "But what's all this helping the scammer stuff—have you forgotten what he put you through?"

"Of course not and that hurts. But the 'Joseph' I fell in love with doesn't exist and there is nothing that will change that. I started to think what would drive a person to do something so horrible and that's when it became clear… surely no one could do this 'scamming' for a living voluntarily—they must be in trouble and have no choice."

"So that's why you want to help them—because you think they didn't mean to hurt you?" Anthony was trying to understand.

"I don't know if they meant to hurt me—it's not about that. They were obviously just trying to get money out of me… although I confess, I don't know how they thought they would do that… I just know that they must be in some kind of trouble to need to do this to get money." She was clearly thinking logically, and Anthony could see her logic.

"Well, I guess there must be some truth in that. How are you going to help them?" Anthony had accepted her 'why' and was starting to move on to the 'how'. Philip was not quite there yet.

"Anthony! Don't tell me you are agreeing with this madness? We need to stop messing around and help the Police catch this bastard!" Philip was near hysterical.

Elizabeth got up—she was feeling stronger by the day—and said she would make them all a cup of tea. Philip collapsed into a chair and Anthony held his hand—Philip the caregiver was suddenly in need of care.

Coming back with a small tray with three teas on it, Elizabeth looked at Philip with affection and patted his hand to indicate things would be OK. She then turned her attention to Anthony's question a few minutes earlier.

"I am going to contact 'Joseph' using WhatsApp on my iPad. He once said that we could chat or call using WhatsApp, but I was used to Facebook Messenger and so we just stuck to that. The Police only found messages between us on Messenger and so won't be monitoring WhatsApp."

"Good thinking," said Anthony leaning in closer in a conspiratorial way, whilst Philip was rocking slightly in the chair next to him, "Then what?"

"Well, I haven't completely decided yet—shall I just come out with it and tell him the game is up or shall I try and coax him into confessing to me?" she was asking for Anthony's opinion.

"I think outright would scare him off and you might never hear from him again. So, some kind of gentle coax I think—not sure how you are going to do that, but you need him to confess feeling safe if you see what I mean."

"And what are you going to do when he admits to being a scammer and tells you to bugger off—how has that helped anyone?" Philip had stopped panicking and was now trying to come up with an argument to dissuade her from this course of action, "At least if you let the Police handle it they can follow up and arrest him."

"But that's the point Philip… they won't really be able to do that will they? … the best they can hope for is to discover his name and location and pass that information to the local police in Singapore—who probably won't do anything or at least not anything serious and then this man will be back scamming within weeks," Elizabeth reasoned.

"And you think you can rehabilitate him to a life of goodness, do you?" Philip had a sarcastic tone.

"Well, I am not saying that, but something about the way we have built a relationship together and the way he talks…. I don't know… just makes me think he might be a decent person underneath. Maybe I can help that person come out," Elizabeth didn't sound as confident about this as she had done and Philip's negativity about it was making her start to doubt this plan. Anthony came to her rescue.

"Philip—stop being such a negative ninny! I think this is very brave of Liz—she could help someone get on the straight and narrow, as well as helping bring closure to her for all this. We need to support her."

Philip shrugged—he didn't like disagreeing with Anthony or Liz for that matter, but he felt strongly about this "Liz—I love you and I don't want to see you get hurt more. I think you are doing the wrong thing." He got up and walked out, leaving Anthony and Elizabeth staring at each other, surprised at Philip's strong stance.

"Don't worry Liz—leave 'her' to me," he said in extra camp mode. "Trust me, by tomorrow he will be on side with your brave plan," and with that he got up, air-kissed Elizabeth and went out after his husband.

Chapter 48
Multi-Tasking

E: Hi Joseph. How are you today? I feel stronger every day. x.

J: Good morning. Great that you are getting over the flu. I am OK—a little fed up.

E: Why are you fed up?

J: I don't know. Just getting a bit homesick, I think.

Penny and Billy knew this was the start of the 'can you pay for me to come back to the UK' conversation and they wanted to get the most out of it.

P: Hi Elizabeth—we are going to take control of the chat for a bit—see what we can get out of him—OK?

E: Hi Penny—yes, sure. Be careful!

Elizabeth quickly opened the WhatsApp app and clicked on the contact 'Joseph' that she had already set up. She typed.

E(WhatsApp): Hi Joseph. I thought I would see if I can use WhatsApp like you suggested a while back.

J(WhatsApp): Hi! Clever you. I didn't think you wanted to try it. I like it better than the messenger.

E(WhatsApp): Well let's see how it goes—I might switch between the two a little until I get used to it.

J(WhatsApp): Thumbs-up.

Penny took control of the Messenger conversation.

E(P)(Messenger): Oh, dear. What is it that you don't like about where you are now?

J(Messenger): Oh, we are back here then—OK! Well, for starters you are not here! E(P)(Messenger): Bless you. But really—what's not to like about Singapore? Why don't you tell me what you see out of the window—I bet it's lovely.

Penny had not picked up on his comment about being 'back here'. He had meant back on Messenger, but she had just taken it to mean back on the topic of Singapore or something. She was focussed on her first attempt at getting him to reveal something.

J(Messenger): You would be surprised. It's not all that lovely here. Anyway. Let's talk about where you are—that will cheer me up!

E(P)(Messenger): I think it's sad that you can't be happy where you are. We all kid ourselves about things to make us think we are happy. I lie to myself all the time.

J(Messenger): Really? About what?

E(P)(Messenger): Well, you know my lovely hair? It's not that colour naturally anymore—I dye it to make myself think I am still young!

J(Messenger): Do you? You have been lying to me all this time—you told me you were a natural redhead! ha-ha—it doesn't matter to me—you are still beautiful!

Elizabeth was sitting back and watching this conversation unfold. Slightly uncomfortable that someone else was representing her. Although she had to admit that Penny had got her tone of voice right. She couldn't see where this line of questioning was going, however.

E(P)(Messenger): As I said—we all lie to make ourselves feel better. You must have some secrets only you know that makes you feel better about yourself?

J(Messenger): Oh, I don't know about that—what you see is what you get with me. E(P)(Messenger): Come on—play the game. I told you a secret about me. Now you tell me one about you...

J(Messenger): OK—well... the pictures I sent you... I am not really that slim anymore. They were a bit old and I have put on weight.

Elizabeth realised that this was a trust-building exercise that Penny was trying to play. She thought it was a good approach but didn't think it was going to get a confession out of him.

E(P)(Messenger): There you go—I bet you feel better now, having confessed that! Ha-ha, I still think you are lovely.

J(Messenger): Perhaps. Anyway, it doesn't matter what weight I am as you are not cuddling me...

Penny was pleased that he had played the game and she thought it was best to leave it there for now. Especially as he was bringing it back round to wanting to see Elizabeth.

P: Hi Elizabeth—I am going to leave it there for now and hand back control to you. E: OK. I can see that you are trying to gain his trust, so I will continue in that vein and let you know if anything comes of it.

P: OK—don't try too hard—it's a slow process. Thanks for all your help so far! E: That's OK—happy to help.

Penny released control of Messenger back to Elizabeth.

E(Messenger): Well, I would love to cuddle you—whatever your size. Sending you hugs now...

J(Messenger): ha-ha—Thanks. We should talk about how we can make that hug real... E(Messenger): One day perhaps. We can dream.

J(Messenger): It doesn't have to be a dream...

E(WhatsApp): Listen Joseph. I need to talk to you about something.

J(WhatsApp): Hi—you are testing out switching between apps today!

E(WhatsApp): Do you trust me, Joseph?

J(WhatsApp): Well, not after that confession about your hair! Hee-hee.

E(WhatsApp): I am being serious—do you trust me?

J(WhatsApp): of course, I do—what is this about?

E(WhatsApp): I want to help you. But I need you to just trust me. I want what is best for you. J(WhatsApp): I don't understand—why are you saying this? Are you OK? Maybe you have taken too many tablets for your flu and need to lie down?

E(WhatsApp): OK—well I will go now. But I just want you to know that I want to help you and you have to trust me.

J(WhatsApp): OK. OK. I get it—I trust you. Go and have a rest and we will chat later. x.

Elizabeth wasn't sure if she had done the right thing. She had gone in a little heavy on WhatsApp, but she had been worried that he was about to ask her for money to travel and the Police would probably have jumped on that and it might have gotten out of her control. Either way, she had prepared the ground for a more serious chat about how she could help him. She knew she would have to confess about knowing he was a scammer in their next WhatsApp chat, and she was a little scared of doing that.

What Elizabeth didn't know, was that despite using the WhatsApp app that the Police had not built an intercept system for like that had with Facebook Messenger, they had still seen the entire conversation she had with 'Joseph' via WhatsApp—thanks to Billy putting the, slightly illegal, monitoring software on her iPad.

Penny and Billy were looking at this conversation and wondering what to make of it. Was it just Elizabeth doing what she said and trying to help them by building trust like they had started to do? They hoped it was that, but given it was via another App, they also wondered if she was up to something. They were going to have to keep an eye on Elizabeth—she might not be as sweet and innocent as they first thought.

Chapter 49
It's Good to Talk

Gloria had been getting on really well. Her initial chat with Gerald had turned him from someone who was mildly interested in 'Evie' into someone who couldn't get enough of chatting to her. Jem, Azi and Gil watched over Gloria's shoulder with several punters and saw how she lured them in with seductive chats—she was a natural.

The irony was that when she wasn't acting as one of her personas, Gloria was actually quite repulsive—She ate like a pig, dressed like a whore and smelt like a combination of strong body-odour and cheap perfume! Despite this, Gil liked her and had gotten over his initial embarrassment. She treated him like a younger brother and even seemed able to defend him against Jem's temper—she had Jem and Azi wrapped around her little finger.

After she had been working there for about two weeks, it became clear that to move the punters to the point where they would 'send money', a verbal conversation was going to be needed. The boys had not really considered this, but they had been running the operation for nearly a month and hadn't yet got to that point with any of the punters—it was Gloria who brought it up.

"So how do I phone this Gerald then—he wants to speak to me—I mean, of course, he does—who wouldn't!"

"Erm, really—can't you just convince him to pay for your travel to see him over the chat?" Azi optimistically suggested.

"Duh—of course not. Would you give money to someone you think you might be falling for, but have never actually talked to? Didn't you think this through?"

"Clearly not," chimed in Jem, walking over from his corner to join in the conversation.

"Sounds like it's the next obvious step though. Are you OK to talk to him, Gloria?"

"Sure thing, babe—I can talk to any man who is desperate for some of the Gloria gifts—innit," Gloria puffed out her chest as usual and spoke with extra swagger.

"OK—well, you can't talk like that! You will have to keep with the persona of 'Evie' that you have been using on the chat messenger."

"Oh yes. Naturally my good man. I will use the Queen's English at all times and ensure a delightful conversation with the gentleman," Gloria went the other way and overacted her version of an 'English Lady'.

The guys laughed and then so did Gloria. They agreed she would do it without them watching over her, so she didn't get the giggles whilst acting the part. They also agreed that using the phone call part of Facebook Messenger was the way to go—partly because after the initial two weeks 'no direct contact' most punters moved to use their own Facebook Messenger apps rather than the 'Expats Reunited' chat service, and partly because Azi and Gil had not managed to activate the phone call part of the messenger module in their website.

So, Gloria arranged to call Gerald and put on a suitable 'English middle-class' voice. The call went very well, and Gerald was taken in by her acting. The guys hadn't heard what she had said, but the next thing they knew Gloria was asking how they wanted Gerald to send 'Evie' her ticket money to travel home—they had success! Jem and Azi were so pleased that their 'business' was going to work, that they wanted to go out and celebrate straight away. Gil didn't really want to join in their kind of celebrating at the club and anyway he had arranged to meet up with Eb, as they had been doing for the past couple of weeks. So, a jubilant Gloria, Jem and Azi all went off to the club and Gil feigned a headache to get out of it.

Gil and Eb had been meeting at a local café and that is where Eb was sitting with two coffee's, waiting for Gil. Gil waved to Eb as he walked across the floor and Eb smiled back. They were both really happy to see each other and their friendship had been growing fast—they both felt like they were the friend they had been missing in their lives. They both had so much in common it seemed—neither had a father around, neither had much money, neither had much control over their lives. But it wasn't the bad things in common that made them friends, it was the opposites—they were both fascinated with their different experiences.

Gil had not been encouraged at school; Eb had been taken under a teacher's wing, Gil didn't have a family meal prepared for him every day; Eb sat down with his Mum and sister every evening, Gil went out whenever and wherever he wanted around Lago; Eb had to tell his Mum where he was going and what time he would be back. As well as being fascinated, they were actually both jealous of each other—they joked that they would like to swap places. In reality, they both knew that Eb had the better life, despite Gil's seeming more adventuress.

Eb's smile soon disappeared as he re-told the story of his Mum's sacking to Gil. When he got to the bit about his Mum not being able to pay what she owed on the loan, Gil shuffled his feet and looked sheepish. He had not yet told Eb that it was his brother Jem who ran the loan business and obviously he had not told Eb about Jem, Azi and his involvement in the death of Eb's father—he wanted to confess, but couldn't find a way that they could remain friends if he did. Gil listened and was truly moved by the plight of Eb and his family—he asked what they would do.

"Well, I think my Mum will have to go and talk to that bloke about the loan—see if she can buy us some more time—he is a businessman and I am sure will see the sense in giving us more time so he can actually get his money," Eb was trying to convince himself as he spoke.

"I wouldn't bank on him doing that—he is unlikely to—he is a tight bastard," responded Gil without thinking.

"Oh, do you know him then?" Eb asked interested.

Gil cursed himself for his slip up. "Oh, er. Yeah, sort of—I heard he was a tough businessman…," hopefully that would cover his tracks.

"I bet—you don't go into the loan business around here without being a bit of a tough nut!" Eb had accepted Gil's cover-up. "And I think I will have to stop all my drama stuff at school and get a job—like I used to."

"That's a real shame—your drama stuff sounded really fun and you seem to be a great actor."

"Maybe, but someone has to put the food on the table and I am getting to the age where I need to be responsible—my old market job is just before school and straight after, so there won't be time to do the drama stuff at the end of the school day—it is what it is I guess."

"Still, you really like old what's-his-face—that teacher—you will miss doing stuff with him."

Eb ruffled his hair up and pulled an old man face, then said in a voice mimicking JG, "Do you mean me, young man? Well, I am not sure you couldn't do a better job of that Shakespeare play—hey? Now let's put our backs into it and crack on—that's the ticket!"

Eb had done this impression before, as well as others and he knew Gil loved it. Gil was in fits of laughter as soon as Eb had started. "You are really great at doing JG—you have got him to spot on!"

Eb was glad that he had managed to lift the gloom that had covered their conversation so far today—meeting Gil was his release from his normal life, and he wanted to enjoy it.

Chapter 50
Showing Her Hand

Philip and Anthony popped round the next morning. They had a late-night as they sat up with a bottle of Rose to discuss what Liz was proposing to do. Philip had argued strongly that the whole thing should be left to the Police, but Anthony was more logical and wordier than Philip—he just kept talking (and topping up his glass) until Philip gave in and agreed with him. They decided that they would help Liz in whatever way they could and, to appease Philip, they would make sure she stayed on the right side of the law as much as possible.

"Liz babe," Anthony was so excited by the adventure they were about to go on that he couldn't help calling her his usual 'babe', "Philip and I have agreed that we are gonna support you in helping the scammer—we think you are being really strong girlfriend and we love that—female empowerment is one of our big things!"

Trying to ignore the over-enthusiasm Elizabeth answered "Well, that's great—thank you both. I am not sure what any of us can actually do, however…."

"I have been thinking a bit and the first thing is that we must use another iPad for talking to the scammer—we can't risk talking to him on your iPad, even using WhatsApp like you were suggesting yesterday—I don't trust the police not to be looking at everything on there," Anthony spoke with certainty.

"Oh, well that's blown it then," replied Elizabeth.

"Why? You haven't already contacted him and confessed, have you?"

"No, not quite. But I did chat with him using WhatsApp and told him I wanted him to trust me."

"Oh, dear—you might have blown the mission before it started! Better have a look at what you said, Liz."

Elizabeth reached for her iPad and handed it to Anthony. Philip looked over his shoulder as he opened WhatsApp and looked at the messages that Elizabeth had sent the evening before to 'Joseph'.

"Hmmm. Well, you didn't totally blow it and we might be able to pull it back—if the Police don't say anything today, then I think we will get away with it."

Anthony got his iPad out and installed WhatsApp. Elizabeth gave him her WhatsApp username and password so he could log in as her. He had been worried that even using his iPad at Elizabeth's (and therefore through her Wi-Fi connection) would allow the Police to see what was being sent from his iPad. But after a quick Google last night he found out that everything on WhatsApp was encrypted and so no one would be able to see what he was sending unless they had installed a tracker on his device, which he knew they hadn't. They might be able to see that another device had connected to the Wi-Fi and even that it was using WhatsApp but not the messages. He must make sure not to leave his iPad at Liz's house in case the Police dropped by and snuck some monitoring software onto it.

"OK—that's my iPad set-up with your WhatsApp account—now you can use it to break the news to the scammer that you know all about him," Anthony handed his iPad to Elizabeth.

"OK—well last night I asked if he trusted me—he said he did, so now let's see if that was true…."

E(WhatsApp): Hi. Are you there?

J(WhatsApp): Hi Elizabeth. Yes, I am here. How are you today? Back on WhatsApp, I see—are you starting to like it more than Messenger?

E(WhatsApp): Look. I need to talk to you about something I have discovered, and it is going to be a big shock.

J(WhatsApp): Oh, right. Nothing wrong with your health, I hope?

E(WhatsApp): No—nothing like that. Just wait and listen, please.

J(WhatsApp): OK—fire away…

E(WhatsApp): I know that you are not who you say you are.

J(WhatsApp): What, just because I said I had put on some weight—ha-ha!

E(WhatsApp): Stop it—you said you would listen.

J(WhatsApp): oh. Yes, sorry. Carry on.

E(WhatsApp): I know that you are pretending to be someone else so that you can make me fall in love with you and then get me to send you some money. I know that you are a scammer. I know your first instinct will be to cut all connection with me and disappear from my life, but please don't. Since I worked it out, I have been through all sorts of emotions, but the strongest one has been a sadness that anyone would be driven to scam people in this way. You may not be 'Joseph' but I think over the past few weeks I have started to see some of whoever you actually are come through and I think you might really be a decent person. So, I think that you must have gone through some tragedy to be doing this—I can't believe you want to, and I think that if you let me help you, then you could stop having to do it. Please, please give me a chance to help you.

WhatsApp showed that 'Joseph' was 'typing'. Then it stopped saying that. Then after a minute, it started saying it again, then stopped, then started and finally stopped altogether. 'Joseph' had obviously tried to respond but couldn't find the right words. Elizabeth knew she was losing him and with it her chance to have some closure on this whole thing, by helping others to avoid a similar fate. She tried one last ditch thing.

E(WhatsApp): Sorry to have sprung that on you. I know you will need time to think about it. I will be here—even if I don't hear from you for a few days, I will still be here. Please give me a chance to be your friend. X.

Anthony and Philip had been perched on either side of her chair, watching every word she had typed. They had not interrupted her or suggested any word changes—she had known what she wanted to say and had done her bit brilliantly. Both the men had wet eyes when she signed off with the kiss and both of them hugged her tightly as soon as she put the iPad down. Elizabeth had felt strong and determined up to this point but now with her friends around her and her desperate plea done, she could allow the emotions in. She sobbed. Anthony and Philip joined in. They all sat there sobbing—hoping, beyond hope that the scammer would see the light and step into it.

Chapter 51
Slow Stakeout

It had been three days since Elizabeth had last communicated with the scammer, as far as Billy and Penny were concerned. There had been that funny message about trusting her on WhatsApp and then nothing. They were a bit worried. Surely another opportunity to progress this case had not slipped through their hands!

Chapter 52
Watch, but Don't Catch

Gloria had gone on to scam five more punters out of airfare money. Quickly disappearing from their Facebook Friends list once the deed was done. Azi or Gil would cut access to the 'Expats Reunited' website for the punter and they would never communicate with them again. The beauty of it was that the punters were just too embarrassed to report it to the Police.

That said, the team knew that the Police had started taking an interest in them. Well, they assumed it was the Police, although they didn't even know if it was Nigerien Police or UK Police. It was Gloria who had first noticed something going on.

"Hey, Gil baby. What is this here flashing thing on my screen?"

Gil slid over on his chair to take a look. "What flashing thing?"

"That thing there in the bottom right-hand corner—watch this space…," she pointed at a point on the screen.

"There is nothing happening."

"Just watchman!" They waited about twenty seconds. There was a brief double flash of a small black line where Gloria's finger was pointing.

"Oh, right. Yeah, I saw that. No idea—probably always been there and you only just noticed it."

"No way, boy—I know what is on my screen and that's new—for sure," Gloria was adamant.

Gil had no idea but brought it up with Azi when he was next at his desk.

"Probably just a computer glitch innit," suggested Azi. Gil was curious. He agreed with Gloria that he had never seen it before—so something had changed. He decided to do a bit of digging around. He went to the Facebook developer's website and looked at all their articles on recent updates they had done or problems they knew about with Facebook Messenger—there was nothing that suggested the chat module had changed or had issues. He did some further Googling to see if anyone on the internet had experienced anything similar. He spent nearly an hour going down rabbit holes only to find that the problem people were talking about were never quite the same as his. Then after about an hour, he found something, and it made him scared. Gloria noticed he had gone as white as a sheet and asked if he was OK. He muttered something about feeling hot and went outside to get some fresh air. If what he had found was true, then they were in trouble—he had to tell Jem and Azi but wanted to be sure before he did.

He went back inside the office and calmly logged into Facebook Messenger as 'Melanie', who was one of the oldest fake personas they had created and so her Facebook account had existed for some time. He opened up a recent chat that one of them had had with a punter and sat staring at the screen—nothing happened and he was just deciding that it must be a glitch when he realised he had not done anything on the chat, so it was not really active as such. He came out of that particular chat, as it wasn't one of his punters and scrolled down the contacts list until he found one of his current punters.

He opened their last chat and sent a message saying "Can't wait to chat with you later when you wake up. x," knowing that this punter would be asleep and so he wouldn't have to interact with them right now. He waited and watched the bottom right-hand corner. Nothing happened for nearly two minutes, but if he was right, then they needed time to realise he had started a chat conversation.

Sure enough, he then saw the little black line blink twice in the bottom right corner. Horrified those he was, he had one more test to make sure. He checked the list he kept of all his punters and found one that had connected with a new persona 'Karl' that had only been created a couple of weeks earlier. As two weeks had passed, they had now exchanged contact details (as per the rules of the site), but he had not started a Facebook Messenger conversation with the punter, a lady called Sarah.

He logged into Facebook Messenger as 'Karl', which none of them had done previously, and started a chat with Sarah. He sent the same message he had for the other one. He waited five minutes and no little black line flashed in the bottom right corner. His research was complete and although still terrified of the consequences, he felt more confident to share his findings with Jem and Azi.

"What do you mean the fucking Police are monitoring our chats with punters?" screamed Jem, leaping up from his chair.

"How has this happened? What are we going to do?" He was about to grab Gil, but Azi stepped in his way.

"Calm down Jem—we don't know the facts yet... Gil—tell us what you know," Azi tried to bring some calm and logic to the conversation.

Gil explained what Gloria had seen and the investigation he had done to confirm what searching the internet had told him—that it was possible to intercept Facebook Messenger chat sessions and change what was being sent and received or even delete messages altogether—in effect, to take control of the conversation.

Jem had listened intently but now was back to roaming around the room and ranting. Azi, on the other hand, was sitting quietly, thinking.

"But what do they hope to do with this monitoring?" he asked no one in particular.

"Fucking shut us down, throw us in prison and chuck away the key you prick!" shouted Jem.

"But what evidence have they got to do that—a bunch of chat messages where, at best, our victims volunteer to send us money..." Azi was looking less worried than he had done initially.

"I mean, it's annoying they are watching us, but they won't get anything from our chat messages to put us in prison—there is nothing 'wrong' in those messages."

"Are you mad? They can do us for extortion!"

"No, they can't—we haven't extorted money out of anyone—just provided some online fantasy," Azi suggested with a raised eyebrow.

"And what happens when they find out these people have sent us money to bring their new lover home and they don't turn up!" Jem couldn't believe Abi was being so calm.

"You tell me what happens...," Azi said coolly.

"I fucking well will! .... The Police will be around here faster than a speeding bullet...," he was about to go on when Azi interrupted him.

"How?"

"How what?"

"How will the Police know to come round here... like a speeding bullet."

"Well, they will get our address from ...," Jem stopped.

It slowly started to dawn on him why Azi was being so calm. "Ah, they don't have our address—just our fake internet accounts!"

“Exactly! No one knows we are even in Nigeria bruv—that’s the beauty of our set-up,” Azi reminded Jem.

“Yes. Of course—I forgot and started to, well you know….”

“Panic?” suggested Azi.

“No, man—just get excited about the Police tracking us down—we are like wanted men—haha!” Jem was trying to cover his panicking up with some bravado to save face.

Azi consolidated the fears of the last ten minutes with a calming declaration, “Those Police can watch all they like—and maybe we can even have some fun when we know they are watching—but they would have to find us to prosecute and even then they would have to catch us in the act of pretending to be someone else to con people out of money—it ain’t never gonna happy bruv—we are Kings of the Catfish!”

Chapter 53
Day One of Waiting

Elizabeth checked Anthony's iPad every thirty minutes or so. She also checked her iPad just in case a message came via that instead.

It was the first day of silence from 'Joseph' she had experienced in a while.

Chapter 54
More Waiting

Billy busied himself with tracking the activities of the other potential victims and watching for any 'chats' that could help them find out more about the scammers.

Penny didn't do anything. She sat and brooded. Only coming out of her mood every now and then to check with Billy if Elizabeth and 'Joseph' had communicated.

Jane Porter looked out of her glass office at the two of them. So much promise—Technology and Psychology combined into one dream team—was her faith in them misplaced?

Chapter 55
"Actor Wanted"

Now they knew the Police were watching them, but couldn't find them, the team were motivated to move forward faster with their business. They paid for some more advertising on the internet and spent more time chatting with the punters as they joined. There was a real buzz in the office.

However, Gloria was still the only one of them to have successfully got money out of any punters. The boys had come close, but the punter always got jittery at the last moment and dropped off the relationship, usually with a lame excuse. It was clear that the difference was that Gloria spoke to her punters with her 'phone calls'—this seemed to be what was needed to build that final step of confidence.

It wasn't that Azi and Gil were not willing to try, it was that they didn't have the skills to carry it off. Their first attempts had failed dismally.

Azi tried an audio call on Facebook Messenger as his most popular persona 'Stewart'.

'Stewart': Hi Pauline. I thought we should talk properly at last!

Pauline: Oh, hi. Is that you Stewart? You don't sound how I thought you would.

'Stewart': Oh, am I sexier? (laugh).

Pauline: Not so much that as—I can't really hear that lovely Yorkshire accent you told me about. You sound a little more, erm... European?

Azi cursed himself for forgetting that 'Stewart' was from Yorkshire and that he had made a big thing about the great accent from the area—it was one of the things that Google told you about men from Yorkshire and he didn't think it would ever come back on him!

'Stewart': Oh, well maybe some of it has gone since I have been in Singapore, but it's still me!

Pauline: Well, it's lovely to speak at last. The only problem is that you have caught me at a bad time and I have to go somewhere. Can we talk another time?

'Stewart': Oh, right, yeas sure—no problem. Let's talk later—really looking forward to it!

Pauline had hung up without saying goodbye and shortly afterwards had 'un-united' from 'Stewart'. Azi realised he had buggered up his first call. Although Azi hadn't let anyone listen in on his call, he was sensible enough to share his experience with Gil before he did his first call, in the hope his would go better.

Gil logged into his 'Chris' account on Facebook and chose a lady called Beth as his chats with her had been really bubbly and fun.

'Chris': Beth! We speak at last!

Gil had double-checked that he hadn't told Beth in earlier chats that he had any particular UK accent—so he was able to go for a general British accent.... Or so he thought.

Beth: Yay—it's my online flirt Chris—so great to speak to you!

'Chris': Ain't it just gal! Ow's ya bin den?

Beth: Ha-ha—good accent! (mimicking 'Chris')—I as bin up and down me apples and pears, ain't I!

'Chris': What?

Beth: 'Apples and Pears'—Stairs! I was just copying the funny accent you put on.

It turned out that Gil had got his 'typical British accent' from watching 'Only Fools and Horses' on TV! The call went from bad to worse, with him trying to deny he was doing an accent and Beth eventually losing patience with him because he wouldn't admit he was putting it on. Another failed phone call.

Jem walked over to their desks to see how their respective calls had gone. He was disappointed with them both, but in fairness, he admitted that he could not have done much better. Pretending to be someone else when you are typing is one thing but acting the part out for real on the phone was something else.

Since his last coffee with Eb, Gil had been trying to think of a way that he could help Eb and his family. Not only did the history with Eb's Dad make Gil feel like they owed Eb some help, but the fact that it was also his brother that was the loan shark made him feel he should have some kind of power to help. He knew Jem wouldn't tolerate him sticking his nose into the Loans business, but now he had an idea…

"What we need is someone who can act," proposed Gil.

"I can act!" said Gloria slightly affronted.

"Yes—But we need a male actor for the women punters—you are good Gloria, but you are not that good!" Gloria took this in the good humour that it was intended and laughed.

"Right, but it's not like we can just recruit someone with acting skills—is it you stupid runt" Jem moaned.

"Well, actually…. I do know someone," Gil looked pleased with himself, but then remembered the next bit, "and in fact, so do you…." He was playing it cool in the hope Jem would as well.

"Go on…," Jem was intrigued.

"You know that woman you were moaning about having to go and visit the other day about her loan?"

"Yes—what do you know about it?" Jem snapped, not pleased that his brother was tracking his every move.

"Nothing really, except that her son is an actor."

"How the fuck is that going to help us?" Jem wasn't getting it.

Gil was careful not to patronise his volatile brother, "I know him a bit from school and bumped into him the other day. He was telling me that his Mum just got the sack from the factory she worked at, for pinching stuff, and now he needs to get a job to help pay back the loan and for food and stuff."

"She lost her job? Well, how is she gonna pay back the loan—ha-ha—Mrs Goody-goody is in trouble—that's how I like my customers!" Jem was warming up to evil thinking.

Gil didn't want to overdo it and land Eb and his family in real trouble with Jem—that would not end well. "How about we give Eb a job here? He can use his acting skills to talk to the punters, which helps this business and then he will have money for his Mum to pay the loan, which means you get that money as well—everyone wins," Gil concluded, feeling pleased with how he had pitched it.

Jem frowned and then scratched his stubbly chin. Jem knew who this Eb was but didn't know if Gil would remember what they did to Eb's father—perhaps

Gil had not made the connection and just thought this Eb was a boy from school. He decided to risk it—"We could give this boy Eb a try and see how it goes. But I warn you Gil—if it all goes wrong, then I will fuck that boy and his family up—you hear me?"

Gil hoped it wouldn't come to that, but first, he had to convince Eb to come and work for his brothers dodgy scamming business—it wouldn't be Eb's first choice he was sure.

Chapter 56
Even More Waiting

It was three days since Elizabeth had that last chat with 'Joseph' and he had not responded at all. Philip pointed out, during his and Anthony's daily visit that they were doing to keep Liz's spirits up, that he had not disappeared from WhatsApp or Facebook and so had not exactly shut up shop and gone into hiding. They didn't know if this was a good or bad thing—either he had just decided to ignore Elizabeth and was concentrating on the other victims he must have or… he was thinking how he could safely accept her help. Elizabeth hoped, against hope, that it was the latter.

Chapter 57
The Double-Dip Problem

Penny and Billy were waiting, with less and less patience, for something to happen between Elizabeth and 'Joseph', but that didn't mean they were not busy. Lots of the other scammer profiles they had been following were very active and they were monitoring their chats with their victims, looking for a way in. Once or twice Penny dived in and paused a message to tweak it or add her own message, with the original plan of getting info out of the scammers.

Mostly the chats between scammer and victim were flirting, as you might expect with chats for any online dating couple. A few had moved to agree to send money, but they were hard to trace because they started to talk on the phone at that point and they couldn't monitor that—they often saw details of a Money Exchange branch in Singapore being sent by Facebook Messenger and it was always the same branch, which confirmed they definitely were the same people doing all these different scams, but that didn't help them to track down their location or any real details about them.

There was one couple where things went further. Again, it was hard to follow because they were clearly talking on the phone as well, so the bits that came through on Facebook Messenger needed stitching together with some guesswork.

There was a man called Paul, who was the victim, and a woman called 'Julia', who they assumed was a made-up persona of the scammer. They were still not certain if scammers only operated personas as their own sex—so 'Julia' could have been a woman or a man. It seemed that Paul had registered on the 'Expats Reunited' dating website and when they looked up his profile it said '*Strong, but lonely farmer who has spent too much time building up my successful business and not enough time on love—wants an interesting, sexy and fun woman to share everything I have'*—so they knew he was kind of desperate, which is exactly what the scammers needed.

They could see from the chats they had intercepted that the relationship was quite a way on and they had made plans to bring Julia back to the UK from Singapore. There were some messages that had the same Money Exchange bank transfer details in them from 'Julia' and then a day later a message from Paul confirming he had transferred £1200 via this service. A few days went by with nothing very interesting and it was clear most of their communication was via phone calls now, but then suddenly a picture of a man that must have been Paul was sent—he was standing outside the big Heathrow Airport sign with a bunch of flowers and balloons.

'Julia' didn't reply to that. Then there were several hours with nothing except one message from Paul saying 'did you get the flight?', which was strange because surely he wouldn't have been at the airport several hours before the flight was due, they thought. The next message a little while later was another Money Exchange bank set of information, but this time it was in Australia.

Penny and Billy were really confused by this and puzzled over it for a while. It was hard to guess what it meant without all the background information. Jane Porter dropped by at the very moment they were struggling and asked how things we going.

"Well, it's funny you should ask that...," said Billy, immediately annoying Penny for starting out with a negative aspect of how they were confused.

"Yes, we have made some great progress with another scammer and victim relationship—we have noticed some real differences and are just working through possible solutions," Penny tried to recover with a positive spin.

"You mean you haven't got the foggiest!" Laughed Jane. "I love a puzzle. Tell me all and let's work it out together," she said with glee, plonking herself down on a free chair.

Penny outlined what had happened between Paul and 'Julia' as far as they knew it. Jane asked, "So what does it sound like has happened?" she was trying to get them to think again.

"Well, sounds to me like he has sent her money for a ticket, she has somehow spent the money and is now in Australia rather than the UK, but for some unfathomable reason he has agreed to send her more money—which makes no sense whatsoever," Billy said flatly.

"OK—so why would he agree to send her more money?"

"Because he is an idiot!" suggested Billy.

A lightbulb came on in Penny's head when Billy said that, "But that's the point… he is not an idiot… so he must still think she is still the real deal and not scamming him… but she already has scammed him and not turned up."

"So, if someone doesn't turn up somewhere, they have agreed to—someone you think you trust—then what do you assume… a. that they are a scammer or b. that they have made a mistake and got lost?" Jane continued to exercise their brains.

"You are not suggesting she got on the wrong plane and ended up in Australia rather than the UK and he is now sending her money to get another plane to the UK from there—are you?" Penny asked with some incredulity.

"Firstly, let's remember she didn't get on any plane—she is still in Singapore with no intention of leaving. Secondly, this Paul is in love and his heart will easily convince him she has made a genuine mistake, no matter how ridiculous it seems, rather than she is conning the love of her life."

"An idiot—as I said," chimed in Billy.

"The head rules the heart Billy—as you will find out one day."

"That is a huge leap, but let's run with it for now…," Penny suggested.

"Why thank you," Jane commented with heavy sarcasm.

Blushing, but carrying on regardless, Penny said, "Whatever reason he is sending her more money, he has sent it to a different Money Exchange and that helps us!"

"You are right," Billy sprang into action, tapping away at his keyboard.

"Does it?" Jane suddenly finds herself playing catch-up.

"Got it—they are using the same account number!" shouted Billy.

"Got them!" shouted Penny.

"Will someone please explain!" Jane was getting impatient.

"Well, whilst the scammers have been using the same Money Exchange branch in Singapore, we haven't been able to trace any payments through that because it is just a single personal account—we talked to the company and they don't release records for individual transactions, which each payment was," Billy explained.

"And…"

"Well, now that they have made a payment to another branch of Money Exchange but using the same account details, Money Exchange will have to transfer the money back to Singapore and that's classed as a multi-transaction, which we can get a warrant for them to release information on—it's under the anti-money laundering regulations that they have signed up to."

"And what will that tell us?"

Penny had been involved in the research they did with Money Exchange on this as well, "Their address—you must provide an address to be able to transfer money from multiple locations—we can find where in Singapore these guys are!"

"Right—let's go and find the duty Judge and get that warrant," Jane sprang to her feet to lead the charge.

Chapter 58
New Employee

"Listen Eb, I might be able to help with your money troubles," Gil came straight out with it when they met for coffee the next day.

"What? I don't want your charity Gil—I will have to get my old job back."

"But what if you could do a job that paid good money, involved your passion for acting and still gave you time to do the drama stuff with JG at the school?"

"Who are you—the genie in the bottle?" clearly Eb thought Gil was delusional.

"No. I mean it. My brother has a company you can work for."

Eb sat up and paid more attention, "OK, but what's the catch?"

"There isn't any catch… well not really…."

"Come on Gil—your acting is not as good as mine… what's the catch?"

"The business is kinda not quite a legit business."

"I'm not peddling drugs to young kids' mate!"

"No, no, nothing as bad as that," Gil protested. "It's more about conning foreigners out of a bit of money—we do it via a dating service—it's called Catfishing."

"Blimey—I didn't see that coming. And you said 'we'—are you part of this?" Eb raised an eyebrow suggesting he hoped the answer was no.

Gil started to get a bit offended. He was trying to help Eb and his family out of a desperate situation, and he was calling Gil's morals into question—especially considering it was Eb's mum's questionable morals that caused her to lose her job in the first place. Then Gil remembered that his morals were in question and no more so than by himself on a daily basis. "Well, yes I am. I am not proud of it, but there are not many choices for a high school dropout with no parents and no money—at least my brother is only taking money from non-Nigerians and people who can afford it."

"Like Robin Hood you mean!"

"Erm, nearly," he blushed.

Eb thought about it for a second or two and decided that he was not in a position to judge or turn down an offer of help for that matter. Anyway, everyone in Nigeria was on the fiddle in one way or another—his Mum at the factory, the kitchen staff at school pinching food and even him and his mates that helped out at the market, they all nicked stuff. This was a bit bigger and more serious, but he didn't have much choice and at least it wasn't against people in the community.

"Sorry, mate. It was just a bit of a shock. Tell me about it. And thanks for thinking of me buddy—you are a real mate."

Now Gil felt bad because actually it was at least what he, Jem and Azi owed Eb's family, he just wished they didn't need Eb's skills to help them get the money and could just give it to him instead.

Gil filled Eb in on the scamming operation and when Eb said with a grin 'Your brother sounds like a right little mafioso boss' Gil took the opportunity to add that Jem was also the loan shark his Mum had been dealing with, which didn't go down well, but again he got over it through lack of choice.

The next day, Eb turned up at the address Gil had given him and was instantly turned off the whole idea. The place looked like a dump from the outside and there were no other businesses or people in this derelict area of town. Just as he was wondering if he was even in the right place, Gil stuck his head out of an upstairs window and shouted for Eb to come up. Eb carefully navigated his way through the broken glass and dirty 'reception' area and climbed the stairs to the second floor where Gil met him.

Gil had managed to get Jem to agree not to say anything about being his Mum's loan shark, as he felt that would make the whole thing awkward. Everyone knew why Eb was there and they decided to just treat him as a new member of the team. As the newest member and a fellow 'actor', Gloria welcomed him most. Eb didn't recognise her from the club and he didn't ask about her past—he felt that the less he knew about the past of this group of individuals, the better.

"Welcome, Eb—great to have someone else good looking and talented around here," Gloria enthused.

"Oi!" said Azi, but knew she was only trying to wind them up.

"Thanks. And thanks very much for giving me a job—I will try my best," Eb stammered out.

"Too right you will," sneered Jem.

Azi wanted to start off on the right foot. He hadn't twigged that this Eb was the son of the man they had accidentally killed in that raid a few years back. He just thought the connection was to his mum and Jem's loan business. Jem and Gil alone knew about the full connection, albeit they hadn't shared with each other that they remembered.

"So, we hear that you are a good actor and can do voices and stuff like that Eb—we really need help with that. Gloria has the woman side covered, but we need someone to cover the man side," explained Azi as if inducting a new team member.

"Oh yes. I certainly have the lady side of things covered my dear—some would say amply?" Gloria put on a posh English voice and pushed her bosoms together as she said the word 'amply', laughing hysterically to herself.

Eb instinctively responded, almost as if he was in one of his drama sessions at school, "Of course madam, you speak very well, and I must say impress me with your charm and wit!" all said in a posh English accent.

Azi, Gil and Gloria clapped and were clearly impressed. Jem was pleased that Gil had found a solution to their problem but remained cooler.

"Not bad little Eb, not bad. Now let's see if you can use that talent to earn us all some money."

Jem slunk back to his corner office and Eb sat down with Gil to start his 'training', with Azi and Gloria chipping in with advice as they progressed. At the end of the session, Eb felt that he understood what was required of him. He still didn't like the idea of what they were doing but kept reminding himself that he didn't have a choice as they needed the money. However, he was pleased that they had welcomed him and also glad that, based on the successful approach Gloria had taken, it would be a good two to three weeks before he actually spoke to anyone—time enough to get to grips with being a professional scammer.

Chapter 59
Rejection

It was day four since she had sent the message offering to help 'Joseph'. Suddenly there was a ping on her WhatsApp app.

J: Sorry. I can't do this. Nothing personal. Sorry.

Elizabeth burst into tears. The build-up of the last few days had all come down to this—he was clearly a scammer and was rejecting her offer of help. Now she would never get closure.

Just then, the doorbell rang…

Chapter 60
The Wrong Country

The warrant came through in double quick time. Judge McCall had been the duty judge and Jane had been worried he would remember their past run-ins and be awkward, but he actually sent a note with it saying 'Go get them!', so perhaps she had found an area of crime which he was passionate about at last. She ran it down to Penny and Billy, urging them to send it through to the Money Exchange legal team immediately.

They got a response within the hour—these guys didn't mess about when the term 'money laundering' was being thrown about. At first, they were confused and thought some of the data must be wrong. The account number they used did have transactions between Singapore and Australia, but they all seemed to be linking back to the master account in Nigeria.

Nigeria had never come up in any of their investigations. Then Billy remembered something about his conversation with Philip, Elizabeth's physio and friend. He looked for the email Philip had sent them after their chat on the phone. Philip had said something like 'he knew all there was to know about this case and would put it in an email'—Billy couldn't remember what Philip had said about Nigeria, but he remembered hearing that country.

"Found it," Billy declared.

"Found what?" asked Jane—she was always having to unpick this pair's brains on this case it seemed.

"The email Philip sent me."

"And Philip is? …"

"The Physio who reported the whole thing."

"I thought we found Paul and 'Julia' via your monitoring research on the scammer persona names?"

"Yes, we did for those guys, but I am talking about Elizabeth and 'Joseph'."

"Blimey Billy, you might let us into your brain sometimes!"

"Sorry, Ma'am. Let me start again… I know we were looking at the Paul and 'Julia' case for the warrant on Money Exchange, but when the result mentioned Nigeria it reminded me, I had heard something about that country in another case—the Elizabeth and 'Joseph' case. So, I was just digging out the email that her friend Philip, who is her physio, sent when they first reported it."

"Right, I am with you now. Thank you."

"And what does the email say," Penny had been growing increasingly frustrated whilst waiting for the boss to come up to speed.

"Hang on…. Blah, blah, blah…. 'Joseph profile matches real person'… blah, blah…. 'a man called 'Joseph Grey' in Lagos, Nigeria," read Billy, "I knew I remembered something!"

"Is that it Billy?" asked Penny.

"No, hang on. There is a link to a newspaper article. Here look," Billy clicked on the link and they all waited as the profile of the real Joseph Grey loaded onto the screen.

They all spent a minute or two reading the news article by Lucy Beck in the 'Lagos News'. They all looked at each other and knew that they had found the 'real' Joseph, or at least where the scammer had got the profile information from. Billy was the first to recover. "So, if this guy is in Nigeria and the payment went to Nigeria, does that mean he is actually using his own details to scam people? Seems like a stupid thing to do."

"It is a stupid thing to do and also we know there are lots of other profiles of people, so he must just be one of many people whose profiles are being used. I doubt he even knows anything about the scamming," Penny said slightly downhearted because she didn't think this got them any further forward. It was Jane who spotted the potential lead this was.

"But now we have two things that link us to Nigeria—the Money Exchange master account and the profile of someone who lives in Nigeria—I think this means that we have been focussing on the wrong country. These scammers have been cleverer than we have given them credit for… they have led us to believe everything was happening out of Singapore when in fact they are based in Nigeria. We need to talk to the Lagos Police!"

Chapter 61
The Perfect Fake Profile

Despite his acting ability, Eb was struggling to pick up the scamming game. It wasn't that he had trouble with the computer stuff, that was easy. It was more the making stuff up that he found difficult. As all the fake profiles on the website were being 'worked' by Azi, Gloria or Gil, Eb had to create some of his own.

He wrote out a profile in the system, but when he read it back it just made the person sound one dimensional and therefore, he didn't think it would attract any punters. Eb was getting a basic wage, but the only way he would make proper money was by completing a scam—a bonus payment per successful scam was how Gloria was paid as well. So, he had to make the profiles into people that women would be attracted to and fall in love with.

It was during one of his first coffee breaks that he hit upon an idea. Gloria was reading an old copy of 'OK!' Magazine. She had got hold of some UK magazines to help her with current UK affairs for when she spoke to her punters. Eb noticed that on the front cover of the one she was reading was there was a picture of Tom Cruise—that's when Eb decided that he didn't need to make things up, he could just 'borrow' existing profiles of individuals that were known to be attractive to women—a perfect solution.

After the coffee break, he took the magazine back to his desk and started to write out a profile based on what he knew of Tom Cruise. He googled some other things about him to fill in the gaps and ten minutes later was very pleased with his new fake profile of 'Tim Sail'. He carried on looking through magazines and by the end of the morning had profiles for 'Chad Hole' (Brad Pit); 'Tud Thief' (Jude Law); 'Manuel Crag' (Daniel Craig); and 'Pugh Give' (Hugh Grant).

Gloria slid across as he sat back looking pleased with himself.

"What are you looking so happy about young man?"

"My fake profiles—I think you will agree they are an attractive sounding bunch…."

Gloria read through the profiles and when she finished, she laughed so hard that she nearly fell off her chair.

"What? It's a good idea isn't it?"

"Well, if you think all your punters are going to be idiots, then yes, it is a great idea," she laughed.

"You think they will recognise that the profiles are pinched from celebrities?"

"Yes, of course!"

"Oh," Eb looked dejected.

Gloria took pity on him. He had tried hard after all. "Listen, we can fine-tune them a bit and it will all be fine. You just need to mix and match a bit—let's say 'Tim Sail' is actually 'Tim Smith' because that's much more of a British name and rather than putting him as five foot four inches, let's make him six foot one inch and black—that way you have used most of Tom Cruises profile, but no one would guess it is based on him—simple see?"

"Oh, right. Yes, that makes sense. Thanks Gloria."

"That's OK my darling. Now the other problem you are going to have with using celebrities is when you start chatting to the punters—you will try and answer their questions as if you are the celebrity—you won't be able to help it because that's the person that is in your mind."

"So how do I deal with that?" he was beginning to realise why his mother always said, 'one lie leads to another'.

"Well, you really need to try and think of the person you are acting like someone you know—then you can imagine having a conversation with them and what they might say. I have lots of sisters and aunties, so I just think of one of them and pretend I am them when chatting with the punter," she explained. "Right, that's so clever!"

"Well, until you are juggling thirty punters at once and you can't remember who you were pretending you were with who! That's why I write down all my profiles and who they are based on in my little notebook. You should do the same."

"Great idea. Now I just need to think about men I know and how they talk. Thanks again Gloria."

Eb tried to think about his Dad and how he spoke to his Mum, but the memories were too old. He didn't really know many other adult men very well, except JG. He wasn't sure how JG spoke to women normally, let alone in a romantic or flirty way. Then he remembered what Su had said about JG and his Mum—she had thought they were interested in each other.

Eb shuddered at this thought, as he had done when Su suggested it, but continued to try and think how he had heard them speak to each other over the last few years. He couldn't quite think of anything particular they had said that might prove useful in his new job. He decided that maybe he should write down all the things he knew about JG and that might help jog his memory. He got stuck again doing that and realised that even though he had known JG a long time, he hadn't actually asked him much about himself.

Then he remembered there had been that newspaper article a few years ago after he had finished building the school and had stayed on to teach. A quick google and he had the 'Lagos News' website open and the article written by Lucy Beck in front of him.

Eb was surprised to discover that JG had been a Marketing Executive in the UK but not surprised about his love of Motorbikes—that was something they had talked about lots. He was also surprised to hear that JG was considered handsome by lots of the local Mums. Maybe Su had been right and his mum did 'fancy' JG—another shudder passed over him. The article had a picture with it and Gloria was just walking past Eb's desk as he had it up large on his screen.

"Phwoar! Now he is a hotty. Who is that?" she fanned herself pretending she had come over all hot.

Eb was a little embarrassed that he knew JG and didn't want further enquiries about him and his relationship status from Gloria, so he lied, "Oh, no one. Just some pictures I have been googling for my profiles."

"Well, make sure you use that one—it's a winner!" and she carried on to sit at her desk, continuing the fanning.

This reaction gave Eb a great idea. He would use JG as one of his fake profiles—he was handsome, had an interesting background and Eb knew a lot about what he did, so could answer questions as if he were him—it was perfect. He had no intention of letting JG, his Mum or his sister know what sort of work he was doing, so there was no danger of them finding out he was using JG's profile. JG had himself said he was not 'looking for love' and so was hardly going to come across the dating website.

Eb wrote the profile up on the dating website system, copying and pasting most of the details from the article, added the photo and published his first fake profile. He then added the other fake ones he had come up with that morning, mixing the details around as Gloria had suggested and giving them better British names. He was very pleased with his work and looking forward to getting some requests to connect.

When he came into work the next morning, he was pleased to see that his brainwave about using JG as a fake profile had paid off. There flashing in his system was an 'Expats Reunited' request from a lady called 'Elizabeth Gresham'. He quickly clicked 'accept'.

Chapter 62
The Real Joseph

Elizabeth got up and was pleased to notice that she got to the front door considerably quicker than she had a few weeks ago when she last had to open it—she was getting a lot better, thanks to Philip's work. She didn't look through the peephole or put the chain on, possibly because she forgot that it is a necessary precaution these days, but possibly because she didn't know who would possibly be calling on her as no one ever did these days and Philip always let himself in. She opened the door wide, stood tall despite a small twinge in her leg to present herself to her visitor in the best possible way and said a cheery 'hello'.

Then she fainted.

When she came around, Philip was standing over her with a concerned but excited look. She could hear Anthony enthusiastically talking to someone in the background.

"But how did you know to come here? And where have you been until now?" she heard him ask.

"Philip. Where am I?" she whispered.

"In your chair at home my love," he answered stroking her hand.

"And who is that I can hear talking?" she tried to raise herself a little to look around Philip.

"It's me darling," Anthony sprang forward and kissed her hand, "Thank goodness you are OK.

"You had a little knock on the way down and we thought you might be out for the count!"

"Anthony—don't be so macabre!" Philip chastised him.

"Well, she went as white as a ghost. No, as if she had seen a ghost," he replied in his defence.

Elizabeth was regaining her full faculties quickly and she said, "Well, that's exactly what I did see… I think," she said with great drama. "At least, not a ghost but someone who doesn't exist! … But I must have been hallucinating."

Another figure stepped forward into the light and in a deep, but smooth voice said, "I am afraid you were not Mrs Gresham."

"Joseph!" she exclaimed and clutched her hand to her chest.

"Oh, she is going again," said Anthony with melodrama in his voice.

"No, I am not! Shut up, Anthony."

"Sorry."

"Now Sir—please can you tell me who you actually are and how you come to be in my home?" Elizabeth asked with more strength and stability than she felt.

Chapter 63
International Policing

Jane, Penny and Billy were all sitting in Jane's office with the speakerphone on.

"Thank you for taking the time to speak to us, Deputy Commissioner—we are honoured you would take such an interest in this case," Jane said in her best and clearest English, and slightly slowly as Brits always do when speaking to non-English speakers.

"It is perfectly alright, commander Porter. I understand the utmost importance of our two countries working closely together to fight this kind of cyber-crime. I and my team are entirely at your disposal," he replied in a very British sounding voice, with perfect English and Jane suspected a better understanding of her language than she had—he had clearly been educated at Oxford or Cambridge!

"That's very decent of you Sir. We shall endeavour to cooperate to the furthest extent of our abilities, in order that both our legal systems gain mutual benefit." She had slightly upped the posh-ness in her voice and was being more wordy than normal—never try to out-British a British person, she was subconsciously thinking.

Penny, who thought of herself as a bit posh and wordy, was fed up with this verbal jousting, "OK, so who should we speak to in your team Sir about trying to find where these criminals operate from please?" Jane frowned at her, but let it go.

"Well, Constable," was he reminding Penny where her rank sat compared to his she wondered.

"We will email over the team and their contact details and you can go from there."

Jane jumped back in and forgot the posh-ness, "That's great—thanks. And will that team be able to follow up any leads for us and attend possible locations of this gang?"

"Ah, well. We may have a small problem there," suddenly the Deputy Commissioner sounded more down to earth as well. "When I say the team. It is actually Constable Sebastian that you will have access to… and then only when he is not on traffic duty."

It was clear that Nigerian police did not have the resources that Jane and her team had hoped, despite the Deputy Commissioners opening statement. But Jane had foreseen this and talked to Penny and Billy before the call, so they had a plan.

"I am sure that Constable Sebastian will be a very useful person to us. Thank you for committing some of his time. I wonder if I might suggest a way in which we could push this investigation forward a little more quickly… my two constables here that have been working on this case for some months would be very willing to come and work alongside Constable Sebastian for a week or so—does that sound like an option?"

The Deputy Commissioner didn't reply for a second or two. He was weighing up the pros of having more officers on the ground to help sort out what was becoming a major issue for the Nigerian Police, against opening up a corrupt and inefficient Policing organisation to two UK officers. He decided that it was worth it, but they would have to make sure they were kept away from certain things.

"That is an excellent idea and a most generous offer commander Porter. When would they like to come?"

"How about they fly out this weekend and start investigations first thing Monday?" this had been her plan all the time and she was glad it was coming to fruition.

Penny and Billy were thrilled about this development in the case and despite Nigeria not being their travel destination of choice, they were excited about travelling. On the downside, as ambassadors for the UK, they had to wear their full uniforms for the whole flight, which made some people stare a little. The upside was that they got a lot of respect from the cabin crew and Billy even accepted the free drinks that they offered—he figured he wasn't technically 'on duty' until the next morning. Penny felt this was going to be a career-defining trip and wanted to keep a clean head—she did however take advantage of the great duty-free prices, buying her Mum and Sister some perfume for Christmas and treating herself to some as well.

Constable Sebastian, a tall gangly youth, with bad acne and an ill-fitting uniform, turned up at the airport to meet them. What he lacked in presentation, he made up for in friendliness. "Welcome to Lagos! I am so excited to have the UK Police here—man I look up to you. It's the British that made me want to be a Policeman. Here let me take those bags—I have a car for you outside."

Penny and Billy felt like VIPs. Until they got to the hotel, which was a two-star at best and looked like it was last decorated in the fifties. Penny very nearly refused to stay there but decided on the British stiff upper lip approach and they checked in. Despite appearances, the rooms were clean, with fresh bedding and towels, so they relaxed a little. They had arranged to meet Sebastian just outside the hotel that evening for a meal and their first briefing on what the Lagos Police knew of the scammers.

Sebastian looked more normal in civvies and weirdly he clearly thought Penny and Billy looked less important in theirs, but he suppressed his disappointment that he wouldn't be seen dining with British Police and led the way to the restaurant. The restaurant was typical Nigerian cuisine with lots of spicy stews and soups—Penny thought it was like being on holiday and embraced the new tastes; Billy thought of his Mum's roast dinners.

As is often the case with young people on their first business trip, Billy drank a little too much and when Penny knocked on his door at seven the next morning, he groaned and just about managed to say he would meet her downstairs in the breakfast area. As is also often the case with young people, he recovered quickly—jumping into the shower, quick clean of his teeth (gargling to clear last night's beer from the back of his throat) and was dressed and downstairs tucking into a full breakfast ten minutes later—Penny was impressed by his recovery.

Sebastian picked them up at eight and drove them to a derelict area of town and parked a little distance from a disused office block. This was the place that his investigations, which mainly involved bribing local people in cafes and nightclubs over the last week, had led him to believe was the centre of operations for the scamming team. Sebastian got out some old looking binoculars, a flask of tea and some biscuits which he hoped his British colleagues would appreciate. The stakeout had started.

Chapter 64
The Fake "Joseph"

Elizabeth wasn't the only connection request that Eb got for his fake profiles, but it was the only one for 'Joseph'. After a bit of chatting back and forth over the next few days with Elizabeth, he worked out that it was because he had used the picture of Joseph sitting on that BSA Goldstar Clubman motorbike and Elizabeth was crazy for the old motorbikes. Perhaps the same thing had put other people off connecting with 'Joseph'.

Eb was getting used to flirting with his punters, who in the main were after an adventurer so he played up to that. Azi and Gil gave him some pointers—simple things like not being too nice as the ladies wanted a 'real' man and talking lots about how they wanted a 'Jane to their Tarzan'—real fantasy stuff was what their punters wanted the whole team told him. So, he used his acting skills and put himself into the mind of being Tarzan or some kind of jungle explorer—it seemed to do the trick as the ladies kept pinging him for more and more chats.

It wasn't like that with Elizabeth though. She seemed more interested in just chatting to someone about everything and anything—she came across as lonely. She was also a little older, according to her profile than most of the other punters. Eb didn't feel right flirting with her. In fact, he found himself channelling JG more and more into his character when he was chatting with Elizabeth—she responded best to that and he felt he was making a real connection, much more so than the other punters.

After a few days, he ran out of things to say to Elizabeth. This wasn't a problem with the other personas he was acting as they were all airhead hero types and you could more or less say anything, and the ladies seemed to swoon at your feet. Then the solution presented itself.

As a result of getting this job, he could work in the evenings and at weekends, meaning he was still able to do the after-school drama sessions and help JG as he had done in the past. This particular day, the drama session had just finished, and Eb was helping JG to pack everything away. JG asked how things were at home, as he always did, and Eb neglected to tell him that his Mum had been sacked and he was working for scammers—he just shrugged and said 'OK'. However, he then did something he never did, he asked JG how he was. Initially, JG was a little surprised at this enquiry from Eb who had never shown any interest in anyone but himself really, but then he put it down to Eb maturing, so he decided to go with it.

Joseph said that it had been a long few days at school recently because it was coming up to exam season and practice papers had to be prepared and extra tuition for those not quite up to scratch yet.

Eb made a mental note 'Long days—hard work'.

Joseph went on to talk about how the play they were in rehearsal for was stressing him a bit because no one knew their lines yet and he couldn't get people to turn up on time. He moaned about this for some time.

Eb made another mental note 'Stress due to other people not working' and 'drama is his hobby/passion'.

Then Joseph stopped talking, which didn't suit Eb's purpose, so he got Joseph onto the topic they hadn't talked about for a while.... Motorbikes. Joseph could talk about motorbikes for hours and Eb made plenty of mental notes. Eb also enjoyed talking about Motorbikes, so it hopefully didn't seem that he was drilling JG for conversation to use when chatting to Elizabeth.

Getting JG to give him things to talk to Elizabeth about worked like a dream—she chatted to him every day without fail and started being really open with him. It was building this 'trust relationship' that Gloria had said was the most important bit. You needed to get your punter to the point that they trusted you so much, that when the time came to scam them out of money it would not enter their heads that you might not be sincere. Eb felt like Elizabeth was coming to that point and it made him nervous. He thought it was because the next step was to talk to her on the phone, but in truth, it was because whilst he had been OK with the playacting part of his job, he was increasingly dreading the actually scamming them out of money part—it just didn't sit right with him and certainly not for Elizabeth who he had become very fond of.

Azi and Gil kept an eye on Eb generally and made sure he was starting to warm up his punters ready for the scam, but were understanding that it would take a while before he got to that point—this is a long scam and it had to be done properly, as they knew from their own experience. Gloria knew that Eb was thinking about his first call and would be nervous—acting out a character behind a messaging app is one thing, talking on the phone as one was a whole different level. She gave him some tips.

"You need to do a light flirt and try to get the conversation round to how great you think they are, and you wish you could talk to them for real. They normally suggest it first, which is the perfect way. Then you just make that first call and go for it. Might be worth having a few notes written down about things you have talked about so that you don't trip yourself up."

"But how do I get from there to asking them for money Gloria?" Eb asked genuinely bemused by this part.

"You don't—they offer. You just keep talking and saying how good it would be to see them, touch them, taste them…," she smiled cheekily and shimmied her whole upper body, "they will soon offer the airfare and then you have them!"

Eb was not so sure. But he gave it a go. The next evening, he determined that he would try to suggest a phone call or better still, get Elizabeth too. It didn't go very well. He started trying to do some light flirting, which was something he didn't ever do with Elizabeth, so it came across a little clumsy—something about him suggesting he was a toy-boy because she was older than him—pointing out a woman's age did not seem like the best way to flirt. Despite that, Elizabeth seemed to respond quite positively and then suddenly she suggested they were more than just friends and images bounced into his mind about getting sexy with this old woman and he panicked, closing down the chat quickly to retreat and re-think his approach.

He nearly buggered it up again and worse the next day when out of the blue SHE called him via the Facebook Messenger Audio phone. He was so surprised that again he panicked and declined the call. He breathed deeply and sat looking at his screen for a while. No one else was around as it was early and after a minute or two, he decided it was now or never, so he called her back. He was so nervous that he totally forgot he was meant to be a man in his early sixties and spoke with his normal youthful voice—naturally, Elizabeth commented on how youthful he sounded and cursing himself for being such an idiot, he quickly made himself sound more gruff and older, blaming a dry throat. He just about got away with it. After that, it was all plain sailing. They spoke nearly every day and sent messages when they didn't—Eb loved talking to Elizabeth and she loved talking to him—it became his daily comfort. But that meant that, again, Eb forgot what

'Joseph's' mission was—to get money out of her. Azi reminded him again one day and he suddenly started getting nervous again. In fact, he wasn't sure he could bring himself to scam the lovely Elizabeth out of money at all—now what was he going to do about that?

Chapter 65
Swapping Stories

It was a stupid question because everyone in the room knew that this was Joseph Grey—the real Joseph. Better questions would have been, 'are you scamming me?' Or 'is your name really Joseph Grey' or 'why aren't you in Singapore?'. But Joseph went with the questions he was asked.

"My name is Joseph Grey. I am British but moved to Nigeria over 5 years ago to help people less fortunate than myself. I come to be in your house because one of those people seems to have taken a wrong turn in life and needs my help, and quite possibly yours, now more than ever."

Philip and Anthony sat in stunned silence. In shock at this surprising turn of events. They didn't know what to think or do.

Elizabeth found herself split in two—it was almost like there were two of her sitting side by side. One of her was thinking 'yes, I get it now. The person he is talking about IS a scammer and they DO need help—just like I thought they did. I don't know what relationship this man is to the scammer, but we can work together to help them'. The other of her could not have been having different thoughts, 'Wow—so this is the real Joseph and he is every bit as good looking as his photos.

His voice is so silky and manly. And he is on a mission to help someone and has chosen me to be by his side [love struck sigh]'. The good news was, that whichever 'her' she was going to be (and it was probably a bit of both if she was truthful to herself), it appeared that she was getting closer to her mission of helping the scammer with the terrible situation she imagined they were caught up in.

"Joseph Grey. This is a little strange for us all, you also I imagine," she opened with.

"Yes, indeed. I do hope that I have done the right thing and not scared you all too much?" he replied with sincerity.

"Well, I am not scared and these two will snap out of it in a minute. I would like to know everything you know and mostly about this person you say you are trying to help—I think I know them, but perhaps in a different way to you."

"He said you were clever, but mostly that you had compassion and he knew you wanted to help—that is what drove me to come."

"And you say you have come from Nigeria—we are a little confused on that point. We thought the scamm… people you are trying to help were in Singapore?"

"Ah, well I think that was the point. And you are right to call them 'scammers' that is definitely what they are. However, one of them means something special to me and he has been dragged into their world by circumstance and I want to get him out of it. I think you do too. His name is Eb."

Philip and Anthony snapped out of it enough to make tea for the guest—there seemed to have been a lot of tea making in this house of late. Joseph was invited to sit down next to Elizabeth and start at the beginning, which he did.

He covered the story of Eb's father being killed in a raid on his workshop when Eb and Su were very young and how the family had struggled, but just about managed to keep going; he was very passionate when it came to talking about Eb joining the school and developing as a high potential student, particularly with computers and drama, and how he and Amelia were hopeful this would give Eb his bright future; he spoke about Eb's Mum being caught up in a bad loan and getting sacked, which led to Eb getting dragged into the world of scamming and how finally, after being used as the 'fake Joseph' without his knowledge, Eb had revealed his betrayal of Joseph. Leading to his current involvement and how he set out on his mission to, once again, help Eb and his family.

Elizabeth listened intently and although tears sprang to her eyes at several points throughout the story, she kept quiet and didn't interrupt. She asked one question at the end.

"So, what can we do to help Eb and his family?"

"I have a bit of a plan, but I need to know what has gone on at this end and if you are involved with the Police."

Joseph perhaps should have checked how much Elizabeth was cooperating with the Police before he told her all the history of what had gone on with Eb, but he had trusted her as soon as he met her. Eb had told him so much about her. In fact, when Joseph first found out what Eb had done and how he had abused his trust, he had insisted on seeing all the old chat messages between 'Joseph' and Elizabeth. Initially, he was horrified to read messages supposedly sent from him to some stranger, but as he read through them and saw Elizabeth's responses, he grew to like her and felt she was someone he could trust. That's why he felt coming to the UK to enlist her help was the right gamble to make.

Elizabeth told her side of the story, with Philip and Anthony chipping in as she went along. She explained how she had been recovering from her accident—she mentioned that her husband had died in the accident briefly, but didn't dwell on it; she told Joseph about how she had been lonely and was recommended to get on the internet to keep in contact with the outside world and how she had been on a course at the local library; she mentioned that although she enjoyed the internet friends she had made, she longed for someone special in her life and that's how she had joined the dating site 'Expats Reunited'—she was a little embarrassed about that part, but Anthony piped in with 'She is a catch for any man!' and the laughter covered the moment; she paused before telling about how she had developed a relationship with 'Joseph'—she was very aware that she was talking about falling in love with the man (or at least the persona for the man) sitting in front of her—Joseph could see she was struggling and helped her by saying he had read all the messages and understood the nature of where the relationship had been developing—she was grateful for him doing that; finally she explained how Philip had been first to be suspicious and at that point Philip and Anthony took over for a couple of minutes, outlining their initial fears and then their test questions and then the News Paper profile they had all found and Philip contacting the Police—Joseph sighed at this point and muttered something about wishing he had never agreed to that interview—Elizabeth took the story back at the point where the Police visited her and they could all see Joseph tense a little at this point—perhaps he had been hoping the Police were not that involved yet for his plan to work.

After this mutual telling of each side of the story, they were all exhausted. Anthony, ever the practical one, suggested they might need some food. He and Philip said they would go and get a takeaway—Joseph sat up at this suggestion, not just because he was hungry, but because he hadn't had decent fish and chips in over five years—he asked enthusiastically if they all wouldn't mind humouring him with this request. Elizabeth was actually enjoying all the excitement and she also had not had fish and chips for a while. The boys were dispatched, and Elizabeth and Joseph found themselves alone, which felt both very strange and very familiar to them both at the same time.

Chapter 66
The Inside Woman

After what seemed like forever and just as Billy was about to suggest they go and find some lunch, someone approached the building. It was a woman and Sebastian said he knew her or at least her kind. They watched for a little longer, before they quickly went to get some lunch, hoping they didn't miss anything in the twenty minutes it took. The next activity they saw was about 5 p.m. when a young man, about five foot eight, with black hair with unusually long curls for a Nigerian man.

He actually looked more like a boy than a man, with acne and a sort of gangly look about him. Like the woman before, he entered the building. Then nothing happened. After an eight-hour stakeout, they were no further forward apart from some photos of the two people they saw enter the building. They decided to call it a day and went back to the hotel for dinner and a fairly early night.

Penny didn't go to bed as quick as Billy and sat in the bar discussing the next steps with Sebastian. He had recognised the woman who they had seen entering the building and she wanted to know more about her. Sebastian agreed to set her up with a coffee the next day with one of the women who he knew from the local club scene that would be able to fill her in.

Billy had a restless night. He knew they needed to find out what was going on in that building and most importantly, they needed to catch the scammers in action. They needed someone to be inside that building. Now Billy was brave but not stupid—he knew there was no way, given the few days they had to be in Lagos, that neither he, Penny or Sebastian were going to be able to infiltrate the scamming gang and gain access. He thought about disguises. He thought about bribing one of the people who worked there (not knowing that Penny and Sebastian were investigating that route already). In the end, it was his love of technology that gave him a brainwave—a drone. He had not brought his drone with him, but he knew he should be able to get hold of one from the main city. With a camera fitted, they could fly up to the office windows and film everything going on inside—simple.

They met for breakfast again and each discussed their plan of attack. They both had a certain amount of scepticism about each other's plan but agreed they would divide and conquer. Sebastian went with Penny to meet a woman he had managed to track down who he assured Penny would know the woman they saw enter the office. Billy went with a colleague of Sebastian's into the city to buy a drone. They agreed to meet back at the stakeout point at lunchtime.

Penny was surprised to be taken to what by night must be a nightclub, but by day was a very run-down old building which stank of stale beer and sex. They met with a woman who did not want to give her proper name but said they could call her Trix. She was clearly a prostitute and was only talking to them because Sebastian bribed her, which was the standard approach. Trix spent some time pretending she didn't know anything about any scamming gang or a woman that might work for them. Some more money was pushed across the bar. "Oh yeah. You mean Gloria. Great hair, fantastic tits—wish mine were as good as hers," Trix suddenly remembered.

"Ah, that sounds like her from what I have seen," Penny had clocked both the hair and the ample chest the day before. "Do you know what she does for them?"

"No, clue, and I ain't saying that for more money," she glanced at Sebastian. "She is cleverer than most of us gals here. So, they probably using her brain for something."

"And do you think you could get her to talk to us?"

"She will talk to anyone for the right amount of money. Do more than talk if you like for a pretty lady like you…."

Penny blushed, but only a little. "Can you get a message to her for us, please? I would say don't tell her it is the Police, but I suspect you will anyway. Perhaps you could just tell her we want some information and are willing to pay for it?" Penny suggested.

Trix coughed and looked at Sebastian. He doled out some more money and she was all smiles and agreed to pass the message on.

Billy was having less luck. The only drones that he could find were very old spec and huge—not very good for covert surveillance! He bought the best and smallest one he could find and also a digital camera that he could strap to it. He arrived at the meeting point just after Penny and Sebastian, carrying a large box with the drone and camera in.

"What the heck have you got there?" Penny looked puzzled.

"Well, it's the only drone I could get really—it might be OK if I can get the camera to zoom well. Otherwise, they are going to get suspicious with a bloody great whirring machine hovering just outside their window."

Billy set it up and they gave it a test flight in the opposite direction from the office. This would also make it look like they were just having some fun with their drone if anyone from the scamming office saw them. It worked OK but made a loud noise as predicted and the camera didn't have a great zoom—they were going to have to chance it. Billy did a trial run as close to the scamming office as he dare and they looked at the footage when they got it back—the windows of the office had clearly not been cleaned in ages and all they could see were the outline of people and office equipment. So that was a waste of money on the drone and camera, and the end of Billy's big plan.

Penny was more hopeful with her plan and it wasn't long before Sebastian got a message from Trix telling them she had arranged for them to meet Gloria that evening in their Hotel. Gloria was waiting for them in the bar when all three of them arrived and she asked for the money straight away. Sebastian may have been young, but he knew how to deal with bribes—he offered to give half now and half later. Gloria tucked the money into her cleavage and smiled broadly.

"Now what can I help you lovely people with?"

Penny felt woman to woman was the right approach here and so she took control, "We have reason to believe that you may know something about a scamming operation taking place here in Lagos?"

"Mmmmhhhmm" was all they got.

"And we think that you might be involved—perhaps knowingly or perhaps not," Penny gave her a look and the chance for Gloria to position herself in the best light.

"Sswwccchh," with her lips pursed was the response this time.

Penny played the ace card, "and if you were to help us, then I am sure we would be able to keep you out of any trouble...."

This was clearly what Gloria had been waiting for, "I want to work in one of those nice hotels in the main city. I need the money to set me up and somewhere to live. I don't need protection as I can look after myself, innit."

She liked the boys she worked with, but Gloria knew she needed to look after number one and if these Police were onto the scammers, then it would all be over soon anyway and so she may as well keep out of trouble and get something out of it. “What is it you want me to do then?” she confirmed she was in.

Chapter 67
A Rumour

"Eb, man. You got to go in for the kill! Come on brother—you can't keep leading these ladies on—put them out of their misery," Azi laughed. He was trying, for the umpteenth time, to get Eb to ask for money for a plane ticket home when he next spoke to one of his punters. Azi knew that forcing him to do it would push him over the edge and all the time they had invested in him would be wasted. But they also needed him to get on with it to pay his keep. Anyway, Jem had been moaning at Azi and was only one step away from having a proper go at Eb.

"Yeah, I know. I know. I promise I will do it this week—I just have to pick the right moment," It was Monday.

Eb had several punters on the hook, but none of them was as developed as Elizabeth. So, she was the obvious choice for going in for the kill. Except that the previous day she had suggested she knew he wasn't who he said he was and now he didn't know what to do—he needed time to think about his next step.

Gloria could see him struggling and started to encourage him not to do it if he didn't want to. She even pointed out to him, quietly, that technically he had not done anything illegal yet and so if they ever did get busted by the Police, then he would not actually be in real trouble. Eb had no idea why Gloria was suddenly pointing this out to him after weeks of her being the best at getting money out of people and therefore the one that he guessed would be most in trouble with the Police. But then Eb didn't know that it was the day before that Gloria had become the Police's inside woman.

To add to his confusion and mixed messages, he was getting from his fellow scammers, Gil suddenly gave him a warning that Jem was on the warpath and to keep out of his way. Apparently, the mafia bosses that Jem ran the Loans business for were getting a bit demanding and he needed more money to keep the whole thing going. Gil advised Eb to get some money from one of his punters and fast, to keep Jem off his back.

Eb went home late, he often worked until gone ten in the evening and walked straight into his mother waiting by the front door with her arms folded and that motherly look on her face.

It looked like he was about to get an earful.

"I heard a rumour today that I hope was just that, a rumour…," Amelia was taking no prisoners he could tell.

"What about?" he said in that teenager sulky way.

"Well, I can't really bring myself to say it… something to do with using the internet for bad things—I don't really understand what or how, but it doesn't sound like the kind of thing I brought you up to do!" She was building up a head of steam now.

"Maybe you shouldn't listen to rumours," he tried.

Smack! She clobbered him on the side of the head. Quite a feat given she was so much smaller than him these days. He reeled and said nothing—suddenly the boy again, not knowing what to say.

"Don't you dare!" she screamed. "You tell me what's going on now or god help me I…. well, I don't know what I will do, but you won't like it."

He didn't like the sound of that, whatever it was. But he couldn't bring himself to confess to his Mum—he wanted to, as he suddenly felt ashamed. But instead, he turned and ran out of the house. Leaving his Mum sobbing behind him.

He ran and ran, the tears stinging his eyes so he couldn't see where he was going. But it wasn't really any surprise when he suddenly found himself outside JG's house. It was nearly midnight and no lights were on, but he needed JG now more than ever—he knew JG would help him do the right thing. He stood up tall, wiped away the tears, although more kept coming, and knocked on the front door. A light came on, then another and quickly JG opened the front door.

"Eb! What's the matter? Come in, come in," Joseph ushered him in and shut the door behind him. It was a small house, with few creature comforts, but welcoming. Joseph manoeuvred Eb through the kitchen and sat him down at the table.

"Is anyone hurt?"

"No," through sobs.

"Is anyone in immediate danger?"

"Not really I guess."

"OK—so let's breathe, have a cup of tea and talk it through—I am sure we can sort it out, whatever it is."

British and their tea, thought Eb, they think it can solve anything.

The tea actually made Eb feel a lot calmer and he stopped crying. JG asked him to start at the beginning and Eb nearly started talking about when his father died, but then realised he meant about the current events—although Eb was clever enough to realise it was all kind of related. Eb told JG about his Mum's loan (which JG knew about apparently) and that his Mum had lost her job (he knew about that as well—Eb didn't know who from)—he went on to say that he had met Gil previous to this (he didn't go into detail on the circumstances of their meeting) and Gil had offered, out of genuine friendship he was convinced, to help him out with money by offering him a job with his brother. Eb then outlined the business of the scammers, being careful not to give too much information about locations and details (they were sort of his friends after all—well Gil and Gloria were—and he didn't want to get them into trouble).

He noticed that JG didn't flinch or show any judgement whilst he was telling him, he just listened intently and with sincere concern for Eb across his face. When he got to the detail about his role and where he had got to in terms of not actually scamming anyone out of money yet, he hesitated because the punter he had to scam this week was Elizabeth and he had used JG's profile to lure her—he felt especially bad about this now. Joseph could see him struggling a little and guessed he might be wondering how to navigate part of his story. "Eb. It sounds to me like you have got yourself in a pickle and need some help. I am happy to help, but I do need to know everything. Even if you think it will be painful to me...."

Eb wondered how JG was able to sort of read his mind but was glad he could.

"The thing is JG... I needed to create my profiles and so I used celebrities, but these were not real enough people. I needed some real people to base them on.... I am afraid I choose you as one of them," Eb looked very sheepish.

"Well, I am not sure that I would be much of a catch for anyone but thank you for being honest with me," he tried to lighten the moment a little for Eb's sake.

"Well, you WERE a hit with this one punter...er, woman. Elizabeth. She can't get enough of you and we talk for hours every day," Eb seemed pleased to tell JG.

“Oh, just the one hey? Ha-ha—only joking. I am sure she is a woman of taste,” keeping it light still.

“Oh, she is. You would really like her Joseph,” Eb started to get enthusiastic and then burst into tears again, “She is so nice, and I have ruined her life!”

“Well, perhaps not yet you haven’t. Now calm down and let me ask you some questions.”

Joseph asked Eb everything he could think of and made some more tea, then some more.

They talked for a couple of hours. Then Joseph stood up and announced, “Right—time for bed. Tomorrow, Eb, we are going to meet your mate Gil—I think he can help us.” Eb lay down on the sofa and was asleep within minutes, only briefly thinking about his Mum before his eyes shut. Fortunately, Joseph was a bit more considerate than that and had called his Mum when he made the first pot of tea, so at least she knew Eb was safe.

Chapter 68
A Plan for "Joseph"

Elizabeth was surprised at how much talking to Joseph felt like talking to 'Joseph' and she quickly swapped them in her brain. Now 'Joseph' was Eb and the man in front of her was both 'Joseph' and Joseph—at least that's how it seemed to her. She also quickly started feeling like the gaping hole in her heart wasn't there anymore. She hadn't exactly fallen in love with Joseph at first sight, but the fact that he was real and so much like the version of him she had slowly fallen for, well it made it all seem like there might be some kind of happy ending at some point.

They hardly noticed that Philip and Anthony had been gone for thirty minutes when they returned, apologising that there were long queues—they had just carried on talking, finding out more and more about their real lives. After the Fish & Chip supper, which Joseph was like a kid in a sweetshop about, they picked up on the topic of helping Eb and his family.

"It sounds like although you have helped the Police, they don't have much to go on and we don't need to worry about them too much," said Joseph.

Philip chipped in, "Er, actually, I am not sure that is so true. I called them earlier today to get an update—well you know what people are like if you don't chase them—and was told that Billy, the constable I originally spoke to, and his colleague Penny, who visited here with him and their boss, were both out of the country on a case."

"How does that impact us?" Asked Elizabeth.

"Well, I did a bit of detective work and found this Billy on Facebook. He posted a picture yesterday of a meal he was having in a restaurant in Lagos—that cannot be a coincidence!"

“That’s great work Philip,” praised Joseph, which pleased Philip enormously, “We are going to need to move fast if they are on the ground in Lagos already.”

“I wonder how they found out about the scammers being in Nigeria—we didn’t know until you turned up,” Elizabeth wondered aloud.

“We may never know. But we need to make our own plans—OK—so here is what I think,” Joseph clapped his hands together and sat forward, ready for business. Elizabeth couldn’t help but be impressed by his assertiveness.

After Joseph had outlined his plan, got some interesting looks and lots of questions, particularly from Anthony and then had re-outlined the plan, everyone said they were ‘in’. Joseph was pleased he had their support, but it wasn’t like they were risking much—He was risking his life in Lagos and, now, an unexpected friendship with Elizabeth—not to mention letting down Eb, Amelia and Su if it failed. It was getting a little late and Philip offered for Joseph to come and stay with them the night. He was about to accept when Elizabeth stepped in and said she wouldn’t hear of it—this whole thing was her responsibility and she was more than capable of hosting Joseph. This was of course only half her motive.

Chapter 69
Smartphone Filming

They met Gloria the next morning, well it was more like lunchtime, but Gloria worked late hours. Sebastian had managed to get an agreement on some of her terms and Penny & Billy wanted to run through with her what they needed. Gloria had a smartphone and was happy to film what the Police needed on that. No need for complicated hidden cameras and microphones, meaning it was also less dangerous for her.

Penny and Billy told her that they needed film and audio evidence of the scammers actually communicating with someone whilst pretending to be someone else and most importantly actually asking them for money. Gloria was confident this would be easy as it happened several times a day now. They told her to be careful and under no circumstances to try and communicate with them whilst she was in the office. If she got caught, she would just have some random videos on her phone, and she could claim she was just messing around. Penny and Billy didn't like the fact that Sebastian had agreed to some of her demands, but there was a bigger picture at play here and they wanted to get the scamming operation closed down fully.

Jane Porter wanted an update and they did a FaceTime call with her to tell her what they had discovered and what their plan was. She was very pleased but concerned it was all a bit risky and didn't want Gloria to get hurt and it comes back on them and the Nigerian Police—typical Police politics thought Penny.

Penny and Billy were sure this was the best approach given the options available to them and Sebastian agreed—he had got clearance from his bosses to do the filming on the basis that they were not actually sanctioning anything—Gloria was to provide evidence to cooperate with the Police in catching a gang of scammers—how she did that was none of their business and so no special warrants or judges needed to be informed—that was the way they like it in Nigeria, very unofficial and low risk to the establishment.

Gloria went off to work and they all just prayed she would not mess it up. Nothing to do now but wait…

Chapter 70
Faking Death

Gil thought he was just meeting Eb for a coffee as they sometimes did before work. He didn't see JG until he got to the table and it was too late to turn and walk away. Gil had not had much to do with JG, but it appeared JG knew him.

"Hello, young Gil. Haven't seen you since the computer classes I ran at lunchtime a couple of years ago—I hear you are putting those skills to some use?"

"Erm, Hello Mr Grey. Yes, I remember those classes. You taught me a lot," he replied as if he were still a little schoolboy.

"Please, call me Joseph or JG like everyone else."

"Listen Gil. I have a problem and JG is going to help, but I need your help as well. It's a bit of a tricky situation," Eb looked hopefully at Gil.

"OK—well you know I am your mate and will help however I can."

"I need to leave.... Erm... your brothers' business," Eb was conscious of talking about scamming too openly.

Gil did not know if JG was aware of what his 'brothers' business' actually was and so he played it a little safe.

"I thought you were happy there and pleased with the money you can earn? It is keeping your family alright, isn't' it?"

"Well, the money is needed, yes. But I wouldn't say I was happy—it's not really the kind of work I really want to do."

"Gil, Eb tells me that he is unhappy at your brothers' business and so he wants to leave. He has explained that this won't be popular with your brother and we think you can help smooth the way—can you help do you think?" Joseph was trying to put Gil into a position where he felt he had power—this was a standard technique for getting people to help others that Joseph had used before when trying to raise money for the school—make people think it's within their power and theirs alone to help you, and they will.

Eb had explained to Joseph the nature of Jem's business but had told him that if they asked Gil to report Jem and Azi to the Police, he would not do it—it was his brother after all. They needed to find a way of getting Eb out without it coming back on him and his family. Joseph had some money and was willing to pay off the loan that Amelia was struggling with, but they knew that Jem wouldn't just let Eb walk away—especially as he was such a good actor and they needed that. It had to be something fool-proof. They all put their thinking caps on.

After a few minutes, Gil said, "Well, I can't think of any way Jem will let you go, short of being dead—and even then, he would probably expect you to turn up for work." He laughed nervously.

"That's it!" exclaimed Eb, "I need to die."

"Hang on a minute Eb—that's a bit extreme. Where will you go and how will you live?" Joseph had got the idea straight away. Gil was a bit slower.

"Sorry, what? What do you mean die?"

"If I fake my death, then he will have to accept I am not going to turn up for work anymore—it's perfect."

"Oh, right. But Mr Gr… JG is right—it's a bit extreme and you will have to move away so he doesn't find out. Even then he might still hassle your family."

"Not if JG pays off the loan as he says he will."

"I agree with Gil—we need to think of something else. Why don't you two chat it over and see what you can come up with? Let's meet again tonight after you finish work and see where we are," Joseph rose to go.

After he had left, Eb was even more adamant about the fake death plan.

"But it's the only fool-proof way of doing it, Gil—I can't think of anything else—can you?"

"Well, maybe I could convince my brother that what he is doing is wrong and try and get him to close the business down," Gil offered half-heartedly.

"Ha! Like that will ever happen. Gil, man—I know you want to help me—you are the only true friend I have. But I can't let you ruin your relationship with your brother. He may be a bit of a thug, but he loves you and has always looked after you—hasn't he."

Gill shrugged in agreement.

“I think the best thing is for us to go into the office today and at some point, for me to say I feel ill. You can make a big fuss about it, so everyone knows and then I will go home a bit early to show how sick I am. Then you come in the next day and say the doctor has visited and thinks it’s terminal. Then a couple of days later you say I died. That’s it—no one will know any different,” Eb had it all worked out.

“I will know, and I won’t be able to tell anyone. Plus, I will never be able to see you again—you are my best and only friend Eb.” Gil got a bit emotional, “But if that is the only way to help you out, then I will.”

Joseph was in no doubt that the ‘fake death’ plan was the wrong approach and hoped that he had put Eb off it enough. After leaving them, he went straight to the local travel agent to book a ticket to the UK as soon as possible—he needed to get hold of the situation fast and had a feeling that this Elizabeth that Eb had spoken so fondly of could be the key.

Chapter 71
Stepping Out

When Philip and Anthony had gone, Joseph stood up and stretched—not in a tired way (although he must be, she thought), but in a sitting too still for a too long way. He suggested they go for a walk—he hadn't walked under a British moon in several years and wanted to take the opportunity. Elizabeth hadn't either and in fact had not been outside at all for many months. She had been getting stronger and Philip had suggested they try a walk to the local park and back several times recently, but she had never felt confident enough. Suddenly, she felt her confidence returning.

As they stepped out of the front door, Elizabeth felt a shiver of excitement run up her spine—partly because she was getting back to her old-self and partly because she felt like a young girl on her first date. Joseph could see that she was a little uncertain on her feet and offered his arm as support, which she willingly grabbed. They walked along, effectively arm-in-arm, like a couple. They talked like it was the first date—they already knew so much about each other, but second hand as it were, and they wanted to hear it all first-hand.

It wasn't cold and so when she did start to shake a little, Joseph seemed to know that she needed a rest and found a park bench. The night was clear, and they sat for ages, covering everything from their childhoods, their careers and then the last few years in detail. She told him everything about her Teddie and he listened with compassion and grace, saying he sounded like a 'wonderful man' when she finished. It felt good talking to Joseph about Teddie and she didn't feel guilty about the feelings she could feel developing for this new 'wonderful man' next to her on the park bench.

It was a little strange to be falling for him so quickly, she thought, but then for her, it wasn't quickly—this was the man she had been falling slowly in love with over the last few weeks. She wondered what it was like for him as he didn't even know about her until a few days ago. She didn't want to scare him off!

They got back to her house just before midnight and Elizabeth realised, she felt a mixture of things—tired, excited, happy and hopeful—the last one for Eb and his family as well as her and Joseph. The spare bedroom had been made up quickly earlier with the help of Anthony and Joseph made his way there now—stopping to return and kiss Elizabeth tenderly on the cheek—maybe he was starting to have feelings for her too. She lay awake in bed for a short period of time, thinking about the last twelve hours and what the next few days would bring—she fell fast after about twenty minutes and had the best night's sleep since her accident.

Chapter 72
Caught on Camera and off Camera

Gloria was excited by her 'undercover' mission and also the opportunity to get out of her drab life and get a better one. She got into the office earlier than everyone else—unknown to the Police, she had borrowed another phone from a friend and had decided to set it up so it could covertly film the guys at their desks. She positioned it on a ledge near the window, where it was mostly hidden by an old blind from the original office occupants—she felt sure no one would see it as they never opened the blinds because of the sun. She also planned to do some free-hand filming with her own phone as agreed with the Police but would make that more fun so that the guys didn't suspect her. She was going to pretend it was her birthday, so she had an excuse to mess about and do the filming.

The guys got to the office and she soon announced it was her birthday and started messing around and trying to dance with Gil. She grabbed Eb as well, but he said he felt ill and wasn't up to dancing. Azi and Jem were happy to let her have a little celebration mess about but steered clear of letting her pull them into a dance.

They all settled down to work. After a while, Eb said something about feeling sick and went home early. Lucky for Eb she thought, maybe I can keep him out of this—she thought he was a good kid.

She thought it was all going well, and she was hopeful she had some good footage. She waited until the guys were busy at the end of the shift and grabbed her other mobile from the ledge. She met the Police as agreed and they sat down to review the footage together. They were annoyed with her at first when they found out she had taken the risk of setting up a second phone, but actually, it would probably help, so they let her off. The footage she had was too weak—either too far away from the screens so they couldn't see what was on them or the audio was not good enough. Gloria was annoyed and Penny and Billy were disappointed. Their grand plan had failed.

Billy and Penny were not so ready to give up though—they told Gloria that she must go back and get better footage—she begged them not to make her, but Sebastian gave her a stern look and told her their deal would be off if she didn't—she knew she was too far in and had to do what they asked.

What they didn't know, was that Gil had seen Gloria pick up the mobile from the ledge and had got suspicious. He had followed her when she left the office and saw her talking to some people who looked like Police to him.

Gil was not the sharpest tool in the box, but he could put two and two together. He realised that the Police must be onto them and that Gloria must be helping them—that phone was probably filming them at work. He felt real anger build up inside at Gloria's betrayal—but then he remembered Eb and his plan to fake his death. Maybe, just maybe, there was a better way out...

Chapter 73
No Need to Die

Eb knew he was a good actor—he could fool these guys pretending to be sick. After the first hour at work, he went to the toilet splashed his face, so it looked like sweat. Then he started coughing at his desk, a bit to begin and then harder and louder. Gloria put her sleeve to her mouth and muttered something about 'germs'. At one point he might have overdone it by coughing openly in Azi's direction, which caused some swearing at him. Finally, he stood up and immediately fell back down into his chair, as if almost fainting. Although not happy with the plan, Gil fulfilled his part of it.

"Eb man, you sound awful and look worse—Azi, can we send this leper home before we all catch our death from him?"

Azi had grunted his approval and with a wink at Gil, Eb had gone home.

Eb had not yet thought how he was going to get his Mum and sister in on this plan. His Mum knew something was up because of the previous night and Joseph's call, but she didn't know the specifics. He decided he had a day or two of illness before his 'death' and so would think of a way to tell them.

Gil didn't feel good about the plan Eb had set in motion by going homesick and was distracted thinking about alternative ways to help Eb. But he was not so distracted that he didn't notice Gloria grab what looked like a mobile from the window ledge near their desks and he followed her after work, suspicious that she was up to something. After seeing her with some people that he was sure were Police he was really angry with her because she was clearly working with the Police. But then his mind turned to how this might help Eb—and without him having to die—fake or real.

He followed Gloria home after her meeting with the Police and just as she was closing her front door, he stuck his foot in the gap. Gloria looked up and he saw fear in her eyes.

"Gil… erm, what are you doing here my lover?" she tried to remain calm and light.

"I think you and I need a chat Gloria, don't you?" he stood his ground. She sighed and let him in. He didn't know the full story and was about to start asking questions when Gloria opened up like floodgates.

"It wasn't my fault. The Police approached me and said I would be in trouble if I didn't help them. They are already onto your brother's scamming business and he is gonna be in trouble—I don't want none of that and so thought I better cooperate. You know what these bastard Police are like—they would sling me in a cell. What I filmed didn't work the first time and now they say I have to do more and closer—I have to! I'm sorry Gil, but you would do the same if you was me," she burst into tears.

Gil sat in silence and waited for the tears to pass—he was not going to comfort her but let her feel her guilt. When she had finished, he spoke.

"You are wrong. I would not have given into the Police as you have—I would have done everything I can to protect my brother, Azi, Eb and you—you are my friends, my family," he sighed. "However, now that the Police are involved and have you helping them, I think there is no hope for us—we will be caught and all thrown in prison. Unless…"

"Yes? What? What is 'unless'? I will do anything to help," she pleaded.

"I love my brother—for all his sins—and I wouldn't do this if I thought it would make any difference to his outcome…."

Gil explained what he had in mind. It actually meant that Gloria would appear to be helping the Police and so would let her off the hook… she was in!

After agreeing on the plan with Gloria, who he hoped he could trust, he quickly went to Eb's house. Eb opened the front door.

"You are not meant to be here until tomorrow—I am not dead enough yet," he joked.

Gil was in no mood for humour, "Never mind that—I have a plan to keep you alive."

At exactly that moment, Eb's Mum appeared, "Keep who alive? What are you boys up to?" They were both about to revert to little schoolboys and say 'nothing Mrs Azikiwe when Gil suddenly realised it was time to behave like men and own up, "We are trying to right a wrong and help Eb, you and Su at the same time." Eb looked shocked and then anxious at what his Mum would say. She surprised him.

“Is this to do with that trouble that Mr Grey is going to England for?”

“What? What do you mean going to England?” Eb was shocked now.

Amelia quickly explained that Joseph had called earlier that day and told her that he was going to England on a mercy mission to try and help Eb with his troubles. He still hadn’t told her what the troubles were, but she knew it must be serious for Joseph to do such a thing. Eb sat down in bewilderment and couldn’t think straight. Gil, growing more mature and dynamic by the minute, realised this was the perfect opportunity.

“Mrs Azikiwe—when did Mr Grey say he was flying?”

“Erm, I think it was a very late flight—near midnight I think he said.”

“Eb—we have to speak to JG before he goes—if he is going to do what I think he is going to do, then he will need our help!” Eb was confused, but he trusted his friend.

“Take the motorbike,” Amelia said. Eb looked confused. “It’s your Dad’s old Honda CB77—I had it done up as a surprise for your Birthday, but you need it now—go!”

Eb and Gil raced outside and round to the shed at the back where Amelia told him the bike was—Eb just had time to think it was a thing of beauty and looked great restored to its former glory, but then they had to go. Eb tore through the streets, trying to remember the best way to get to the airport—he had never actually been right into it but knew where it was. They got there in just under 15 minutes—Gil holding on as the pillion passenger. They left the bike at the entrance and ran inside—it was a small airport and they found JG about to go through to departures—if he hadn’t stopped to buy something to eat for the flight, they would have missed him. He was surprised to see them.

“I guess your Mum told you I would be here. Well, there is no point in trying to talk me out of it—I am going to England to see if I can convince this Elizabeth to help in some way—I have no idea how she can, but I have to try,” JG seemed bigger and stronger than Eb had noticed before.

Gil showed the way, again, “I know how she can help.”

“Really?” said Joseph and Eb in unison.

Gil told them about Gloria and her mission for the Police. Then he told them how she had failed so far and the opportunity that gave them, but they had to move fast—JG’s timing on going to the UK was perfect, but he would have to win over Elizabeth quickly. Gil explained that Eb would have to act the best he ever had. He missed out on the bit of the plan where he would sink with the ship.

It seemed like too many things depended on each other for the plan to work, but Eb and Joseph agreed it was the best plan they had. Joseph walked through the departures gate with a promise to convince Elizabeth to help. Eb waved hard until he couldn't see him anymore, hoping he would again one day. Gil breathed for the first time in the last few hours—he had suddenly gone from young office boy to master schemer and it was exhausting.

Chapter 74
Incoming Call

Elizabeth was ready for the role she had to play. She knew she would be speaking to 'Joseph'/Eb on the phone and although she was nervous, she felt that she had lots of support with Joseph, Philip and Anthony around her—plus she knew that Eb was on her side now.

They all sat at the table, with the iPad propped up facing Elizabeth and Joseph. The iPad started to ring and the message 'Incoming call from 'Joseph' appeared on the screen—she pressed the 'answer' button and waited...

Chapter 75
It's in the Can!

Gloria had sent a message the next day to say that she hadn't managed to get any footage that day and she would try again tomorrow. Although frustrating to Penny and Billy, they were glad she hadn't just disappeared—their surveillance of the office told them she had still turned up for work.

The next day, they got a message to say she had got some excellent footage and would meet them at the bar that night after work.

This was it—they were closing in!

Chapter 76
The First and Last Act

Eb turned up for work the next day as normal. Gloria a few minutes after him. They looked at each other, perhaps for a moment too long and then went straight into their act.

"So, you're not dead then boy?" Gloria cackled in her normal raucous laugh.

"No—not yet—must have been something I ate. I feel fine now," Eb said a little forced—he needed to tone this down to appear natural and normal.

"Well, good job too," said Azi, "cos if you don't get some money out of that punter you have been warming up for the last century, then Jem is gonna blow!"

"OK. OK. I can do this—trust me—we are gonna be celebrating by the end of today," he resisted the temptation to wink at Gloria at the cleverness of his double meaning reply. He also knew that today would be a tough day for Gil—not just because Gil would need to act better than he ever had, but also because he was in effect condemning his brother, Azi and himself to a terrible future.

Everything was normal—Jem in his corner doing whatever CEO's did in their corners, but always watching them; Azi cracking on with his punters, hoping to overtake Gloria's record for most money scammed; Gloria pinging her punters to keep the façade going, her logic being that this might all go south and she needs this job after all; Gil staring at his computer, trying to act natural and failing completely; and Eb slightly over-acting with lots of tapping on his keyboard and noises suggesting he was working hard.

"Right—this is it—I'm calling her," Eb said with confidence to the whole room. They all knew to hang back when a phone call was going on—no one liked an audience—but they all craned their necks a little to see Eb close his first scam.

"Darling—so lovely to hear your voice! Sorry, we haven't spoken for a while, I have been a little under the weather," Eb using his best 'Joseph' voice and English phrases.

"Joseph—my sweet Joseph. I miss you when we don't talk. When can we be together," Elizabeth almost whispered back.

"Steady," Anthony nudged Elizabeth, "Don't rush him into it!"

Azi did a hand pump and gave Eb a thumbs up—this girl was ripe for the plucking! Gloria and Gil smiled, but for different reasons—the first step was taken.

Eb ignored external mini-celebrations around him and continued, "Well, I have some time owed to me from work and have saved a little money—can I come and visit you?"

"I thought you would never ask—when can you come?"

"Well, in a day or two if I can get the flights and they are cheap enough," 'Joseph' replied. Azi had taught him well—pretend you are willing to spend your own money on tickets and then go back the next day saying they are too expensive. But Eb and Joseph had other ideas.

"Can you look them up now? I am so excited," Elizabeth fed her line with an appropriate amount of excitement.

Eb looked over at Azi, knowing he was listening and knowing he would think this an unusual approach—punters didn't normally go so fast. Azi shrugged and gave Eb the thumbs up, as Eb and Gil had known he would—eager to get the deal done.

Eb made an act of looking up flights and they all had to control their laughter—this was normal office banter when you had to pretend to punters you were doing something.

"Right. Hang on.... Just getting the flights page up now... OK. Erm.... Oh. That's not good."

"What? What's wrong—no flights?" Elizabeth said anxiously.

"Well, there are but not at a price I can afford. I think we may need to put off a visit until I have saved up some more money," Eb said sombrely. Azi was beaming—this boy is good, he thought.

"Oh, Joseph—I can't wait! How much are the tickets—I can help out—I just want to see you," Elizabeth got a thumbs up at her end from all three men sitting around her—she was relaxing into her role.

"Oh, well I am not sure about that—I didn't mean for you to offer. I want to see you too, but don't want to waste your money...." Eb counted five down on his fingers as Azi had taught him. Azi, Gloria and Gil were all doing the same in their head—there was always a little buzz when you were in the finale of the scam and they all felt it for each other.

Elizabeth nearly overdid it with her reply, but had to lay the ground for later, "Joseph! I have lots of money that I don't really need and can't think of anything else I want to spend it on other than getting you here! Tell me the price my love and let's do it."

The normal price to give for a ticket from Singapore to the UK was seven hundred pounds. It actually cost more than this for a standard flight, but over time they had found out this was the figure most punters were comfortable with—any less and they didn't believe it, any more, and they got jittery about sending the money. It seemed seven hundred pounds was a figure their punters could stomach.

To his surprise, Azi ran over to his desk and wrote on a bit of paper '£900'. Eb looked at Azi and shook his head with a surprised look. Azi made gestures as if to say, 'go on—she can take it'. It was a departure from the script agreed with Joseph and Elizabeth, and Eb was worried it would make them think something was wrong—he needed to think quickly. Then he realised this actually played into their plan for the next step—he quickly wrote on the scrap of paper 'Double-dip!' and Azi instantly understood what he meant and gave the thumbs-up sign.

"Oh, my love. You are so sweet. Only because I want to see you so much too…. The price is seven hundred pounds for tomorrow—is that too much?" 'Joseph' poured it on thick.

"To see you, I would pay double that."

Azi was nearly wetting himself and even Jem had wandered over, not quite believing how well Eb was doing with this woman.

Elizabeth followed her script, "Shall I just buy you the ticket to make it quicker?" A small panic always arose when punters offered this—of course, it made sense if they were paying for them to just do it online via the airline's website and put the ticket in the name of the other person. The next step was always difficult to play, they all knew and were keen to see Eb do it well.

"That would be great—let me just look at the details… erm…. Oh, hang on. It says that at this short notice I will have to show my credit card when I pick the tickets up at the airport. So, you paying is not going to work." Pause, pause, pause, "I guess you could send me the money and I can use my card that way?"

Without hesitation, to uphold her eager persona, Elizabeth said, "Yes, that's fine. How shall I get the money to you?"

When everyone heard those words, they knew they were home and dry. The rest was done by Facebook Messenger, sending over the account details etc.

'Joseph' made a few last cooing noises of love and affection to Elizabeth and promised to send her the details when he had booked his flight. He finished the call.

They all whooped, and Gloria and Gil danced around in celebration. Azi high-fived Eb and said, "You're one of the team now!" Eb smiled and looked pleased with himself—for reasons different than they thought. Jem walked over to Eb, everyone watched and quietened down a little.

"Well, Eb. I thought you were never gonna close that bitch, but it looks like you proved me wrong—now do it again a hundred times over!" and he slapped Eb on the back in a congratulatory way. Everyone cheered.

"Was I OK? Not too much?" Elizabeth sought confirmation she had played her part well.

"Babe you was the best," Anthony.

"You did great Liz," Philip.

"That was a brave and courageous thing you just did Elizabeth—I was in awe. Thank you," Joseph said with sincerity.

"When will they call back do you think?" she asked.

"Not sure, but we need to be ready. And remember, it hopefully won't be Eb that calls—so don't be surprised."

They all settled down and carried on with the day. Eb had sent money details to Elizabeth and she had sent the money straight away. He confirmed to the room that it had arrived.

"Shame you didn't go for the nine hundred—she was gagging for it mate," said Azi.

"Yeah, I know. But I think we can get this one on the double—dip," Eb replied with confidence.

"Ha! You get your first punter closed and already you want more—that's my boy!"

Gloria inserted her lines, "You should do my version of the double-dip—it's quicker than Azi's." She playfully smirked at Azi.

"Now come on Gloria—you know mine works best. Waiting until the day of travel and doing the wrong plane con is tried and tested," Azi defended his approach.

“Yes, if your persona is an idiot—but ‘Joseph’ isn’t is he. She ain’t gonna fall for that. Do mine Eb—it’s the best.”

They needed to get Azi wound up so he would overcommit—they knew Gloria was the best bait for this, but Eb needed to tickle it along a little.

“Oh, I don’t know that I can do it, Gloria—it’s hard and you need to be really convincing—I would mess it up.”

“That’s true—it takes a REAL talent to pull it off—never mind then, you BOYS stick to your old ways….” That look at Azi again.

“Hang on, hang on. I didn’t say we couldn’t do it—did I.”

Azi stood up and rose to the taunt as expected, “We could make it work.”

“How much?” Gloria goaded.

“Fifty,” Azi stood his ground.

“Deal.”

“Azi—I can’t do it—I’m not good enough!” Eb pleaded. Wait, wait, wait.

“But I am!” Azi was in full boast mode.

Azi shoved Eb out of the way and went onto Eb’s computer, “Right—it’s this Elizabeth woman—right?”

“I have to capture this spectacular failure about to happen!” Gloria laughed and started filming. Azi was too full of himself to worry about being filmed—he even stuck his tongue out at the camera and shouted, ‘I will get an Oscar for this performance!’.

The iPad rang and Elizabeth tensed—this was it. It had to go well—they only had one shot at it.

“Hello again, Joseph.”

Azi cleared his throat and did his best impression of Eb being ‘Joseph’, “Hello, my love.”

Elizabeth was tempted to say ‘have you got a sore throat’ but resisted. Azi felt he was such a good actor that no one would notice the voice difference.

“I have come across a bit of a problem, my love,” Azi was trying to remember how he had heard Gloria pitch this approach.

“What is it? You are still coming tomorrow aren’t you?” Elizabeth added an anxious tone to her question and got an encouraging smile from Joseph.

“Well… I got the money, which is great thanks. But it appears that the last ticket at that price has gone….” Wait, wait, wait.

“Oh. Are there not any tickets left for tomorrow then?”

"There are.... But they are more expensive...." Azi was feeling comfortable now—he could feel he would get the double-dip and show Gloria who was king!

"OK—well I am excited about seeing you now. How much more expensive?"

Normally they would try to double the money at this point, but Azi wanted to show off and was remembering Elizabeth's earlier words about having lots of money, "Well, it's another eight hundred pounds...," he looked straight at the camera Gloria was filming him on and pulled a face and stuck up his middle finger.

Eb, Gil and Gloria couldn't believe their luck. "Oh, that is quite a bit more." Azi suddenly thought he might have overdone it and was going to lose his bet. Of course, he didn't know that he could have said any figure and Elizabeth would have agreed—the money wasn't ever going to come anyway.

"Well, I can afford it and I so want to see you my darling Joseph—I will send it to the same account—later today—OK?"

"Thank you, my love—you are the sweetest," Azi pretended to blow kisses at the screen whilst flicking the V at it, "I will let you know the details as soon as I book it," he said, knowing this was the last time she would get any communication from them.

"Bye, my darling—see you soon. Mmwaahh," Elizabeth added a kissing sound and closed the call.

It was their turn to whoop and celebrate in England this time—As long as they had caught it all on film at the other end, their plan should work. Philip made them all a celebratory cup of tea.

Azi jumped up, punched the air and held out his hand to Gloria for his winnings. She had stopped filming and went to her handbag to get the money, carefully placing her phone—now a precious piece of evidence—inside. She gave Azi the money, reluctantly congratulating him on his win. The last thing Gloria, Gil and Eb needed to do was finish the day as if nothing out of the ordinary had happened—it was the hardest part of the whole plan.

Epilogue
A Month Later

Penny and Billy flew back out to Lagos for the court case. Jane Porter had wanted to come, but with the success of the case being made big in the UK press, she had stayed in the UK to front that up. Penny and Billy didn't mind not getting the limelight, they had both got promotions out of this win and were now seen by their colleagues as the front line of cybercrime in Norfolk and beyond. Jane knew that she would get the pick of her next role as The Chief Constable wouldn't be able to refuse her anything—he was looking good at a national and even international level and the Police were about to put away a major menace behind bars.

Jem and Azi had been assigned a lawyer but didn't hold out much hope. The prosecution had got hold of that blasted video that Gloria had taken of Azi doing the double-dip on a punter and they had the records of the transaction from Money Exchange, tying Jem's name into the whole thing. The raid of their offices later that day, had seized everything and that's how they found Gloria's recording—it had just been bad luck. Too wrapped up in what was going to happen to them, they hadn't blinked when they heard Gloria was being shipped off to some women's prison.

In fact, Sebastian had been as good as his word and they had changed her identity and relocated her to another part of the city—she was trying to lead a life on the straight and narrow, but old habits die hard. Jem and Azi had not been able to talk to each other since the raid, but clearly, they had both decided that their last act of brotherly love for Gil was that they would keep him out of it. Luckily, Gil and Eb had left the office early to celebrate, at Gloria's insistence, and were not there during the raid.

Gil had visited them both in prison whilst awaiting trial and Jem had told him where his small stash of 'savings' was hidden. They didn't talk about what Gil would do, but he had grown up a lot recently and would make his way.

Amelia and Su never really did find out what had happened and why Joseph had run off to England, but they were happy to hear that things had been sorted. Gil came round often for dinner and was starting to take a shine to Su, which annoyed and pleased Eb in equal measure. Amelia never found out that Gil and Jem were brothers, but one day Gil told her that he had managed to sort out the loan problem and she didn't owe anything anymore.

In fact, Gil had met with the mafia boss that Jem had dealt with and paid most of Jem's savings over to them in return for leaving the loan shark business behind them—with Jem about to be imprisoned for a long time, the mafia were happy to cut their losses.

The surprise of the restored motorbike as a birthday present ruined, Amelia came up with another idea, but she needed Joseph's help. He had remained in the UK, where apparently, he had met a lady who he had known somehow for a while—Amelia was over the moon for him—but was coming back soon. She spoke to him on the phone and he agreed to support her idea—in fact, it turned out that Joseph's new lady friend was also a big vintage motorbike enthusiast and she said she wanted to put some money into her idea. On Eb's birthday, after a wonderful meal that Gil and Su had prepared (with lots of giggling from the kitchen!), Amelia took them all for a walk to find something.

Suddenly Eb realised they were in the area of his Dad's old workshop and when they got close to it he was pleased to see it had been cleaned up and appeared to be operating as a motorbike restoration garage again—it was not until he got really close that Amelia pointed out the sign above the door 'Dev Azikiwe and Son'. Amelia, with Joseph and Elizabeth's financial support, had managed to get the garage back and Gil, Su and her had been fixing it up.

Gil had worked harder than anyone in getting it all set up and had told Amelia that he would commit his life to work alongside Eb to make it a success—whilst it would never take away his guilt for his involvement in Dev's death, in this very workshop, he felt it was a good start at making amends. Eb would have to work hard, especially with Gil as an apprentice, but he was going to take up his father's legacy and do the thing he had loved doing with his dad. He didn't know how to thank his Mum, but the tears she could see and the joy in his heart she could feel as he hugged her was thanks enough.

Philip, Anthony and Joseph had spent the last few weeks helping the Police to piece together everything—being careful not to drop Eb or Gil in it. Elizabeth had played the part of the duped woman beautifully and the police were left thinking they had been the clever ones. During this time, Elizabeth and Joseph had continued their late-night strolls to the park and then beyond—Elizabeth had got stronger and stronger and come alive again and Joseph felt a gap in his heart was being filled.

After only a few weeks, it became clear that Philip' services were no longer needed—with no reason to be in Elizabeth's life so much, Philip and Anthony were a little fed up, which is why Elizabeth and Joseph turned up with a new pug puppy for them, which they immediately named Eb!

With Joseph by her side she didn't feel like a victim and in fact wanted to carry on helping other people who found themselves in impossible positions, as Eb and his family had. That's why they decided to go back to Nigeria and make a difference—it was all Joseph had ever wanted to do and it gave Elizabeth a focus for the future. They would do great things together.

Eb and Gil met Joseph and Elizabeth at Lagos airport. Eb had wanted to pick up Joseph on the Honda CB77 motorbike, but they needed a car for the two of them and their luggage. By the looks of the amount of luggage Elizabeth had, she was planning to stay for some time. Eb had been nervous about meeting Elizabeth, as she had him—they had a relationship of sorts, albeit built on false foundations. When he saw her walk-through arrivals, he ran up to her and prostrated himself at her feet, which caused everyone around to stare. Elizabeth was unfazed and she knelt down and lifted his face to meet her eye.

"You brought me my Joseph, my love, a new passion for life—it is me that should be bowing down to you. Please Eb—stand up and greet me as a friend," she had tears in her eyes as she spoke.

Eb had not known such compassion and slowly rose, tentatively reaching out his hand to shake Elizabeth's—she ignored his hand and pulled him into a full embrace. Eb was not sure what she did, but at that moment, he felt cleansed and knew life was going to be better from here on out…